Earth to Betsy

**Center Point
Large Print**

**This Large Print Book carries the
Seal of Approval of N.A.V.H.**

Earth to Betsy

Beth Pattillo

CENTER POINT PUBLISHING
THORNDIKE, MAINE

For my mother,
Molly Morrison Pattillo,
with love and thanks.

This Center Point Large Print edition
is published in the year 2007 by arrangement with
WaterBrook Press, a division of Random House, Inc.

The text of this Large Print edition is unabridged. In other
aspects, this book may vary from the original edition. Printed in
Thailand. Set in 16-point Times New Roman type.

ISBN 13: 978-1-58547-877-4

Library of Congress Cataloging-in-Publication Data

Pattillo, Beth.
    Earth to Betsy / Beth Pattillo.--Center Point large print ed.
      p. cm.
    Sequel to: Heavens to Betsy.
    ISBN-13: 978-1-58547-877-4 (lib. bdg. : alk. paper)
      1. Women clergy--Fiction. 2. Large type books. I. Title.

  PS3616.A925E17 2007
  813'.6--dc22

2006020509

Rule for Women Ministers No. 1: Don't take the Lord's name in vain on church premises—especially on the Monday morning after Easter.

I push sweaty clumps of hair from my forehead, draw a deep breath to prevent any wayward oaths from escaping my lips, and tug at my nonexistent waistband. *Note to self:* never go to battle in low-rise pants, no matter how stylish they may be.

Wardrobe malfunction or not, I will vanquish this enemy. I am woman clergy; hear me roar. Or as the case may be, watch me install a new toner cartridge in the church's ancient relic of a copier.

With a deep breath, I jam one end of the cartridge in its slot and force the other end toward its final resting place. The copier, though, is possessed. I've known this for the past six months while ignoring the resident demons that jam the paper, staple documents at random, and disable the duplex feature. But my denial, as usual, has proven a more effective strategy in the short run than in the long one. I've been wrestling with this cartridge for the better part of the last hour, and now I abandon coaxing for pure brute force. One way or another, I will make this work.

With an ominous crack, the toner cartridge splits under the pressure, sending out a shower of fine black powder. It stings my eyes, and I inhale a generous dose for good measure, clogging my lungs. Coughing, I drop to my knees, not the victor but the vanquished.

A strangled sound from the workroom doorway tells me that my defeat will not go unnoticed. I wipe my eyes with the back of my hand, and when my vision clears, I see a distinguished older gentleman standing a few feet away, trying to cover his amusement with a look of concern.

His eyes meet mine, and I'm expecting some serious southern chivalry as I've seen so often from the men of Nashville. A clean hanky. A gallantly extended hand to help me to my feet. Instead, he steps back, clearly afraid that the powdery black substance will spread to his impeccable seersucker suit. He eyes me with something like disdain, though it's clear he's trying hard not to show it.

"I'm here to see the minister," he informs me as if he doesn't notice my predicament. I've met his type before. In his eyes I'm just a functionary, one of the little people God put on earth to make his life run smoothly.

He taps his watch. "I don't have all day. Could you announce me, please?"

Clearly he's mistaken me for Angelique, my administrative assistant. It's happened before, usually when I answer the phone with a simple "Church of the Shepherd. This is Betsy." It's appalling, really, how some people treat secretaries. Of course, it's always such fun when I get to set them straight as to my identity. I'm particularly looking forward to the expression that will develop on this guy's face when he discovers

6

I'm the minister he's here to meet.

A truly scathing put-down springs to my lips, but before it can escape, I see Angelique standing in the doorway behind the Mystery Gentleman. She's grinning from ear to ear and holding out a wad of tissues with a fiercely manicured hand.

"You look like you've been cleaning a chimney, *Reverend*," she says with glee, stepping past the man and coming toward me. "I told you we ought to call the repair guy."

I wipe my eyes with the tissues and look down with dismay at the toner stains on my glittery pink shirt and trendy gray pants. I bought them for my Big Date tonight, and now I have less than an hour to race home, de-tonerize, and find something else to wear in the black hole that is my closet. Honestly. All I intended to do was sneak into the office on my day off and get a head start on my sermon preparation for next week. Instead, here I am, covered head to foot in the world's most indelible substance and being served a side order of chauvinism by this refugee from a Tennessee Williams play. The chauvinist in question, though, is the one who's flushed now. He coughs and then looks politely away while I wipe my face. *Ha!*

"We can't afford the repair guy," I remind Angelique. As a graying, downtown congregation, Church of the Shepherd operates on a bottom line that's pretty close to the bottom. Angelique just shrugs her shoulders, which are amply revealed by the fashionable portrait neckline of her sweater. I'd ask to borrow it for my date, but I don't have the . . . um . . . equipment to keep it in place.

"The repair guy would have been cheaper than replacing your outfit. Plus, the church would have paid for it."

She's right. I hate it when she's right. But now that I've been promoted to the position of interim senior pastor, I'm determined to prove that I can handle the job. The way Sunday offerings have been declining over the past few weeks, we won't make our budget projections for the year. We don't need any added expenses.

"By the way," Angelique adds, "The Judge is here to see you."

I groan. Great. The Judge *and* this mystery guy. At this rate I might be ready for my Big Date by next week. I glance at the clock on the wall. Less than fifty minutes to go.

Since I became the interim senior minister, I've had a steady stream of people through my office voicing unique and, in their eyes, extremely urgent complaints. The retired Reverend Squires, a newer member of the church who still hasn't figured out what to do with his spare time, wants me to start special programs for people who qualify for AARP. I think polka dancing and bridge tournaments figure prominently in his expectations. Bernice Kenton, whose face has been stretched tighter than her Lycra exercise pants by her plastic surgeon, wants me to bring in a yoga instructor three times a week. And Jed Linker, longtime church custodian, wants more money just to keep the building from falling apart. And maybe a pension, if it's not too much trouble.

You see, Church of the Shepherd is in a bit of a quandary. It's a dinosaur, one of the last of a dying breed of downtown Nashville churches. While other congregations have relocated to the suburbs where all the young families (i.e., potential parishioners) now live, we cling to life here on the corner of Broadway and Fifth. Our worship attendance continues to slide, and little by little the church has closed off sections of the building to cut down on the cost of upkeep. Even the Family Life Center, built during the eighties in a vain attempt to lure people in from the suburbs, has been shuttered. None of the athletically inclined yuppies of the day ever ventured as far as the sanctuary.

I look down at my clothes again.

"I couldn't be more covered in toner, could I?" I ask Angelique. She nods, so I continue to scrub my face with the remains of the wadded tissues. "The Judge, huh? Well, better get it over with."

At this, the Mystery Gentleman clears his throat. Angelique and I both swing our heads toward him. I've enjoyed leaving him standing there, but he hasn't gone away as I was hoping.

"That wouldn't be Judge Blount, would it?" he asks with an ingratiating smile. "I know him well."

Great. This guy will probably turn out to have been the best man at The Judge's wedding.

"Well, let's not keep The Judge waiting, then," I say

through clenched teeth and a forced smile. "If you'd like to follow me?"

Head high, shoulders back, I lead the Mystery Gentleman from the workroom to my office, ready to do battle with a lot more than just a toner cartridge.

Now, just because I've been made interim senior minister doesn't mean I get the big office—the one with its own bathroom and separate sitting area. Nope, I'm still here in the associate-minister digs with my one little slice of window, a desk chair with a missing caster, and a severe lack of bookshelves. I wince at the chaos of paper and Bible commentaries on my desk, but when I see the dozen red roses in a crystal vase on the credenza, I have to smile. They came with a card—*Looking forward to tonight. David*—along with copies of exegetical notes for Sunday's sermon text. A guy like my David, one who sends you flowers *and* helpful preaching material, is definitely a keeper.

The Judge, having made himself at home in my office, is sitting in one of the two chairs facing my desk, as he does on a regular basis. He doesn't glance my way when I circle behind my desk and sit down, since he's too busy shaking hands with the Mystery Gentleman. The pair of them are clearly friends, but there's also an undercurrent of testosterone here, a jockeying for position, despite the fact they've both been cashing Social Security checks for some time now.

At length, they remember that I'm in the room.

"Miss Blessing," The Judge growls, eyeing my toner-tinged face with a frown. "I see you've met my friend Arthur Corday."

The Judge refuses to acknowledge the fact that I am an ordained minister by continuing to refer to me as "Miss" rather than "Reverend." I tried correcting him for the first month I was here, but like the slow, steady drip of water on a rock, he wore me down. Now I'm just glad when he doesn't refer to me as "that woman."

"Mr. Corday." I rise out of my chair and extend my hand across the desk as if meeting him for the first time. He shakes my proffered hand despite its toner-intense state and again flashes that honey-dripping southern smile.

"A pleasure, Reverend Blessing."

He's all charm now that I've been elevated out of the secretarial caste, so I'm guessing he wants something.

"I'm surprised to find you here, Arthur," The Judge says, still virtually ignoring me. His jowls quiver so much when he speaks that he reminds me of UGA, the Georgia Bulldogs' mascot. Is it a coincidence that The Judge is an alum? Probably not. "I told you we weren't interested in your offer."

Aha! I wasn't wrong about the underlying scent of male competition. Intriguing.

Tap, tap, tap.

I look up, and there's Earlene, one of the church custodians, standing in my office doorway.

"We've got a Big Problem," she says in her gravelly, Marlboro-tainted voice. How that deep, resonant voice got into that rail-thin body of hers, I'll never know.

I swallow a groan and force a smile. "I'm afraid I'm in the middle of something right now, Earlene." But the presence of visitors in my office is no match for whatever Earlene has on her mind. In the past couple of months, almost every mechanical, electrical, or structural thingamajig in the entire building has gone haywire. First it was the leaky baptistery. Then it was moisture in the steeple. That was followed by a series of unpleasant discoveries: fruit flies in the sanctuary (someone left an orange underneath the communion table for no discernible reason), leaks in the roof of the education wing, and potholes in the parking lot that could swallow small children.

Earlene frowns. "It's the doors."

"The doors?"

How could we have a Big Problem with the doors? The Judge and Arthur Corday exchange looks.

"The sanctuary doors," Earlene says, popping her gum. "They're so warped I can't get them all the way closed. They won't lock."

And that is definitely a problem, because like any downtown church, we run a continual risk of vandalism and petty theft. Since the sanctuary doors are approximately fifteen feet tall and have to be ordered from France, Earlene is right to classify it as a Big Problem.

"Have you talked to Jed?"

Jed, the head custodian, can fix almost anything, usually with a toothpick protruding from one side of his mouth while he does it.

"I can't," Earlene says. "We're not speaking right now."

Earlene's "can't" is really a "won't." Every six months or so, she and Jed, who is technically her supervisor, have a huge blowup and refuse to acknowledge each other's existence.

"Earlene," I say with my best Voice of Authority, "you have to talk to Jed. You can't do your job properly if you don't." Although doing her job properly has always been a dicey proposition for Earlene. On the other hand, she's truly a good human being and has a gift for dropping down-to-earth spiritual insights like bombs in the midst of our conversations. Earlene's what we in the church like to call a mixed blessing.

Her forehead furrows, a sure sign she's peeved. "Do I have to?"

Sometimes I feel more like a preschool teacher than a senior pastor. And I really wish I didn't have an audience for this test of my conflict-management skills. "Yes, you have to."

Earlene's not happy, but at length she nods and turns to leave. "You might try some vinegar for getting that blacking off," she says over her shoulder, delivering a parting shot to show me that I'm not holding all the cards. But I refuse to rise to the bait. I turn my attention back to the two men in front of me.

"Sorry for the interruption. You wanted to talk about some kind of offer, Mr. Corday?"

"A proposition for Church of the Shepherd, really," Arthur Corday says. He's practically dripping sincerity. In some ways, I prefer The Judge's open contempt to the false congeniality oozing from this man.

"What kind of proposition?"

"Arthur represents a local real estate development firm," The Judge interrupts. "They want to make an offer for the church." Clearly the two men have discussed this previously, and The Judge isn't too happy about Mr. Corday's proposition.

"They want to buy the congregation?"

The Judge scowls. "Don't be deliberately obtuse, Miss Blessing. They want to buy the land. Downtown real estate is at a premium." He frowns, and his jowls hang heavily on each side of his face.

"That is an intriguing proposition, Mr. Corday."

"Please, call me Arthur. I was hoping to pique your interest . . . if you find the seven-figure range intriguing."

Arthur Corday's words make me forget about the toner. And breathing. My eyes must be gleaming with avarice, because The Judge says, "Don't get the wrong impression from Miss Blessing, Arthur. The leadership of this church would never consider selling the building."

Unfortunately, The Judge is right. These folks had their chance to flee to the suburbs in the 1970s, and they didn't take it. But I'm excited about the prospect of relocating. The chance to cash in our chips and start over in a suburb like Franklin, where land—and families with young children—are plentiful, fills me with glee. With the kind of money Arthur Corday's offering, along with what's left of the church's once-sizable endowment, we could make a good start toward building our own little Fort God on the edge of someone's cow pasture in Williamson County. Young families would flock to Church of the Shepherd—pun intended. Instead of changing toner cartridges, I could be doing the real work of ministry.

Ring, ring, ring.

The shrill sound of the phone at my elbow almost shoots me out of my chair. I try to ignore it, but I'm genetically incapable of not answering a ringing phone.

"I'm sorry, gentlemen. Excuse me for just a moment." Angelique wouldn't put through a call right now unless it's important.

"Yes?"

"Betsy, I'm sorry to interrupt you, but your mom's on line one. She says it's an emergency."

Even the streetwise Angelique frequently falls prey to my mother's guile. When the good Lord was handing out the gift of manipulation, my mother got in line twice.

"It's okay. I'll take it." Because the one time I don't, it will turn out to be a real emergency. "Gentlemen, excuse me for just one moment."

I punch the button for line one. "Hi, Mom. What's the matter?"

"Betsy, you're never going to believe this."

My mom frequently starts conversations this way. Usually, her story-news-harangue has to do with someone I've never met. I know more about her friends' children's in-laws' sciatica and hospitalization for drug rehab than I ever cared to.

"Believe what, Mom? Are you sick?"

15

"Me? Sick? No, of course not. It's Mabel Grant's stepdaughter's husband. He's walked out on her."

"He walked out on Mabel?"

Sorry, but I can't resist baiting her just a little. I'm due a little recompense for listening to these endless tales that seem to come right off *All My Children.*

"No, of course not. His wife. He walked out on her for another woman. Just left, right out of the blue."

Due to our family history, two-timing husbands who desert their wives hold a particular fascination for my mother. I try to interrupt her, but there's no stopping her in midrecital. So instead I paste a concerned look on my face and hope that The Judge and Arthur will think I'm listening to an account of an actual emergency.

"Can you believe that?" my mom asks.

"These things happen," I say, soothingly, because that's been my job since my dad left home—soothing my mom.

"That doesn't make them right."

Well, I can't argue with that.

"Mom, I'm sorry, but I've got to go. I have some people in my office."

"Oh, of course." Her voice trembles a little, just to let me know what it's costing her to hang up the phone. "But aren't you supposed to be getting ready for your date with David?"

"I will. As soon as I finish up here." Panic. Rapid heart rate. Thanks, Mom. Fortunately, The Judge and Corday have gone back to their private discussion and are ignoring me again for the moment.

16

"Please wear something nice," my mom says. "And don't forget to put on lipstick. Didn't you get a nice new shade when you had that makeover? This might be your last chance."

My mother has been giving me the lipstick admonition since she bought me my first tube at thirteen. With the diligence she's shown over the years to keep me properly painted, she could have solved the third-world debt problem.

"Mom, I'm only thirty. I'll get married when I'm ready," I snap. And then I feel bad, so I say, "I won't forget about the lipstick," as my mea culpa. Although I probably will forget, makeover or no. I'm really bad about remembering stuff like that. "Bye, Mom."

"Bye, dear. I love you."

"Me, too."

I hang up the phone, and my hand pauses for a few extra seconds on the handset. She does love me, in her own warped way, but I'm really tired of serving as her emotional crutch. When I went away to college, I had hoped she'd find a new man and he'd fill her life. No such luck. She just kept on micromanaging me and my sister, Melissa. Only Melissa requires far less micromanaging than I do, since she's like Mary Poppins— practically perfect in every way. Melissa's pregnant with her second child and is currently on bed rest. Even though she spends the day flat on her back, she somehow manages to do legal research for her law firm while knitting a complete layette for the baby.

How can I ever compete with that?

Arthur Corday sees that I'm off the phone and clears his throat. "Reverend Blessing, would you at least take my offer to your administrative committee for their consideration? I'm afraid it's only good for thirty days, so you'll need to act quickly. If the church decides not to sell, we'll need to pursue other options."

Disapproval emanates in waves from The Judge, but at the moment I don't care. Corday's offer is a lifeline to a drowning man (or church, as the case may be), and it wouldn't be fair not to let others in on this decision. At least that's how I justify it to myself. It has nothing to do with how leading a successful relocation might induce the church to call me as the permanent senior pastor. If God's purposes and my professional advancement just happen to dovetail nicely, who am I to argue?

"I will certainly bring it up with the committee as soon as possible, Mr. Corday . . . er . . . Arthur. We're scheduled to meet on Wednesday."

The Judge scowls. "You may bring it up, Miss Blessing, but I will certainly make my feelings on the matter known."

"I'm sure you will, Judge," I half say, half sigh. Glancing over his shoulder, I see the rapidly advancing arms of the clock on my wall. My pulse jumps accordingly. Lucrative offer for the church or no, I'm not missing this date.

I stand up, and the men follow suit. Sometimes you have to use a southern gentleman's innate manners for your own nefarious purposes.

"Arthur," I say, extending my hand for a farewell

shake, "thank you for coming to see me."

His smile is just this side of sincere. "It was my pleasure, Reverend." He holds my hand just a little too long, and when he finally releases it, I resist the urge to wipe it on my pants.

I usher the men out the door, and when they're gone, I grab my purse from the desk drawer. Further battle with the copier will have to wait. Right now I have to get ready for a night out with the man of my dreams.

Chapter 2

Fortunately for me, the policeman who hangs out with a radar gun on Twenty-first Avenue must have business elsewhere today, so I press the accelerator of my trusty Honda Civic a little harder than usual. I don't know why I agreed to a date at 5:30 p.m. on a Monday. Well, the fact that the man of my dreams is a fellow minister who has a building-committee meeting at 7:00 probably had something to do with it. It was either join him for the early-bird special or wait another long, interminable week before I see him again. That's the problem when you and the man of your dreams are both at the disposal of a church 24/7.

I take the turn into my driveway on two wheels, jerk to a halt, and check my watch. Fifteen minutes to go.

On the porch I fumble to get the key in the lock. My apartment is part of an ancient bungalow near Vanderbilt University. The house has been subdivided into enough apartments to qualify it as a rabbit warren, but it has far more soul than the cookie-cutter clusters of new apartments in Bellevue and Franklin, so I cinch my figurative belt a little tighter when I write my outrageous rent check each month.

Inside, my living room is its usual shambles. While I manage to stay fairly organized at church, on the home front, it's a losing cause. Pizza Perfect boxes and old copies of the *Tennessean* are the closest I get to designer home accessories. Honestly, I'm lucky most days if I can find the remote.

I fly around the room, grabbing armfuls of trash and heading for the kitchen. Of course, the garbage can is overflowing, so I shove it all under the sink, close the cabinet doors, and pray I'm not providing sustenance for any visiting rodents. Cleaning accomplished, I dart to the bedroom and fling open my closet door. Somewhere in there must be something suitable, although, if there were, I wouldn't have felt the need to go shopping for what I'm wearing right now.

The phone rings, and I can't afford to ignore it now that I'm the senior pastor. I check caller ID and squeal with delight when I see the international dialing code. It's my best friend in the whole world, LaRonda Mason, calling from South Africa.

"Ronnie! I can't believe it. It's you!"

"None other."

LaRonda's only been gone for three weeks, but it feels like a lifetime. She's working in a school for AIDS orphans in Johannesburg that her church here in Nashville helped to fund. This is the first time she's called, and I'm dying to talk to her and hear about what she's been doing. But talk about timing.

"How is everything?" I ask. I want to focus on her answer, but I can't help glancing at my watch. Ten minutes left, and I'm still covered in toner.

"It's . . . fine. I guess."

From the tone of her voice, it's not fine. LaRonda hoped that moving to South Africa would help her find her own path, not the one predetermined by her father, the founding pastor of Mt. Moriah Church. He expected LaRonda to fill his shoes once he reached retirement age, and she did—until she realized that living her father's dream wasn't making her very happy.

"Okay," I say, abandoning my quest for another outfit. "That was definitely an 'It's not fine' type of 'fine.' Dish, honey."

I can do this. I can be a sympathetic listener to my best friend half a world away and simultaneously prepare for the Biggest Date of My Life. Maybe I'll just work on the toner thing while I've got the receiver pressed to my ear.

"To tell the truth, Betz, I didn't think it would be this difficult."

I swallow my first response. What did she expect? A room at the Hilton? We're talking AIDS-stricken orphans, here. Okay, that's not fair, but I'm still peeved at LaRonda for taking off for South Africa so quickly. We barely even said good-bye.

"What's the problem?" I head for the bathroom where I reach into the cupboard for a facecloth. At the sink I turn on the faucet and then brave a quick peek in the mirror.

"Well," LaRonda says with uncharacteristic hesitancy, "to tell you the truth, I don't think people here like me very much."

"Ugly American syndrome," I say in between swipes with the facecloth. The toner's starting to come off, but I'm getting an unholy glow from all the scrubbing. "Give it time, Ronnie. Let them get to know you."

"Betz?"

Her voice is so quiet, I automatically stop scrubbing.

"Yeah?"

"What if I made the biggest mistake of my life, resigning from the church?"

I toss the cloth into the sink and sit down on the toilet. Ronnie's put her finger on the problem. When it comes to being a woman minister, you're you-know-what-ed if you do and you-know-what-ed if you don't. Somehow, serving a church will never be entirely satisfactory. But, then, neither will not serving one.

"Ronnie, I think you've got to give it time there. See where it all leads. Maybe you'll decide to come home, or maybe things will change and you'll decide to stay. Just take it one day at a time."

I'm proud of myself for being in any way supportive of LaRonda staying in South Africa when all I want is for her to come home as soon as possible. It would make my life so much easier. For instance, she would probably know a better way to get this toner off my face.

LaRonda laughs. "When did you get so wise?"

Tears gather in my eyes. "Since I started hanging out with you."

We're both quiet for a moment. Then she says, "I guess I'd better go. My calling card's almost used up. I didn't even get to ask you about your big plans with David."

"It's okay. He'll be here any minute. I'll e-mail when I can and give you all the gory details."

"Okay."

"Bye."

"Bye."

And as I hear the click of a disconnecting telephone in one ear, I hear the ringing of my doorbell in the other.

My Big Date has arrived.

After years of lonely Saturday nights interspersed with excruciating blind dates, I, Betsy Blessing, am about to be courted by the man of my dreams. And this in spite of having toner stains around my hairline and wearing an outfit LaRonda refers to as Old Faithful—tailored khaki pants and a blue sweater set. The prospect of the evening ahead, even if it's a Mundane Monday instead of a Date Night Saturday, is enough to make a grown woman giggle. Or purr. Or both.

I can't believe we're here at La Paz, where the guacamole is a sacrament escorted to our table by a twenty-something hostess in a tight sweater. Fortunately, I know David well enough to know that he won't give the hostess's figure a second glance. The menu—now that's another story. Until he's dithered sufficiently over his choice of entrée, he won't pay any attention to me. Once he's settled on his choice for dinner, though, he'll focus all the charm and intelligence in those big brown eyes right where they belong—on yours truly.

Let the games begin.

"Your server will be with you in a sec," chirps the hostess as she cuts her eyes at David. She's regarding his clerical collar with interest—not an unusual occurrence, as I've learned since I've been back in Nashville. Now that we've found true love and are officially on our first date, though, I can't laugh it off so easily.

"Mmm," David mumbles as he peruses the list of quesadilla options, oblivious to the hostess's last, lingering look. Even if I wore a clerical collar—and in my denomination, we don't—men would never find it as sexually appealing as women seem to find David's.

Figures.

Rule for Women Ministers No. 2: All of the work, few of the perks.

"What are you having?" David asks, peering over the top of his menu. I scramble to open mine and give it a quick once-over. The truth is, even if this is my favorite restaurant, my stomach is so tied up in knots, I'm not going to be able to eat a bite. A real date with David at a normal restaurant, not just dinner with a friend or him escorting me to a charity function. No, this is garden-variety dating, just the way other couples do, the ones I've been envying all these years. I know David is the one for me, but I'm not in any rush to the altar, despite what my mother likes to refer to as my advancing age. I'm only thirty, and as old-fashioned as it may sound, I want to be courted. Heaven knows I've waited long enough for a little romance.

"I think I'll have the shrimp enchiladas," I say, and David nods sagely, as if I've just translated a tricky bit of the Dead Sea Scrolls from the original Aramaic.

Then he frowns. What does that frown mean? My heart skips a beat.

"Or maybe I'll have the taco salad," I say, dithering. Yuck. I hate that note of uncertainty in my voice. Just because David and I are officially an item does not mean I have to turn into an echo chamber for his opinions and preferences. Not that David would want me to. It's just something women seem to fall prey to in the early stages of a relationship, no matter how liberated they are.

Our waiter appears, and I'm forced to interpret the subtext of my entrée choice on the spot. "The shrimp enchiladas," I say, deciding that it's better to assert my independence. I may be in love, but I remain a complete, worthwhile, and independent person.

"I'll have the steak fajitas," David says without any existential qualms whatsoever and hands the waiter his menu. Then his attention finally, blessedly, turns to me.

When I'm with David, I should carry a voltmeter, because I'm sure the electricity that shoots through me would register at an impressive level. For years I denied my feelings since I didn't think he felt the same way. But recently a miracle occurred, and David and I became an item. I try to ignore the angel chorus singing hallelujahs in my ears and turn my attention to David.

"How was your day?" I ask. It's a question I've asked him countless times, but it has a different ring to it now. A more proprietary tone, since I have the vested interest of a significant other in his response. I'm dying to tell him my big news about Arthur Corday and his seven-figure offer, but I also don't want to spend the evening talking about work, so I decide to wait.

"My day? It was great." He's glancing around the restaurant like a fugitive on the FBI's Most Wanted list. David's not normally a nervous person, so little prickles of apprehension shoot up my spine. What if he's already decided it was a dumb idea to risk our years of friendship with the uncertain promise of a romantic relationship? What if he wants out already? Is the courting over before it's even begun?

"Are you looking for somebody?" I ask.

"What?"

"You seem a little nervous, like you're expecting to see somebody."

"Oh? Really?" He tries to look innocent, but that tell-tale flush creeps up his neck. David's a terrible liar, and everyone knows it. Especially his congregation. His neck is like a giant truth thermometer that can be read at ten paces.

"David? Is something going on?"

The flush overshoots his neck and spreads across his cheeks. He laughs like a bad actor in summer stock.

But he doesn't deny it.

So it's true. He's going to dump me on our first official date. The knots in my stomach would make Houdini blanch. "Listen, David, you know, I've been thinking—"

But before I can summon the words to cut and run before he does, the strangest thing happens. David gets out of his chair, comes around the corner of the table, and drops to one knee beside me.

"Did you lose a contact?" I try to ask, but the knot in my stomach vaults into my throat, and my words come out in a high-pitched squeak more suited to Alvin and the Chipmunks.

"Betsy," he says as he takes my right hand in both of his. All around us the other diners have swiveled their chairs to better view the spectacle at Table 11.

"David? What's going on?"

His hands are sweaty but warm, and I don't think he would publicly humiliate me by announcing to the whole restaurant that I'm too repulsive to date. At least not while he's on his knee. Then one of his hands leaves mine, and he puts it in his pocket. When he draws his hand back out, he's holding a black velvet box.

I'm hyperventilating. I swear I'm hyperventilating.

"Betz, I know it's our first date, but I don't see any point in putting off the inevitable." He smiles that smile I feel right down to my toes every time he trains it on me, and for several enjoyable moments I'm mush.

"The inevitable?" I repeat.

Around us, the other restaurant patrons are murmuring excitedly among themselves. As if in slow

27

motion, David brings the box up to my hand so he can use the fingers wrapped around mine to open the lid.

"Ouch!" I cry when he accidentally catches the skin on the back of my ring finger in the hinge.

"Sorry." He raises my hand to his lips and kisses it, and it's all I can do not to slide off my chair into a puddle on the floor.

"Betsy, I don't need any more time to know you're the one I want to spend the rest of my life with." He turns the box so I can see the contents, and nestled on the velvet is a diamond engagement ring. A badly cut, pear-shaped diamond on a milewide gold band, surrounded by little pink things that look like they came out of a gumball machine.

It's the most hideous ring I've ever seen.

"Betz, will you marry me?"

He looks at me with those big brown eyes, and a hole the size of Cleveland opens up in my midsection.

This can't be happening. All I wanted was a date.

"Betz?"

Does my horror show on my face? I need to smile. I must smile. So I do, but it feels as if my lips are being forced upward with a cattle prod. The ring just sits there in the middle of the velvet box in all its Technicolor glory. David's hand shakes a little. He's been on that knee a long time. The other diners start to murmur. It's not every day you see a preacher in a dog collar proposing at La Paz.

This should be the happiest moment of my life, but the tears that start to fall have nothing to do with joy.

It's what I wanted, eventually, but it bears no resemblance to my hopes for this evening.

"Beggars can't be choosers," I hear my mother's voice whisper in my ear. She said it when Harold Grupnik was the only one who asked me to the prom, and I'd resent her for it still if it hadn't had the death knell of truth behind it. For heaven's sake, I'm getting *David* out of this deal. What does it matter if the details aren't perfect?

I blush and hope David will chalk it up to embarrassment and not shame. I'd much rather he think I'm shy about accepting his proposal in front of all these people than have him realize the depth of my disappointment.

"Compromise, Betsy," my mother's voice adds in my ear. *"You don't have your sister's natural beauty, but your intelligence is very attractive in its own way."*

David leans forward, and now he looks concerned. And there's such love in his eyes that I feel like a complete idiot. What am I doing? This man loves me. That's more important than the most fabulous courtship in the history of courtships. He doesn't need to woo me; he's already got me. As usual, I'm so busy getting in my own way that I can't take what's being offered.

"Of course, David. Of course I'll marry you."

He smiles and relief washes across his features. At that moment I realize that he was actually worried I might turn him down. A wave of warm affection washes over me, and I resolve to put my momentary doubts behind me.

"Kiss her!" a man two tables over calls out, and David grins.

"Why didn't I think of that?" he murmurs as his lips move toward mine. I smother a giggle—or rather, David's lips do—and the restaurant breaks out into applause.

A lot of applause. More than there should be, really.

When David lifts his head from mine, I look over his shoulder to see that the doors to the party room have been thrown open, and wave after wave of familiar faces flow forth. My parishioners. David's parishioners. Friends from divinity school. And my mother. *My mother?* And right behind her, my father. I'm stunned. My parents haven't been in the same room since their divorce fifteen years ago. Even when my sister, Melissa, had her daughter, our parents took turns going to the hospital.

"Mom? Dad?"

"It's an engagement party, honey!" My mom, always a great one for stating the obvious, practically shoves David out of the way so she can pull me out of my chair and hug me. Her hair is even blonder than the last time I saw her. A cashmere sweater and modest pearls give her the air of old money, an image she cultivates without any actual financial backing to support it.

"Are you surprised?" she asks. "I bet I really threw you off track with that phone call this morning."

Surprised? How about stunned? appalled? My dad reaches me a split second after my mom. He's so tan he's almost orange. Tracy, his new wife, must be dousing him with that spray-on stuff again.

"Nobody's ever going to be good enough for you, sunshine, but I guess he'll do," he says and plants a peck on my cheek.

My mom scowls. "Not now, Roger," she snaps.

"Don't you mean 'not ever,' Linda?" he fires back. "You may not like it, but I'm still her father."

And then, over the din, I hear the strident voice of David's mother, Cecilia Swenson. The last time I saw her was at our divinity-school graduation, when she wept like a baby at the sight of David in his cap, gown, and master's of divinity hood. (Thankfully, I wasn't there to witness her histrionics a couple of years later when he got his doctor of ministry degree.)

"Over here, Jeremy. I want a shot of this." She pushes past the well-wishers with her Lee Press-On Nails and a shake of her Farrah Fawcett hair. My folks recede into the crowd, and a flash goes off in my face.

"David, get down on one knee again," Cecilia orders him. "We missed that shot."

A shadow passes over David's face, but he does as he's instructed. I'm too stunned to do anything but passively cooperate. The flash goes off again.

"Now, take her hand. You forgot to put the ring on her finger."

David slips the ring from the box and shoots me an apologetic glance.

"David, what's going on?" I hiss.

"It's a surprise," he whispers. "My mother wants to—"

His explanation is interrupted when Cecilia calls out another set of instructions, and the photographer continues to snap away. I feel like J. Lo at a movie premiere—minus the fashionable clothes, hair, and makeup—when David's mother finally spills the beans.

"Isn't it great, Betsy? How many girls would give their right arm to be featured in *Budget Bride* magazine?" David's mother beams. "Lucky for you that your future mother-in-law is the managing editor."

David's fingers tighten around mine. "Please, Betz?" he says under his breath. "It means so much to her. And the magazine will pay for everything."

My eyes meet his, and with a sinking feeling, I know I'm going to agree. Not because I care that much about making his mother happy, but because I want David to be happy. That's how it is when you love someone. I have David now. I can afford to be noble and gracious.

Also, I'm afraid of what will happen if I say no. I remember when David was engaged before—to Jennifer, the glamorous Cindy Crawford look-alike.

"It's fine," I whisper. "Really. It'll be great."

The lines on David's forehead dissolve into relief. "Thanks," he says. "With all the stuff going on at church to rebuild the sanctuary, and with you trying to be interim and associate at your place, it's the only way we can make this happen on such short notice."

He stops and cups my cheeks with his hands, looking deeply into my eyes just like I used to dream of him doing. "Betz, I don't want to wait any longer than necessary to marry you. To be your husband," he says with a purposefulness that makes my knees weak. Then he zooms in for another kiss. The flash is going off again, but at the moment I don't care. The whole world can be as imperfect as it wants to be as long as David keeps kissing me.

"It came from eBay," Cecilia informs me amid the bustle of my surprise engagement party. The photographer snaps a few closeups of my garish engagement ring. "Such a steal," Cecilia purrs.

Her words douse the faint flicker of hope that I might find a gentle way to suggest to David we exchange the ring for something more, well, tasteful. I can't believe I'm going to spend the next forty-plus years of my life wearing an engagement ring that looks like an Easter basket. I bet the person who sold it to him is still laughing.

"It means a lot to me that he picked it out himself," I say demurely, because it's never too early to build a good bridge of communication with your future mother-in-law, no matter what knockoff of *Modern Bride* she edits.

"Oh." A brief look of consternation flits across her features. "Himself. Well, actually, I had my assistant Veronica do that for him. You know David. He's hopeless when it comes to shopping. Plus, Veronica's been scouring eBay for months for the cheapest ring possible. It's going to be a whole sidebar for the feature story."

I try to ignore the stab of disappointment in my midsection. Probably a lot of guys have help buying an engagement ring for their girlfriends. I just wish David's ring consultant hadn't been a twenty-year-old administrative assistant who thinks pink ice is the height of fashion.

"Please thank Veronica for me," I say to Cecilia. But what I really mean is, "A pox upon her and her unborn children."

Okay, that's probably a bit harsh, but I'm a little too overwhelmed at the moment to be a model of graciousness. I was expecting dinner for two, not a party of forty.

I see nothing of David for the next hour. Well, that's not strictly true. Since he's quite tall, I see his head across the room. I'd hoped to spend a good portion of the evening in his arms. Instead, I spend it in the arms of parishioners from his church—St. Helga's Lutheran—and mine. I had hoped to spend the evening enveloped in the combined scent of David's cologne and shrimp enchiladas. Instead, I'm surrounded by the smell of designer imposter Opium, Cecilia's perfume. She buys it in bulk to save money. The closest I get to shrimp enchiladas are a few tortilla chips with some green tomatillo sauce. By the time I've received everyone's well-wishes, I'm famished, my feet hurt, and my mother and Cecilia, beneath a thin veneer of civility, are vying for control of my nuptials.

"A June wedding will be pushing it," my mom says to Cecilia, "but we can pull it off."

June? Did David and I set a date without my knowing it?

"Look, Mom, this is all fairly sudden—"

"It's April, but I don't think it's hopeless," my mom continued, undaunted. "Betsy should have a little pull when it comes to booking the church."

For the first time since I announced my intention to become a minister, my mother seems pleased with my decision. At long last, my profession has its use.

"Maybe we should all take a deep breath—" I don't get any further this time than I did before.

"Definitely June," Cecilia says. "My copy deadline for the feature article will be July 1, so we'll be cutting it close. But that's the only way to make it into the December issue."

December issue? "Won't a summer wedding look strange in a winter issue of the magazine?"

Cecilia looks at me as if I've sprouted two heads. "Oh no, dear. It will be a Christmas wedding. We already have the theme—Low-Cost Winter Wonderland." She flashes her enormous smile—scary because of the gleaming porcelain veneers on her two front teeth—and laughs. "Isn't that great?"

"Great," I lie through my teeth and look frantically around for David. This is his mother; he can be the one to get us out of this mess. But David's having his ear bent, twisted, and mangled by Isaac Johansen, the resident curmudgeon in his congregation. Isaac doesn't look as if he's going to let up anytime soon.

David's church is in the process of rebuilding their sanctuary after last year's tornado, and Isaac has been making his life miserable with his demands. Across the room of party-goers, our eyes meet, and I instantly feel calmer. Of course he's not going to let his mother hijack our wedding, just as I'm not going to let mine use it as an occasion to dish out payback to my father. After all, we're the bride and groom. We're in charge. Everyone will calm down once the newness of our engagement has worn off.

"Regular trips to Goodwill," Cecilia is advising me when I tune her back in. "Twice a week at least."

"Goodwill?" I echo, confused. My mom's looking a little green around the gills, but the prospect of having her daughter featured in a national magazine clearly outweighs the discomfort she feels over going the budget route.

"Of course," Cecilia says. "You have to be in the right place at the right time. Because somewhere out there right now is a bride who's about to be jilted. She'll want to get rid of the dress. You have to be ready to pounce."

Ready to pounce? Doubtful. Ready to flee into the night? Absolutely.

Chapter 3

Angelique stops me the moment I walk into Church of the Shepherd the next morning, and I can tell she doesn't have good news. Well, at least whatever it is might take my mind off my surprise engagement.

"Booger is asleep in the sanctuary again," she says, standing back because she knows what my reaction's going to be.

As the newly appointed interim senior minister, I'm finding out what that "other duties as assigned" on my job description truly means. Things like running to Kroger for grape juice when we're short for Communion on Sunday morning or ordering parts I can't even pronounce for the HVAC unit.

Booger Jones also comes with the senior-minister territory. He may be homeless, but he's a member of the church, a regular attendee who came down the aisle during the invitation hymn just like everyone else. But Booger using our pews as his personal Motel 6 is an ongoing problem. He refuses to sleep at any of the shelters, preferring to find his way into Church of the Shepherd in the wee hours so he can spend the night in peace. According to the property committee, I'm supposed to find out how he's getting inside, but I haven't been very diligent about it. The whole thing makes me uncomfortable. And to tell the truth, there's something about Booger that brings out my inner Bill O'Reilly. We've done everything we can to bring him back into society, but just when we think he's had a breakthrough, he sabotages himself.

On the plus side, he usually leaves the men's room off the sanctuary cleaner than he found it.

I don't want to deal with Booger this morning, but it's easier to take out my frustration on him than on my brand-new fiancé. I understand why David sprang the surprise engagement party. We're both far too busy to plan a wedding, and I'm totally flattered that he wants to rush me to the altar. Okay, to be honest, I assured him repeatedly that everything was fine, that I didn't mind, I'm delighted that his mother has it so well in hand, et cetera, et cetera. But being reasonable (or a doormat, depending on your point of view) means I'll be traipsing down the aisle in white velvet and faux fur in the middle of June. We both wound up nodding meekly while Cecilia outlined her plan for transforming the sanctuary of Church of the Shepherd into a snow scene via the generous use of packing peanuts.

"Are you sure, Betz?" David asked me last night when he dropped me off at home after the party. "I know it won't be quite what we might have chosen, but neither of us has time right now to plan a wedding. The most important thing is being together. I don't want to wait any longer than necessary."

"Neither do I," I assured him, even though it wasn't completely true. But I've seen enough of those travesties people call weddings to know that the trappings are not the important part.

This morning, however, I'm not feeling at all reasonable or doormatish—again, depending on your point of view.

"I'll roust Booger," I tell Angelique. Shoulders thrown back and ready for battle, I head for the sanctuary.

I find it interesting that a place that feels so holy when it's full of people feels a little scary when it's empty, even in the light of day. I locate Booger immediately. His snores would rival the lower registers of our impressive pipe organ.

"Booger," I say in an irritated tone as I nudge his shoulder with my finger, "you have to wake up."

He snorts and swats at my hand. "Five more minutes, Ma."

In the eight months since I arrived at Church of the Shepherd, I have not had a lot of interaction with Booger. But I've been around him enough to know that he's not dangerous. He's homeless because he's an alcoholic, and even in the short time I've known him, he's shuttled back and forth between rehab and the street several times. Fortunately, he's not a mean drunk; in fact, he looks and acts more like Santa Claus than a street person.

"Booger, you've got to wake up." I poke his shoulder again. "Really."

He snorts, scrubs his face with his hand, and then opens one eye. "Mornin', Preacher."

"Good morning, Booger." Honestly, I really don't have time for this.

"You're a lot prettier to wake up to than Dr. Black." He chuckles as he sits up and stretches his arms over his head. The pungent smell of the streets almost overwhelms me, and I try not to gag.

"I'm happy you noticed the difference," I say with a forced smile. Dr. Black is the recently retired senior minister. It was his abrupt departure that vaulted me from mere associate to the senior position. But I'm only temporary. In a few more months, they'll have found a man to step into the pulpit, and I'll be back to the usual associate-pastor duties: recruiting teachers for children's Sunday school and making sure the supply room is stocked with construction paper and markers. Important duties, true, but not exactly why I got a master of divinity degree.

"Look, Booger, they're putting pressure on me to keep you from sleeping in here." I can't look him in the eye while I lower the boom, so I let my gaze drift to the Tiffany stained-glass window over the chancel. It depicts Jesus as a shepherd, carrying a lost sheep over his shoulder. He doesn't seem to find his burden heavy, but I can't say the same for his followers in this congregation.

"Ah," Booger says, "the property committee isn't brave enough to confront me themselves, so they send you to do their dirty work."

With a sigh, I sink down on the pew next to him. Okay, not exactly next to him, but in his general vicinity. After a few minutes you get used to his smell. "I'm worried about you spending the night here, too, Booger, but not for the same reason as the committee."

He cuts his eyes at me. "And what worries you, Preacher, about a drunk sleeping on your pews?"

I rub my temples with the tips of my fingers. "They're not my pews, Booger. They're all of our pews. And I'm worried you could get blamed for something you didn't do." I look him in the eye. "What if someone breaks in here and steals something? It's happened before."

Booger scrubs his forehead with his meaty paw. "Well, if I was sober, I'd run 'em out of here right quick."

"And if you weren't, you'd never notice. And the next morning the police would be the ones standing over you, not me."

Booger harrumphs, but he knows I'm right.

"I wish it could be different, Booger." I take a deep breath, a little nervous at what I'm about to say. "Are you ready to go back to rehab? We can work on another placement."

I know it's a futile question. For Booger to bottom out would mean something far worse than camping out in the sanctuary.

"Naw, Preacher. I'm not ready to dry out just yet."

"Okay." There's no point in pushing. I've at least learned that much. But I'm also feeling guilty for kicking him out, so I ask, "Do you want some breakfast?"

"I'd appreciate that, Preacher."

And that's how I wind up raiding the refrigerator in the church's industrial-size kitchen. The appliances are practically state of the art—the gift of a now-deceased member—but the kitchen's very rarely used. The occasional wedding reception and quarterly fellowship dinners aren't enough to do it justice. It's representative of Church of the Shepherd as a whole. We have a huge facility that would serve a congregation five times our size. Well, once upon a time we actually were five times our current size.

The walk-in refrigerator contains exactly two open boxes of baking soda to control odor. I have better luck in the freezer, where I find a stash of heat 'n' eat sausage biscuits used by the early-morning men's Bible study. They love eating these things out of sight of their cholesterol-conscious wives.

"How about a few of these?" I ask Booger.

"Sounds good. I'll make the coffee."

Making coffee is Booger's usual Sunday-morning job, at least when he's sober. He's on the doorstep at seven o'clock, waiting for one of the custodians to open the building. Once inside, he fills the two pots—one for decaf, one for regular—and lays out the packets of sugar, sweetener, and creamer. He arranges the cups, makes sure there are enough plastic stirrers, and stacks up a pile of beverage napkins. I wish more of our members were as diligent in their volunteer efforts as Booger. Of course, when he's hung over, the coffee may get switched (which leads to a lot of caffeine teetotalers flying higher than a kite) or he forgets to plug in the pot.

So that's where Angelique finds us—in the kitchen having coffee with our sausage biscuits. I'm relieved to see her because I'm beginning to feel a little awkward with Booger. When I have to interact with him, I mostly try to figure out a way to escape as quickly as possible. Thankfully, Angelique accepts a cup of coffee, turns up her nose at the biscuits, and settles in with us for a time-honored, church-staff tradition—shooting the breeze.

"So," she says, tapping her long nails on the table, "how was your Big Date?"

Clearly it's a mistake to involve your administrative assistant in your personal life, but since Angelique's partly responsible for David seeing me in a new light to begin with, I can't freeze her out now.

"Big Date?" Booger asks, smiling. "Well, well, Preacher. And here I thought we were an item."

I know I'm blushing just like David does. We're like the poster children for obvious embarrassment. Maybe it's something we picked up by osmosis in divinity school.

"It was . . . fine," I say. For whatever reason, David's mother overlooked inviting Angelique to the festivities last night, and I'm dreading telling her what happened because her feelings are going to be hurt.

"The biggest date of your life was fine?" Angelique arches an eyebrow.

"Well, it was . . ."

"Yes?"

"Oh, Angelique—" And I crumple. My disappointment wells up inside me and spills out. "It was awful." I tell her and Booger everything. About how I was looking forward to being romanced. To being a real girlfriend for once. I tell them about David dropping to one knee. About the horrible engagement ring and his mother and the nightmare budget wedding looming in my future.

"Where is it?" Angelique demands to see the ring, her indignation on my behalf clearly cloaking any disappointment she might feel about being left out. God bless her. Guiltily I fish the horrible ring out of my pocket. I just couldn't bear to put it on my finger this morning.

"Here it is." I hand it to her as if it's a dead rat.

Angelique takes the ring, pinches it between her thumb and forefinger, and holds it up to the light.

Booger's jaw drops. "Preacher, that's the ugliest thing I've ever seen."

You know your ring is bad when a man whose idea of fashion is using trash bags for outerwear thinks it's awful.

"What was he thinking?" Angelique asks, appalled.

I sigh. "He wasn't thinking anything. His mother's assistant bought it on eBay."

"Sight unseen?"

Despite the tears that threaten, I have to chuckle at that. "I wish. No, there's no excuse for this except bad taste."

"What does David think?" Angelique asks.

"He must think it's fine. He gave it to me, didn't he?"

Angelique eyes me with her customary shrewdness, a surprisingly hip expression given her pierced nose and the diamond winking back at me. "It's more than how hideous the ring is, though, isn't it, Betsy? Something else is bothering you."

Who is she? Dr. Phil? Of course Angelique's right, but I don't want to admit it because my feelings are so petty. And they're also really strong.

"Okay, honey," Angelique purrs. "Out with it."

I sigh. "It's just—"

"Just what?"

"It's just that I remember the ring David gave his first fiancée."

"His first fiancée?" Booger snorts. "How many has he had, Preacher?"

I swallow. "Just the one—and me," I add lamely.

"What did *her* ring look like?" Angelique asks. She inflects the feminine pronoun with enough disdain to soothe my vanity.

"One carat, square-cut diamond with four baguettes on each side," I say. "From Tiffany's."

Angelique and I observe a moment of ritual silence at the mere thought of such a ring.

"This Tiffany," Booger asks, "is that his old fiancée?"

Angelique and I smile. "Tiffany's is a jewelry store in New York. His fiancée's name is—" I stop myself. "I mean *was*. His fiancée's name was Jennifer."

Booger wipes his mouth with the back of his hand. "So what you're saying is that he bought this other girl a better ring."

"Yeah," I acknowledge glumly. "That's what I'm saying." And I also recognize how much it's bothered me since the moment David opened that black velvet box—not the trademark Tiffany blue one with the white ribbon that Jennifer received, but the black velvet one with the nightmare Easter-basket ring.

If my ring is low budget, what does that make me?

"And his mother's in charge of the wedding?" Angelique probes further. "How did that happen?"

"Well, David doesn't want to wait. And neither of us has time right now to plan a wedding."

Booger chuckles. "So, Preacher, you get to boss everybody else around at their weddings, but you can't

45

be in charge of your own?"

Angelique glances at her watch and winces. "Betsy, I forgot. You've got a meeting in five minutes."

"Meeting? What meeting?"

"The Judge wanted to see you again before the administrative-committee meeting tomorrow night."

My stomach, replete with highly processed carbs and saturated fat, drops like a stone. The Judge is clearly prepared to do what it takes to prevent the church from even considering Arthur Corday's offer.

I wipe any stray crumbs from my mouth and tuck the napkin in my empty coffee cup. "Well, if The Judge is coming, I'd better get there first before he starts alphabetizing my files for me."

Booger takes my cup from me and then accepts Angelique's with an outstretched hand. "Ladies, this is certainly the best breakfast scenery I've enjoyed in a while."

We laugh, flattered, because Booger can be quite charming when he puts his mind to it. "Have a good day, Booger," I say. "Be careful out there."

"Always," he says with a wry smile. I return his qualified smile with one of my own. Because the truth is that Booger's days on the streets are, in fact, dangerous. And once he leaves for the day, I'll try not to think about him too much. It's just too hard. If nothing else, sparring with The Judge ought to take my mind off Booger.

With a sigh I slip on my new engagement ring and head for my office. Somehow, getting everything I want isn't turning out quite as I expected.

Chapter 4

I am frequently reminded that voice mail is one of God's good gifts. I make it to my office before The Judge does, so I take a moment to listen to my messages. My mother called from the airport to say one last good-bye. She and my father even managed to share a cab from the hotel since they both had early flights, although from there they went to their separate ends of the country. Mom lives in California now, and Dad and Tracy live in Florida, so a continent between them is just about right.

David called too.

"Just needed to hear your voice, even if it's prerecorded," he says. "I've got another meeting with the fire marshal today."

Poor David. He's worked so hard to keep the rebuilding of the sanctuary at St. Helga's on schedule, and I know he's exhausted. But if this meeting goes well today and the fire marshal signs off on the final inspection, the end of David's agony could be in sight.

"Besides," the last part of David's message says, "I wanted to call you for the first time officially as your fiancé."

The last message is from David's mother.

"Betsy? It's Cecilia. Listen, we need you to meet us at the discount bridal salon this afternoon for a photo shoot. Two o'clock. And don't worry about your hair and makeup. We'll take care of that."

About the last thing I want to do today is dress up in a puffy white dress that makes me look like a deranged tooth fairy wrapped in polyester masquerading as satin while Cecilia's photographer, Jeremy, documents my humiliation. But I also don't have a phone number for Cecilia, so I can't call and cancel. I grit my teeth and take a deep breath, an interesting exercise because it's hard to draw in a lot of oxygen when I have my jaw clamped like a Rottweiler with a mouthful of fresh bacon. I just have to keep reminding myself to rise above it all, that David and I are ceding the wedding plans to his mother so we can be married all the sooner.

"The end justifies the means," I mutter, easing the tension in my jaw ever so slightly. Unfortunately, my muttering is audible to The Judge, who, when I look up, is standing in the doorway of my office. I, of course, realize five seconds too late that he's there.

"Is that your ministerial slogan, Miss Blessing? Somehow I'm not surprised to hear it."

In his seersucker suit and white buckskins, he reminds me of Boss Hogg. The Judge retired from the bench last year, but he has yet to make the adjustment successfully. Most days he starts out by drinking coffee with his courthouse cronies down at the Riverfront Café. Then he wanders over to Church of the Shepherd for his daily inspection of the staff and premises. Angelique is brilliant with him. She doesn't mind talking to him for hours on end, and somehow she still gets the newsletter out by Tuesday and the bulletin printed by Friday. Once she even finagled The Judge into helping her fold the stewardship letters for the annual pledge campaign.

I, on the other hand, have never figured out how to handle the man. For the most part, I've found ignoring him to be an effective strategy. When that doesn't work, inward fuming seems to do the trick. *My* inward fuming, of course, not his. The Judge will never have an ulcer because he never holds anything inside. He pretty much expresses every thought or feeling that passes through his head.

"Ministerial slogan? I wasn't aware I was supposed to have one." Although, as slogans go, "The ends justify the means" would sum up a lot of church life. I don't have a slogan, but I did have to come up with an image for ministry in divinity school. While others got really creative (Minister as Ritz cracker—goes great with anything) or intellectual (Minister as Woody Allen—a participant-observer in church life), mine was more practical. If I recall correctly, it was Minister as Baby-sitter. And I meant it in a good way. I had some deep theological explanation of how God entrusts a minister with the care of his children, just as parents entrust a baby-sitter with the care of their children. I thought it was a brilliant analogy. My professor just asked if I had any interest in working in the nursery at his church on Sunday, because they were in need of some additional staff.

Deep sigh.

"How are you today, Judge?" I smile my brightest, most congenial smile in hopes of putting him in a more receptive mood. He's here to register his objection to Arthur Corday's proposition—again—and I need to muster all the goodwill and patience I can.

"I've been better, Miss Blessing. I've been better."

"Sorry to hear that."

"Well, you're in a position to do something about it." He moves into my office and settles his girth into one of the chairs on the opposite side of my desk. I can tell from the way he wiggles backward to find a comfortable position that he's planning to be there awhile.

"I have to do what I think is best for Church of the Shepherd," I say, "and I'd be remiss in not taking Mr. Corday's offer to the committee."

"We don't need the committee's input to know that this is the wrong thing to do."

As in any conflicted situation, my pulse picks up its pace until I can hear it thrumming in my ears. Panic forms a considerable ball in my stomach. It's an automatic reaction born from my innate need to please whatever authority figure happens to be in my vicinity. Over the past few weeks since I was named the interim senior minister, I've made some strides taming this automatic response, but I haven't conquered it yet.

"I think you know I disagree with that," I say. "This is an amazing opportunity for this church. One that should be fully explored."

The Judge scowls. "An amazing opportunity? For what? To close Church of the Shepherd?"

"We wouldn't be closing. We'd be relocating. That's a very different thing."

"To you, perhaps. But to those of us who built this church"—he pauses for dramatic effect—"it would be the death knell."

Now, I'm not completely cold-hearted. I lay awake staring at the ceiling for a long time last night, wondering and praying about Arthur Corday's offer—mostly to take my mind off of David's proposal and my imminent low-rent nuptials. I know the sale of the building would be traumatic for some of the older members, but I'm also enough of a pragmatist to know you can't have a church with no members. And if nothing changes, that's exactly what will happen. Deaths outnumber births in this congregation a hundred to one, and if we do nothing, the church will eventually close one way or another. At least this way something new will be born in the midst of loss.

"It's not your job, Miss Blessing, to make decisions about the future of this church. You are the interim minister. By definition that means you won't be in charge for the long haul. Don't overstep your bounds."

Okay, now he's making me mad. And that certainly helps with the whole ball-of-panic-in-the-stomach thing. A shot of adrenaline gives me an extra measure of courage.

"I'm doing what I think any good minister would do, Judge, interim or not."

He bristles, and a faint tinge of pink washes across his cheeks. He's not used to being thwarted, particularly by uppity young females.

"Very well. You can bring it to the committee, but I

51

can assure you it will go no further. No one's interested in moving to the suburbs."

"I am."

"Let me amend my statement. No one who matters."

That's about as much plain speaking as a clergy gal can take on any given day. I stand up and move around the corner of my desk. The Judge's upbringing dictates that he get up from his chair as well, although it takes a moment to lever himself to a standing position. I move toward the door, and he follows.

"This will be over by tomorrow evening," he assures me.

"Maybe. Maybe not. We'll hear what the others have to say." I wish the meeting were tonight, because I know The Judge will spend the next thirty-six hours lobbying the other members of the committee to come around to his way of thinking. I, on the other hand, will spend the next thirty-six hours letting my future mother-in-law, who has all the taste of Tammy Faye Bakker, plan my wedding.

"I'll see you tomorrow evening, Judge," I say as he shakes my hand.

"Indeed you will, Miss Blessing. Indeed you will."

Just when I thought my inaugural battles at Church of the Shepherd had been fought, I find out they were only preliminary skirmishes. The real war is still to come.

Dearly Beloved Discount Bridal occupies the better part of a discount strip mall thirty minutes up Interstate

65 in Hendersonville. The other retail establishments include a housewares outlet and a confectionary that specializes in irregular candy. I'm pretty tempted to stop in for some candy—irregular or not—for a blood-sugar boost, but there's no time. Cecilia awaits.

"I thought you wanted me to look for a dress at Goodwill," I say as she propels me toward the dressing area in the back of the store. She was pacing back and forth in front of the entrance when I drove up.

"Oh, we're not actually going to buy a dress here. We just need some shots for the photo spread. Different styles, different ways to save money on the gown."

"How about I just wear my clerical robe? That would save a bundle."

Cecilia is not amused. She purses her lips just like my mom does, and I know it's time to dial it back a notch. What is it with mothers and the lip pursing?

One of the great spiritual teachings of the Christian faith is the concept of surrender. Okay, maybe it's not getting much play in the American church today, but trust me, it's there in the Christian tradition. I decide to practice it for the next hour. And that's how I find myself standing in front of a three-way mirror wearing what can only be described as a dress suitable for Scarlett O'Hara on acid. The antebellum hoops alone encompass most of the metro Nashville area, and the lace must have employed scores of third-world factory workers. I mean, I've heard that dresses like this exist, but I've never actually seen, much less worn, one.

"I can't breathe," I gasp as Cecilia cinches me as tight

as Mammy ever pulled Scarlett's corset. The only nice thing I can say about this dress is that the boned bodice gives me cleavage I've only dreamed of. Too bad David's not here to see it. It's the one area where I might be able to outshine the legendary Jennifer who was, to put it politely, a bit flat-chested.

"Excellent," Cecilia says as she plops an enormous brimmed hat on my head. Truly, I look like Scarlett on her way to the picnic at Twelve Oaks. All I need is a vase to throw at Rhett Butler, and I'm in business.

Jeremy's setting up lights and screens and all sorts of other photographer-like equipment.

"What about my hair and makeup?" I ask. "Shouldn't we do that before I put the dresses on?"

"Oh, that." Cecilia waves a dismissive hand. "Had to cut that from the budget." She walks over to me and pinches both my cheeks, hard.

"Ouch!"

"Voilà! Instant color."

Instant bruising, more like it.

"Okay, I'm ready." Jeremy thrusts a hideous bouquet of silk flowers into my hands. The thing was clearly designed for a bride in an "interesting condition," as they used to say, because it could easily disguise a pregnancy at nine-and-a-half months. With the dress and the bouquet, I'm now roughly the size of a float in the Macy's Thanksgiving Day Parade.

"Cecilia? Are you sure about this?"

For the first time I notice that the sales staff of Dearly Beloved are crowded around the dressing area like spectators at a bullfight. Like I need an audience for this humiliation.

"Tilt your head," Jeremy instructs me, and then there's an explosion of light that blinds me. "Great, great," he coos as he continues to set off nuclear explosions a few feet in front of me.

"Wait, wait." I shield my eyes with my hands. "I can't see."

"That's okay, dear," Cecilia reassures me. "You don't need to see."

And maybe she has a point, because if I'm blinded, I can pretend I don't notice how extremely hideous I look.

Two hours later my humiliation is complete. In addition to Scarlett O'Hara, I've been incarnated as a low-rent Laura Ashley poster child—complete with large pink cabbage roses on the sailor-collared gown—and Little Bo Peep. At least they didn't make me hold a shepherdess's staff. The only bright spot in this experience is that I won't actually be wearing any of these dresses at my wedding. The downside is that all of America will witness my humiliation in the pages of *Budget Bride* magazine.

By the time we're ready to leave, the manager of Dearly Beloved Discount Bridal has finished fawning over Cecilia. She's so excited to get the free advertising that she doesn't care when we don't buy anything.

"Cecilia, are you sure my lack of makeup won't be a problem?" As photo shoots go, it wasn't quite what I was expecting. I was hoping to have at least a fighting chance of looking pretty.

"We'll Photoshop whatever we need to," she says.

"Okay," I agree, but I'm less than confident. "Well, I guess I'd better get back to work."

"Oh no. Not yet. We have to pick out your housewares."

"Housewares?"

"Yes. China. Stoneware. Flatware. You know, housewares."

"Look, Cecilia, I really need to get back and get started on my sermon for Sunday. I don't have time to go to the mall and register right now."

"Oh, we're not going to the mall, Betsy."

And at that moment I realize we're standing in front of the entrance to Chintz & China, the discount housewares store next to Dearly Beloved Discount Bridal.

"Here?" This store is more commonly referred to as "Chintzy China" because only desperate bargain shoppers could overlook the mammoth chips and dings in their merchandise.

"Yes. I've got the most brilliant idea for saving money. Mismatched china."

"Mismatched china?"

"It will be fabulous. You'll see," she says and grabs my wrist, towing me into the store.

I'll be the first to admit that I have no inner Martha Stewart, but I'd always pictured browsing the displays at Dillard's someday with my fiancé, building a solid foundation for our future by selecting just the right Wedgwood or Noritake.

Well, I have to admit that in my fantasies my mother was standing beside us and giving her opinion. Because I've known from the playpen that she would want to have input on something as important as the china and silver I would start my married life with. When Melissa married, she and Mom spent a month dithering between two flatware patterns. Given my history with my mom, I always figured it would take us closer to six months to come to an agreement.

"Cecilia, I can't do this without my mom," I say. "She'd be so disappointed."

Cecilia glances at her watch and purses her lips again. "I'm sorry, Betsy, but there's just not time. I told your mother she'd need to change her flight if she wanted to be here for this." She turns those fierce brown eyes on me. "I suppose I could call David and tell him how uncooperative you're being."

"Okay, okay." None of this is worth bothering David about, not when he's so stressed about the rebuilding at his church. I'll just register here today for purposes of Cecilia's photo shoot and then unregister tomorrow. I cross my arms in front of my chest in at least a small display of resistance. "But I'm going to do the real registry with David at Dillard's. This is just for the magazine."

"Of course it is," Cecilia says, all smiles now that I've capitulated. "It's like a big game of Let's Pretend."

Ha! The only thing I want to pretend is that the past twenty-four hours never happened.

"Come on, then," Cecilia says, and trailed by Jeremy and his camera equipment, we begin our assault on the unsuspecting housewares.

Chapter 5

I return from Hendersonville later in the afternoon with the trunk of my aging Honda Civic stuffed with what could only politely be called china thirds. Somehow we went from registering for purposes of the photo shoot to my actually purchasing the monstrous collection of housewares I'm now toting back to Nashville. No two plates, bowls, or cups actually match, and while that Shabby Chic woman could probably have put together a collection that could grace the cover of *House Beautiful*, my efforts look more appropriate for the *Refugee Monthly*. To add insult to injury, Cecilia finagled me into charging this travesty of good taste on my credit card.

"We'll reimburse you," she chirped as I handed over my plastic to the salesgirl. "Of course, really, it's very little to pay considering all the fabulous things the magazine will be footing the bill for. But we definitely need shots of your stuff laid out on an actual dining table."

Somehow six hundred dollars of unwanted place settings doesn't seem minor to me. It seems more like a goodly portion of my next rent payment. But I relented when she made noises about calling David to see if she could put it on his credit card instead. He has enough to worry about with the fire marshal today.

I glance at my watch. Actually, David should be done with his meeting by now, so I call him as I take I-65 toward downtown. I was due back in the office fifteen minutes ago to meet with the planning committee for the ladies auxiliary. They're preparing for the annual mother-daughter banquet next month. The fact that none of their daughters still attend Church of the Shepherd never dampens their enthusiasm for the event. I just hope they won't want to do an encore of last year's so-called fashion show. I've seen the pictures, and bare midriffs with faux bellybutton rings for the senior set should not be required viewing for anyone. Particularly when their stomachs are full of institutional chicken divan.

"St. Helga's. This is David."

Corny as it is to say, just the sound of David's voice makes the world seem a little brighter. "All alone again, huh?" I ask.

David's administrative assistant is home sick more often than she is at work. Although, to be brutally honest, I think her sickness has more to do with excessive consumption of adult beverages than her usual complaint of a sinus infection.

"Yep. I'm on phone patrol. What's up?" I can hear the tension in his voice, and suddenly my need to tattle on Cecilia plummets. He really is stressed over this whole rebuilding thing.

"Just wanted to hear your voice too," I prevaricate. "Rough day?"

"The fire marshal is the son of Satan."

Now David and I both know he doesn't mean that literally, so don't take it that way. But if you've ever had dealings with the fire marshal's office, you get the metaphor. Fire marshals are like mothers-in-law. They're intent on poking and prodding into all the hidden corners of your building—or your life. Purely for your own good, of course.

"He didn't approve the plans? I thought the architect swore they would pass."

"Oh, the new plans passed okay. We have fire doors for our fire doors and sixty-two possible exits from every pew in the new sanctuary. No, he decided to take a stroll through the rest of the building and see what caught his fancy."

"Shoot."

"I considered that an option, but I'm not ready to start a prison ministry yet."

"Very funny. What did he find?"

"He took issue with the stove hood in the kitchen."

"You're kidding."

"Nope."

"But the kitchen's not in the part of the building that was destroyed. What does that have to do with the sanctuary?"

"It has to do with him signing the papers so we can worship in it."

"Well, how long will it take to replace the hood?" It couldn't be that complicated.

"We've got to come up with sixty thousand dollars for a new hood because it's got to be vented up through the entire building. It wasn't done right when they first built St. Helga's, so now we're talking significant structural work."

I'm silent because I have no idea what to say. Even with the insurance settlement, David's church has been pushed to the brink of insolvency during this rebuilding process. Some members couldn't stand the pain of the loss, so left. Others couldn't take the financial pain that rebuilding would inflict on their bank accounts, so they left too. The rest of the congregation did their best, but without any resident deep pockets, St. Helga's is tapped out.

"Betz, how in the world am I going to stand up in front of these people and tell them we have to come up with that kind of money?"

His desperate tone scares me because I've never heard David sound defeated before. Tired, yes. Frustrated, sure. But not like he's lost all hope. I'm suddenly very glad I gave in to Cecilia and kept David out of the dress-and-china mess. In the grand scheme of things, it really isn't that important.

"What are you going to do?" I ask.

"I have no idea."

And I don't have any idea either. This isn't a problem that can be fixed with a bake sale or a spaghetti supper.

"Have you told the building committee yet?"

"Isaac was here when the fire marshal dropped the bomb."

"Great." Isaac Johansen has been against rebuilding St. Helga's from the beginning. At least, he's been against rebuilding unless they can afford to pay for everything up-front. "Thou shalt not go into debt" is Isaac's eleventh commandment. That must be what he was bothering David about at the engagement party last night.

"But you've already scheduled the dedication," I say. "Why didn't the fire marshal say anything about this before?"

"The fire marshal is like God. All is mystery until he's good and ready to reveal something."

Oh yeah. That's a better analogy than my mother-in-law one. "Can I do anything?"

David sighs. "No. I was going to see if you wanted to go to dinner tonight, but now . . ."

"It's okay," I reassure him, despite the sting of disappointment. I hardly saw him during all the hoopla last night. Come to think of it, we still haven't had our official first date. "We'll do it another time."

"Thanks, Betz. I appreciate your being so understanding."

I twist my tacky engagement ring around my finger while at least maintaining contact with the steering wheel. "Hey, what are fiancées for?"

And though I may sound carefree, a traitorous little voice is whispering in my ear like one of those devils who sits on the shoulder of a cartoon character, saying, "He would never have cancelled a date with Jennifer just because of a crisis at church." I have no way of knowing whether that's true, but my insecurities have never needed truth to provide fodder for my imagination. Because I can remember many dates Jennifer broke with David (since he usually wound up at my apartment wanting me to nurse his wounded pride), but I can't remember any time he ever put her off when they'd made plans.

Stop it, Betsy, I admonish myself. *You're the one with the ring on your finger. A tacky, eBay-purchased travesty of a ring, but a ring nonetheless. And a fiancé who needs you to be supportive and understanding, not racked with insecurities.*

"We'll meet up soon," David says.

"Sure." What can I do but be agreeable? I swallow all the complaints I was planning to spill about his mother. "Let me know if I can help."

"I will. We'll go out Friday at the latest, Betz. I promise."

"Sure. Okay. Well, I'll talk to you later, I guess."

"Okay. Bye."

And I hear the click that signals he's hung up. I close my cell phone, drop it in my purse, and put both hands back on the wheel. Unfortunately, the only driver's seat I'm in right now is the one of a beat-up, ten-year-old Honda loaded down with a cache of mismatched china.

The ladies are waiting for me in my office when I roll into Church of the Shepherd a good thirty minutes behind schedule. Edna Tompkins, president of the ladies auxiliary, has ensconced herself in the most comfortable chair. She's wearing a sling due to an injured shoulder, but it doesn't seem to be slowing her down a bit. (I'm not sure, honestly, if she still needs the sling for medical reasons or if she continues to wear it to disarm her opponents, so to speak.) Her two cronies, Bernice Kenton and Margaret Devereaux, perch nearby on the two straight-back chairs.

The irony of the existence of the ladies auxiliary never ceases to amaze me. Once upon a time, when the men used to run Church of the Shepherd, the ladies formed this group so they could have some control over their butter-and-egg money, as they called it. They gave to missions, both local and global, and ran their own meetings since they weren't allowed to participate in the "real" church meetings or serve in any leadership roles. Now, though, as church membership has declined, the men have ceded most of the work and a good portion of the leadership to the women. There's really no need for the ladies auxiliary anymore, but I'm not going to be the one to tell these ladies. I value my life too much.

I've only been at this church since last August, but already Edna Tompkins and I have a history. A few weeks ago, though, she and I came to terms. I'm helping her get admitted to Vanderbilt Divinity School so she can, at long last, pursue her thwarted call to ministry. In return, Edna has decided to be my new best friend. Frankly, it was easier when Edna was my sworn enemy. For the past several weeks, she's spent more time in my office than The Judge. Now that Edna's true vocation has been unleashed, she's like an F5 tornado with no eye, and I'm like Dorothy caught up in her mighty force.

"There you are, Reverend Blessing." Edna's come a long way in a short time in her acceptance of me as a woman minister, but she's not all the way there yet. I can tell this by the way she's pursing her lips. If a male minister runs late, most folks assume he's out winning souls to Christ or helping the poor or something. If a woman minister is late, folks think she had a fashion emergency or was sidetracked by some shiny bauble. (Well, okay, there may be the tiniest bit of truth to the shiny bauble thing . . . but I digress.)

"Sorry," I mumble breathlessly as I stow my purse in one of my desk drawers and sink into my chair. "Bit of a wedding crisis."

Edna looks as if she's annoyed, but she's trying to hide it. "Oh yes. Well, I suppose it will be difficult to plan your wedding while serving as our pastor." I can tell that she's dying to say something else, but, bravo for her, she keeps her tongue in check—for the moment.

"So how can I help you ladies with your plans?"

Bernice is Church of the Shepherd's resident socialite as well as the secretary for the administrative committee. She also has an unfortunate addiction to plastic surgery. She always looks surprised, as if her mother pulled her pigtails too tight. Margaret Devereaux has pretensions to social greatness but has never cracked the upper echelons of Nashville society. Every once in a while she visits Our Lady of the Mink in Belle Meade, a high-society church where the elite meet to worship, but sooner or later, she winds up back here at Church of the Shepherd.

"We have the most marvelous idea for the program for the mother-daughter banquet," Edna enthuses. "And we think you'll find it especially timely."

"Me?" Uh-oh. That sort of remark is never a good omen.

"Oh yes," Margaret says, nodding her sleek blond helmet of hair in agreement. Margaret, who has to be at least seventy years old, has the hair of someone forty years younger. "We're going to have a bridal theme—Weddings of Yesteryear. We're all going to model our wedding dresses. And you'll be the *pièce de résistance,* Betsy, when you come out as the final model in *your* wedding dress."

"Well, that's certainly an unusual idea," I say, stalling for time. I don't want to be anybody's *pièce de* anything, especially in a dress that's likely to come from Goodwill.

"Our daughters love the idea," Bernice adds. And I'm sure they do. Despite the fact that she's approaching forty, Claire Kenton Morgan has the hips of a prepubescent girl. And Elizabeth Devereaux Mitchell wore Vera Wang when she married. At least, that's what church legend says. There are also rumors that her figure was EDA—eating-disorder assisted.

I'd really like to ask if they've thought about the feelings of the women who can't fit into their wedding dresses, but once that question passes my lips, I'll be Officially Involved in the planning process. And I have enough to do without sinking into the quagmire that is the annual mother-daughter banquet.

Plus, if I end up modeling my wedding dress, my mother will want to come back to town for the festivities. In fact, she'll probably want to model her own wedding dress. She, of course, is one of those women who can still wear hers and look cute as a bug, as we say in the South. She's still bewildered about why my father left her when her girlish figure hasn't. She prides herself on the fact that she never let herself go. I, on the other hand, let myself go at approximately age six.

"So we have your blessing, Reverend?" Edna asks. It's a very strange sensation when a woman who's been your nemesis is suddenly looking to you for approval. Like looking into a fun-house mirror, knowing it's your new reality.

"Sure . . ." I say, because I'm not ready to die in this ditch. As a minister, I have to pick my battles, and this is not one worth fighting. Except for one teensy caveat. "Although I'd prefer not to model. I'm sure you'll have plenty of lovely ladies without my participation."

Hmm. That came out a bit self-aggrandizing, which I didn't intend.

"Oh, but we can't do it without you," Edna says. "That's the whole point."

Now I'm pretty sure no male minister has ever modeled his wedding tuxedo in a church fashion show, but I guess that's yet another difference between male and female clergy. No matter how many funerals we perform or sermons we preach, we lady preachers will always be judged like we're candidates for *Glamour* magazine's fashion "Dos and Don'ts."

"Really, Edna, I think it would be best for me to sit this one out. I don't even have a dress yet, and the banquet's just a few weeks away."

"I'm sure you can come up with something by then," Edna replies with the blithe indifference of someone who refuses to accept no for an answer. The other ladies nod in agreement.

"So it's settled," Margaret says and stands up, all the better to show off her Chanel suit. At least, I assume it's Chanel because almost everything she wears is.

"But—"

Like the card-carrying members of the ladies auxiliary that they are, these three know how to get when the getting is good.

"Good day, Reverend," Edna calls over her injured shoulder as they hightail it out of my office.

"But . . . but . . ." I'm still sputtering even though I know I've been played by three ladies with more than two hundred years of combined experience manipulating the pastor.

Great. I think about the dresses I've worn so far today. The deranged Scarlett O'Hara. The sofa-upholstery cabbage roses. The shepherdess. I wonder which of them would show to best advantage beside Vera Wang. Although apparently I'm not even going to be allowed the dignity of a second-rate dress from Dearly Beloved Discount Bridal. With a sigh I pull my purse back out of the desk drawer and head through my office door.

"Where are you going?" Angelique asks when I walk by her desk. "Didn't you vow to get your sermon finished earlier in the week this time?"

"I will, I will. First I have to go to Goodwill."

"Do you have a donation to drop off?"

I snort. "Not exactly. More like a wedding dress to acquire."

"You're kidding, right?"

Sadly, I'm not. My only comfort is the thought that any dress I find in a thrift store is sure to match my engagement ring perfectly.

Chapter 6

The administrative committee of Church of the Shepherd holds most of the power in the congregation. They're authorized to make decisions between the quarterly meetings of the church's official board, and they basically set the agenda that the board rubber-stamps. So preparing for an administrative-committee meeting is akin to girding one's loins for battle. Even though I may be armed with the sword of truth and the breastplate of a seminary degree, these folks are seasoned church warriors. Their battle scars are just cleverly concealed by their deceptively pleasant demeanors.

The Judge serves on the committee in his capacity as chair of the elders, the spiritual leaders of the church, and, as you know, he's no fan of Arthur Corday's offer. Edna Tompkins has a spot on the committee since she's president of the ladies auxiliary. Since she's my new Best Friend Forever, I think I can count on her support.

That leaves four others. First, there's Peyton Driscoll,

the chairman of the congregation. He's a retired attorney, a devoted golfer, and a longtime crony of The Judge, so I think we know where he's going to land on this issue.

Mac McHenry is chair of the deacons, the service arm of the church. He's an aging hippie with a long gray ponytail, an organic farm, and a passion for building Habitat for Humanity houses. Since he usually sides with the poor and oppressed, I'm not sure where he'll come down on this issue.

Two more complete the committee. There's the aptly named treasurer, Ralph Pennybacker, and the secretary, Bernice Kenton of the surgically sculpted face. I have no idea what the two of them will think of the idea of selling the property. So Mac, Ralph, and Bernice are the people I will have to persuade if I want to accomplish the daunting task of moving the church to the suburbs.

Now, at this point I have to confess something. This is my first administrative-committee meeting since I was named interim senior minister. Of course, my luck being what it is, I don't get the luxury of a warmup meeting where we tackle something easy like, say, world peace. No, my first shot at leading the administrative committee has to center on persuading people to pull up stakes and move.

In divinity school my Practice of Ministry professor always admonished us not to go into any church meeting without already knowing what the outcome would be. Of course, the fact that this professor never actually pastored a church always made me suspicious of his counsel. What's the old saying? "Those who can't do, teach."

So in the absence of adequate preparation for this meeting due to frantic but unproductive wedding-dress shopping at Goodwill and similar thrift stores, I make sure I'm the first to arrive in the boardroom. At least I can take the chair at the head of the table, a strategic move not to be underestimated. I've learned through hard experience that she who controls the head of the table controls the course of the meeting.

The Judge arrives hard on my heels and scowls when he sees that I've claimed the prime spot. He greets me with a firm handshake that leaves my fingers semicrippled and then takes the chair to my right. One by one the rest of the board members file in—Edna, Bernice, Peyton in a golf shirt and visor, and Mac in paint-stained jeans. Ralph is the last to arrive. He mumbles an apology and opens a huge file containing the church's financial statements. He's famous for bringing that huge accordion file to every meeting. If you want to know how each and every cent has been spent at Church of the Shepherd in the past twenty years, Ralph's your man. Ralph is also the only other person in the room besides me who is under sixty.

We begin the meeting with a prayer—by me, naturally, because why would a layperson pray when you have a perfectly good preacher you're paying to do it for you? Then Peyton begins to move through the items on the agenda, approving the minutes of the last meeting—Bernice is asked to correct the spelling of *harassment*—and then yielding the floor to Ralph to give his incredibly detailed financial report.

"As you can see," Ralph says, "the lack of a permanent senior minister is having an effect on the offering. No disrespect intended, Reverend Blessing."

He delivers this news with Eeyore-like relish, because he still hasn't forgiven me for not going to his company Christmas party with him. One of the great blessings of having David for a fiancé will be that Ralph's mother will have to quit trying to set me up with Ralph. I twist my unsightly engagement ring around my finger, grateful at least for its power to ward off matchmakers.

"None taken," I assure him, but I wish he'd found another way to put it. "Church offerings always drop whenever a congregation is between ministers," I say, but even though everyone sitting at this table is aware of that fact, none of us—even me—can quite let go of the sneaking suspicion that having a woman in the pulpit can't be helping matters.

"We'll need to revise the budget," Ralph adds, "to reduce expenditures. It will most likely mean cuts in staff—immediately, if not sooner. Payroll has to be turned in by the end of the week."

Their heads all swivel toward me. Now I'm pretty sure Ralph doesn't mean cutting me, since I'm the only minister left at this point, and someone's got to get up in the pulpit Sunday morning and preach. And believe me, it's not going to be any of them. Still, my professional insecurities set alarm bells clanging in my head.

"Staff cuts?" I say. "We're pretty bare bones as it is."

The current roster of employees at Church of the Shepherd includes me, Angelique, a part-time bookkeeper, the choir-director-slash-organist, and the custodial staff. Jed's the head custodian, and Earlene, Lester, and a guy named Frank are his subordinates, a fact that he never lets them forget for a moment. They're also paying the recently retired Dr. Black through the end of the year. That fact alone eats up a low six-figure amount of the budget.

"It will have to be one of the custodial staff," Peyton says. "That's the only place there's wiggle room."

"Wiggle room" is churchspeak for "chopping block."

While I don't want the church to struggle, this piece of news can only bolster my argument that we need to seriously consider Arthur Corday's offer. Do we want to be like all the other inner-city churches, marking time as they make the long, slow decline into eventual death? Wouldn't it be better to cut our losses now and make a fresh start?

I clear my throat and sit up straighter in my chair. "I may have an answer to our financial dilemma. We've been approached by the representative of a local real-estate developer about the possible sale of the property," I begin.

No one looks shocked, which means The Judge has been hard at work.

"An offer which we don't even need to consider," he interjects. But I persevere.

"The representative, Mr. Corday, has named a price

73

that would mean a fresh start for Church of the Shepherd in a new area of town. I can't help but think that God may be calling us to consider the brave step of relocating.

"Let's be honest," I say, deciding that I might as well sin boldly. "Ralph's financial report only confirms what we already know. This church is in a decline that cannot be reversed. Our demographics have changed substantially in the past thirty years, and people just aren't willing to make another commute on Sundays to attend church downtown."

"First Baptist doesn't seem to have that problem," The Judge counters.

"Yes, but they also never allowed themselves to slip the way we have. Plus, well, they're Baptists." Like a lot of others in the Protestant community, we suffer from Baptist envy.

"Would a move really help?" Peyton asks with a skeptical grimace. "If we can't draw people where we are, would we do any better in the suburbs?"

"That's where the people are now," I answer. "With our more traditional worship, we can appeal to the under-thirty-five set."

"I don't want one of those jeans-and-Jesus services," Edna says.

"It wouldn't be. Younger folks are looking for mystery, for ritual. Smells and bells are in fashion again."

"Smells and bells?" The Judge frowns like a ferocious bulldog.

"Well, we're talking incense burning and church bells

74

ringing. But I meant that metaphorically. People under thirty-five like all the high-church stuff. Formality is back in vogue."

"Why should we move to the suburbs if we already have what they're looking for right here?" Peyton counters.

"Location, location, location. It's not enough just to have the right stuff." I try not to lean too far forward in my chair so my eagerness for Arthur Corday's offer doesn't show too blatantly. But as I talk, I can feel my own excitement growing. If we move the church, we really could do something new and exciting. We could reach people we'll never reach from our little corner of downtown.

"Being downtown was enough in the old days," Peyton says.

I take a deep breath. I knew it wasn't going to be easy to get them to even consider the offer, so I can't get discouraged by their resistance.

"The only people left downtown are bankers, lawyers, state employees, and the homeless. Along with a few tourists and the occasional urban pioneer who buys a loft on Second Avenue. How can we grow a congregation out of that? That's why we should at least entertain Mr. Corday's offer. Besides, what harm can it do to simply talk to him?"

"Because once the door is opened, it's much easier for someone to push us through it," The Judge says.

"Nobody will push," I insist.

"Of course they will," he snaps. "These things have

a way of taking on a life of their own. Holding out hope and possibility and then refusing to let people grasp it is cruel, Miss Blessing. There's no other word for it."

What The Judge is saying contains just enough truth to make me bristle. "It's far crueler to do nothing and watch this church die."

"We're in no danger of dying," he retorts. "True, we're not as financially healthy as we used to be, but we can maintain." He taps his fingers on the conference table in staccato agitation.

"Maintain? Shutting down the building bit by bit isn't maintaining. It's just one more step in our decline."

"Perhaps someday we will need to move, but it's hardly necessary yet."

"Perhaps it wouldn't hurt just to talk to this Mr. Corday," Edna ventures, clearly trying to be supportive of me.

"I can call him tomorrow," I volunteer, latching onto the faint crack of light shining from behind the door that The Judge is trying to slam shut.

"What kind of property could we afford if we did sell the building?" Ralph asks with a frown.

"How many Habitat houses could we finance?" Mac interjects.

"I'm not sure I'd want to make the drive to the suburbs every time I wanted to go to church," Bernice adds, prompting me to wonder how an extra ten miles would be a terrific hardship in a Mercedes sedan.

"We're a long way from making such a momentous

decision," I emphasize. "But shouldn't we at least be open to new possibilities? God works through new things as well as the tried and true."

"God also wants us to sell everything we own and give it to the poor," Mac replies. "But I don't think we're in any danger of honoring that command."

"Can I at least arrange a meeting with Mr. Corday?" I ask. "In the meantime I'll see what kind of property might be available down in Williamson County. If there's nothing that would suit us, the whole discussion will be moot."

"I'll help with scouting property," The Judge says.

My heart sinks because that will make the whole experience the ministerial equivalent of shopping for a wedding dress with my future mother-in-law—only with acreage instead of yardage as the standard of measurement.

Still, I'm smart enough to get while the getting is good. I at least have the committee's tacit permission to entertain Mr. Corday's offer. As my mother, who is a great spouter of platitudes, always says, "The longest journey begins with a single step." Or maybe it's, "We have nothing to fear but fear itself." In any event, I now have something to worry about besides becoming the Queen of the Budget Brides.

Now I get to star in *Moses II: The Sequel* and lead Church of the Shepherd to the Promised Land.

Chapter 7

Gossip at our church travels at warp speed, so I shouldn't be surprised when Booger turns up at my office door by 8:00 a.m. the next morning.

"So you're going to sell out, huh?" He walks toward my desk and plops down in the chair inhabited yesterday by Edna. He looks more sober than I've seen him in a while, but whether it's from abstinence or the shock of the news, I don't know. How Booger already knows what happened at last night's meeting when he doesn't have a permanent address, much less a telephone, is a mystery to me. Perhaps there's some sort of inner-city grapevine that drums out the news or sends up smoke signals.

"We aren't making any decisions right now," I assure him, closing the Bible commentary I was using to prepare Sunday's sermon. Somehow this week's passage—"Ask, and it will be given you"—seems both appropriate and distressing. A double-edged sword.

"Would you really sell the building?" Booger asks, his eyes not meeting mine, which launches an explosion of guilt in my chest. We both know that most days the only thing between Booger and a total descent into the Dark Side is this church.

"Whatever happens, Booger, you'll always be part of this congregation." My words sound good, but we both know they're not exactly true. I'm ashamed for saying them when I know they're meant to alleviate my own guilt more than anything else.

"Will I, Reverend Blessing? Then you have greater faith in this flock than I do."

Tears sting my eyes as I'm forced to acknowledge that if we head out for the Promised Land, some of us will be staying behind in Egypt.

"We'd pick you up on Sunday mornings, Booger, and drive you out to the church."

He reaches into his pocket and pulls out a filthy handkerchief, with which he proceeds to wipe his face. His liver-spotted hand trembles noticeably. "Sure, sure." But he's clearly unconvinced.

"The church is going to die anyway, Booger, if we don't do something. Every Sunday the congregation gets smaller. Not to mention the offering shrinking as well. At some point the well will run dry. And then it will be too late to sell and start over somewhere new."

"Who says you're supposed to start over at all?"

"God wouldn't want this church to die."

"Why not? Everything else he's ever created does."

And despite my master of divinity degree from Vanderbilt, I can think of no rebuttal to Booger's argument.

"I have to think of what's best for the whole church. I'm sorry, Booger."

Please, God, don't let him start crying. I don't mean to be self-centered or insensitive, but I can't handle it today. Cecilia will be here any moment to take me to look at irregular wedding invitations (please let that woman go back to New York soon!), and I'm still exhausted from the administrative-committee meeting last night. But that's usually when someone from my congregation really needs me—the very moment when I feel as if I have nothing left to give.

"Look, Booger, it's going to be okay. Really." I feel like the meanest of the mean when I pull my old standard of standing up and moving toward the door so he'll get up and follow.

"Sure, sure." He's got his guard back up after that brief moment of lowering it and being snubbed for his efforts. "I'm sure you'll do the right thing, Preacher." Booger sticks out his meaty paw, and I shake it. I feel as if I've just told Santa Claus he's a fake.

Booger looks me straight in the eye, and this time I'm the one who looks away. Because I can't deny that in my heart this idea of moving the church to the suburbs is all mixed up with my own dreams for the future.

"Everything's going to work out, Booger. You'll see."

"You bet, Preacher." He says the right words, but he walks away without the usual awkward hug—awkward on his part because he's skittish about being touched, awkward on my part because I'm skittish about getting too near someone who only showers on a quarterly basis.

"Betsy? David's mother just called," Angelique says as we pass through the reception area. "She'll be here in three minutes and wants you to be waiting out in the parking lot for her."

Of course she does.

The day has barely begun, and already I'm looking forward to the end of it. My only consolation is that

David's supposed to meet us at the printer, so at least one friendly face will be there.

Cecilia's presence is the only thing that keeps me from flinging myself into David's arms when we rendezvous at Bertie's Samples and Spares, and I'm pretty sure he feels the same.

"Hey, Betz." He gives me a quick peck on the cheek, which is not the full frontal kiss I'm longing for. But at least he looks as though he'd rather sneak me off into a dark corner instead of pick out wedding invitations. Since Monday's surprise engagement party, I have been properly kissed by my fiancé zero times. This, I think, is not a good way to begin an engagement. I'm sure there should be significantly more lip-locking.

"Hi." I have to be content with David draping his arm across my shoulder in lieu of kissage. As trade-offs go, I could certainly do worse.

"Well, let's get to work," Cecilia says and ushers us into the print shop.

Bertie's smells like the aftermath of an industrial accident, all chemically and unnatural. We're not two steps in the door before Cecilia starts quizzing me about how to word the invitations.

"Formal? Chatty? Maybe a poem about winter?" she prods.

"I'm sure just the usual will be fine," I say with a sidelong look at David, who nods in agreement. "You know, 'Parental Units A and B invite you to share their joy . . .' and so forth."

"No poem?"

I can tell she's disappointed. "I don't think so. What do you think, David?"

He raises his eyebrows in male alarm. "I think I'll just leaf through some of these sample books," he says and trots off to a nearby counter to leave me to do battle for invitation verbiage that won't completely humiliate the two of us. You know, I used to be really critical of brides who allowed their fiancés to get away with ducking most of the wedding decisions, but now that I'm on the other side of the officiant's book, I'm becoming less judgmental with each passing moment.

"We'll need At Home cards as well," Cecilia says.

"At Home cards?"

"You know, 'Mr. and Mrs. David Swenson will be at home following their honeymoon at 2525 Oak Street.' Whatever David's address is. So people know where to send the late presents."

My spine stiffens. Okay, two things bother me about that statement. First, I might not want to be known for the rest of my life as Mrs. David Swenson, since I do possess an identity of my own apart from my future husband's. And second, I would never, ever live in David's studio bachelor apartment. His refrigerator is a penicillin factory. Ew.

"I'm going to keep my maiden name," I say.

"Just professionally, you mean."

"Um . . . well, no. I meant personally, too."

Her eyes narrow on me like Patriot missiles tracking an incoming Scud. David's flipping through a big sample book and missing the whole exchange. We haven't discussed this—we haven't had a chance to discuss anything about this wedding, really—which is why I don't want to get into it with Cecilia at the moment. From the steam starting to pour out of her ears, though, I don't think I have much choice.

"I just feel more comfortable doing it that way," I say.

"*You* feel more comfortable?" Cecilia arches an almost nonexistent eyebrow that's been plucked to the verge of extinction. "How on earth could spurning your husband's name and family make you feel more comfortable? Don't you respect David?"

Okay, I realize that people have different takes on the whole keeping-your-maiden-name thing. Some folks are laissez faire while others see it as an affront to the very structure of the family. Some even go so far as to suggest that it will lead to the downfall of civilization as we know it. But since millions of people on this earth don't even *use* last names, I can't see that it will irreparably rend the fabric of society if I choose to be known after my marriage as Betsy Blessing instead of Betsy Swenson.

"You could hyphenate," Cecilia says in an attempt to be conciliatory, but I can tell it's killing her. Her face is more pinched than usual, as if her extremely pointy-toed pumps hurt even more than mine do.

Here's my take on the whole hyphenated-last-name thing. Betsy Swenson-Blessing. Or Betsy Blessing-Swenson. The Blessing-Swensons. I can't imagine imposing a moniker of that size on any future children

I may bear. I mean, first grade is hard enough without having to learn how to spell a last name that's twice as long as everyone else's. Plus, there's no way there would be enough spaces on the SAT form for my kid to get his or her name to fit.

"We don't have to solve this right now," Cecilia says with a dismissive wave of her hand when I don't respond to her hyphenation idea. "You two just browse through the books and see what you like."

Gratefully, I flee from her presence and join David at his sample book.

"What about these?" David pushes the open book in front of me. "They're nice."

And they are lovely invitations. Quite lovely, in fact. Just what I would choose if I had the freedom to do so. Heavy cream-colored paper. Beautiful black calligraphy. Classic elegance. In fact, they're way too nice to be sold at Bertie's. I flip the book closed and glance at the cover: *Designer Invitations*. I open it back up to the invitation David liked and glance at the fine print next to it. Two words leap out at me: *Vera* and *Wang*. Who knew she did invitations, too?

"I don't think these are *Budget Bride* material," I say with regret—and a small sigh. Then I glance at the price table beneath the fine print. "Definitely not in our price range." It's unfair of Bertie to have these fabulous invitations sitting out here in full view of God and everybody when most of the patrons are here to see how far they can stretch their dollars.

David harrumphs. He's trying to be a good sport, but

I can tell he's in a bad mood about something, most likely the fire marshal. "Look, Betz, how long is this going to take?" He starts to riffle through the other pages in the sample book, but I pull it away. And I bristle. He's not the one who had to play Scarlett and the shepherdess—or carry all that china in from the car.

"You're the one who said we should let your mother handle everything," I answer more sharply than I intended, but the whole Cecilia thing has me teetering on the edge. "So don't get humphy on me now."

David's frown fades, and the warm light I've always adored returns to his eyes. "I know, I know," David says, squeezing my hand. "I got us into this. I'm sorry, honey. I'm just a little stressed about my meeting." He glances at his watch.

Hallelujah! That's David's first official use of an endearment. There's a buzzing in my ears, and I feel a little short of breath.

"I'm sure whatever invitations we end up with will be fine," I say, because once again I've been reminded that all the window dressing of a wedding isn't what's important. What matters is the marriage, not the pomp and circumstance.

"Oh, you found something," Cecilia says, appearing over our shoulders. Then she pauses. I look at her, and I can see the wheels spinning in her head.

"Cream? For a winter wonderland?"

She's got to be kidding. Surely she's not going to hijack the invitations with this winter theme too.

"Maybe just a plain white," I say, trying to head her

off at the pass, but she's already whipped open another sample book and is thumbing through it as if she's an FBI cryptographer looking for the key to a secret code.

"No. No. No." She rejects the offering on each page.

And then I can almost see the light bulb come on over her head.

"We shouldn't be here," she says, slamming the sample book shut. "We shouldn't be here at all."

I couldn't agree more.

"Where else would we get cheap wedding invitations?" I ask with all the innocence of a baby fresh from its christening.

"Look, Mom, I've got to get back to the church," David says. "I'm meeting the architect to try to figure out how to vent the stove in the kitchen so we can get our occupancy permit. Assuming we ever raise enough money to pay for it."

"Do you have to go right now?" I ask, but my question falls on deaf ears. Or at least distracted ones. Cecilia puts her arm around him and starts walking him toward the door.

"That's fine, dear. You have important work to do. Betsy and I understand. We can take care of this."

Hey, what about me? I've got work that's just as important as David's. We're both senior pastors, aren't we? Even if my tenure is just temporary.

"Sorry, Betz," David says and kisses me again on the cheek. And he is sorry. I can see it in his eyes, which makes me feel marginally better. Or at least it does until he says, "Look, I'm going to have to work late tonight.

And tomorrow's no good either. I have a funeral to do, and the eulogy isn't finished. Can I take a rain check on dinner?"

What am I going to say? No? A parishioner's funeral is always going to take precedence over our dinner plans. Fortunately, the regret in his voice and the way he threads his fingers through mine while he's talking softens the blow a little.

"It's okay," I say. "I'll go with your mom wherever it is she has in mind."

"Great. I'll call you later. Promise."

Before I can pin him down about when I'll see him again, he's gone. I watch him through the print-shop window as he slides into his ancient Volvo.

"He's a good boy, my David," Cecilia says with pride. "Very dedicated to his church."

And I, by implication, am not, since I'm the one still standing here in the middle of Bertie's Samples and Spares.

"Okay, Cecilia. If this isn't where we should look for invitations, what do you suggest?"

Her face lights up like a kid's at Christmas. "It's so perfect. I can't believe I didn't think of it before. You'll have the cheapest invitations ever."

I'm sure I will. She's so pleased with herself that I know it's got to be bad, because so far the atrociousness of her taste has been directly proportional to her joy in exhibiting it.

"Office Depot," she announces.

"Office Depot?" I echo, uncomprehending.

"Yes. We don't need to pay for printing. Office Depot has blank invitations you can buy and run off on your computer."

"My computer?"

"We'll save a bundle. Come on."

Chapter 8

Have you noticed how relentlessly helpful the sales-clerks at Office Depot can be? I think their supervisors must hold stopwatches on them because they usually assault you within ten seconds of crossing the store's threshold. When I need to find something fast, this briskly efficient customer service is a benefit. I can get in, find what I need, and get out in record time. Just like a Navy SEAL—only I emerge with a ream of ink-jet printer paper instead of a hostage freed from terrorist captivity. Sometimes, though, I come here to soothe my battered soul among the gel pens, ClearVue binders, and random desk accessories. When I'm indulging in office-supply therapy, I don't want to be bothered.

Today, though, for the first time in the history of Office Depot, no helpful salesperson materializes at my elbow. Of course not, since this is a Navy SEAL day, not a soothe-your-soul day.

"Hmm, now where would those invitations be?" Cecilia trots off across the store in pursuit of her quarry, and I'm helpless to do anything but follow. Unfortunately, I get the teensiest bit distracted by a rack of Sharpies in fashion colors. By the time I catch up with her, she and an enormous salesperson named Raymondo are debating the relative merits of beige invitations with gold edging versus white invitations with silver trim.

"But the white suits the winter wonderland theme perfectly," Cecilia says as I step up next to her.

"This gold, though, says first class all the way," Raymondo argues. He looks as if he should be discussing nickel defense packages with the Tennessee Titans linebackers, not debating the merits of wedding invitations with my pushy future mother-in-law.

"Winter wonderland has to be silver," Cecilia insists.

"Sure, if you just want the same old, same old. If you just want to be one of the crowd. A sheep."

Again, I can see the wheels kick into gear inside Cecilia's head. And the click when she makes her decision is almost audible.

"Yes, yes. I see what you mean. The gold would set it apart."

Why Raymondo can suggest beige with gold and get away with it while David and I are chastised for mere cream is a mystery to me.

"We'll take five boxes," Cecilia says.

We will?

"Um . . . Cecilia?"

She looks over her shoulder at me, and it's clear she's forgotten I'm even there.

"I'm not sure about the invitations," I say. But my hesitation doesn't register on her radar screen because she and Raymondo are piling boxes of invitations into a shopping basket.

"These are perfect, Betsy, and Raymondo is right about the color scheme. We're going to have to start from scratch."

I wasn't aware we'd gotten past scratch in the first place. "I'm sure my mother might have some thoughts—"

Cecilia stops in her tracks. "But your mother's not here, Betsy," she says with a sad, gentle smile that makes me feel like an orphan.

"No, she's not, but—"

Cecilia grabs my elbow and pulls me close, tilting her head toward mine as if we're girlfriends confiding our deepest secrets. "I talked with your mother the night of the engagement party, and, really, we've got carte blanche. She was perfectly agreeable. In fact, she seemed really eager for you and David to be featured in *Budget Bride.*"

Cecilia's argument has the ring of truth. If there's one thing my mother values above doing something the genteel way, it's getting people to notice what she's doing in the first place. Her daughter's wedding featured in a national magazine, even a lower-end one like *Budget Bride*, will definitely be a feather in her cap. A long, glamorous peacock feather in an otherwise molting headpiece.

"Okay, Cecilia," I concede. They are, after all, merely invitations. Not Holy Writ. "Let's go ahead and pay. I really need to get back to work."

She smiles in triumph, and I try not to let it irritate me.

"They'll be great, Betsy. You'll see. In fact, I'll have Veronica do them at the office as soon as I get back to New York."

"What about the wording?" I ask as Raymondo rings up the stack of boxes. We've already established that the wording is going to require some tricky negotiating.

"The wording?"

"On the invitations. Like we were talking about earlier."

Cecilia flips her hair back with one hand, a gesture about thirty years too young for her. "Oh, don't worry about that. I'll take care of that."

I bet she will. "You know, Cecilia, I think I'd like to do the invitations myself." I can't believe I'm saying this, and yet it's the only way I can make sure they don't say something incredibly cheesy, like "Two hearts / Destined to be one / Like the sky and the sea / Like the moon and the sun." I don't want my wedding invitations to sound like a disco anthem.

"Well, if you're sure . . ."

"Absolutely."

"Will that be cash or charge?" Raymondo asks.

Cecilia just stands there, motionless, and I realize she's waiting for me to whip out my credit card.

"The magazine—" she starts to say, but I cut her off.

"I know, I know. The magazine will reimburse me." I just hope they do so in a timely manner because too much more of this, and I'm going to be over my credit limit.

Finally I've signed the sales slip, and we emerge from

Office Depot to the roar of five o'clock traffic pouring down West End Avenue as people abandon their jobs for the dubious pleasures of a commute on the Nashville interstates.

"I'm catching a plane for New York first thing in the morning," Cecilia says as we walk to the car. "But I'll be back with Jeremy to shoot the mother-daughter banquet in a few weeks."

"Great," I say, but I really mean "grate"—as in "on my nerves." *Marrying David is worth it,* I chant to myself as I stow the large plastic sack with the boxes of wedding invitations in the backseat of Cecilia's rental Geo. Even printing out several hundred wedding invitations on my computer is worth it if I can have control over at least that much of my wedding. With a sigh I climb into the passenger's side, and Cecilia, fittingly, climbs into the driver's seat.

Rule for Women Ministers No. 3: You're not the right woman for the job unless no one else actually wants to do the job.

"You have to fire Earlene," Peyton Driscoll informs me when I reluctantly answer the phone that night. It's nine o'clock, I'm still recovering from my Office-Depot-wedding-invitation trauma, and I'm ready to be done with Church of the Shepherd for the day. Clearly, Peyton, in his role as chair of the congregation, does not share my sentiment about evening hours.

"Why Earlene? Why not Lester?" I ask, although I already know the answer.

"You heard Ralph. Someone has to go, and Earlene is the most expendable."

"We'll have to convene the personnel committee before we can do that," I say, stalling for time. If I play my cards right, I can buy her another couple of months. Since she's single and raising her two grandchildren while her daughter does a stint in the Tennessee Prison for Women, Earlene needs somebody to stand up for her.

"I'm as fond of Earlene as anyone," Peyton says, "but we can't spend money we don't have."

Now, I'm sorry, but it sticks in my craw that while Dr. Black is enjoying retirement and drawing a salary until the end of the year, a woman exactly his age who has worked at the church three times as long as he did is about to be let go. And her future will not be filled with golf foursomes at Belle Meade Country Club followed by martinis at the clubhouse.

"Betsy, if you're going to be the senior minister, you're going to have to do all of the job, not just part of it."

I roll my eyes and poke at the hole in my faded Vanderbilt Divinity School sweatshirt. It's so easy for people like Peyton to justify letting go a longtime employee as a business decision.

"I think we should wait," I say, knowing that waiting won't make a difference. But I have to try anyway. When it comes to the ultimate chain of command at Church of the Shepherd, the senior minister has to bow to the will of the administrative committee.

"You have until five o'clock tomorrow," Peyton replies. "And we don't need to meet because the custodial staff doesn't fall under the purview of the personnel committee. You as the senior pastor have authority to hire and fire them."

"Me?"

"Yes, you, Betsy." I can hear him impatiently tapping something. Like a pencil. Or his devil's pitchfork. (Kidding—sort of.)

"I wasn't aware I had that sort of authority."

"Well, for you it's probably best only to exercise it at the direction of the administrative committee. But Dr. Black was fully empowered to manage the support staff."

"All the support staff?"

"The custodians, the office staff. Everyone but other ministers."

So apparently the only person I can't fire is myself. An interesting setup, really, if you view it in an existential sort of way. Though somehow I doubt Peyton would appreciate the philosophical conundrums of Church of the Shepherd's personnel policies.

"Five o'clock tomorrow," Peyton reiterates. "See that it's taken care of."

Click. No "Good-bye," no "Have a nice evening." I wonder if Peyton ever talked to Dr. Black that way. I doubt it, but then you never know. Sometimes the relationship between two people isn't what you assume it might be.

Speaking of relationships that aren't what you'd

assume them to be, I wish David would call. I knew he wouldn't tonight even though he said he'd try. I understand how busy he is. But who knew that being engaged would be this lonely? Things will change soon; I'm sure of it. Cecilia's leaving tomorrow, the fire marshal can't be impossible forever, and David will have to be involved in the wedding plans at some point. Won't he? I'm really longing for him tonight, longing for him in a new way. Not that old feeling of an unfulfilled dream, but a new, more vivid sensation of needing to have his arms around me while he whispers words of reassurance and comfort in my ear. I don't need him to carry my load for me, just keep me company while I'm doing it.

On that disturbing note, I take myself off to bed where I can dream of impossible things like prospective mothers-in-law who prefer Tiffany to Target and church offering boxes that overflow with cold, hard cash.

Managing other employees isn't nearly what it's cracked up to be. At least, that's my assessment after a few weeks as the senior minister of Church of the Shepherd. I'd always envisioned pleasant, smiling people going about their jobs with brisk efficiency and warm, good-hearted cheer. Instead, I'm always prodding, pleading, and nagging to get stuff done, like the mother of multiple hormonally impaired teenagers. Angelique is normally the rock around here, but even she's off her game this week, so when I roll in the next morning, she's slamming files around her desk and muttering at her computer—the one she loves so much that normally she calls it "Mr. Pitt." As in Brad.

"What's wrong?" I ask, and I'm rewarded with a scowl for my efforts. Since bringing her coffee when she's in this kind of mood is the better part of valor, I make a beeline for the workroom. We have the ubiquitous BUNN coffee maker, beloved by offices everywhere, but the bane of my existence. I hadn't been at Church of the Shepherd a week when Angelique forbade me to make coffee. That may have had something to do with the brown river that flowed across the workroom floor like the mighty Mississippi when I overfilled the coffee maker just a tad.

"The usual?" I call out from the safety of the workroom, but Angelique merely grunts in reply. I'll take that for a yes. Angelique and I each have our own special mugs. Mine says "Preacher Girl," and hers says "Touch This and You're Dead." That should pretty much tell you how our office works. When Dr. Black was here, I was more the go-between since the two of them were the high-strung ones. I have to say it's a relief not to be caught in the middle anymore, although since I have to fire a longtime employee by the end of the day, I guess there are worse things than being a go-between.

"Ange, I need your advice," I say when I hand her the cup of coffee I've carefully prepared.

"Advice?" Her eyes narrow. "About what? How to fire someone?"

"How did you know?"

"It doesn't take a genius to know what's going on

around here," she says with a sniff. "And you could have told me sooner."

"I only found out last night."

"Well, I know I haven't quite mastered Mr. Pitt, but I thought you'd at least give me a probationary period or something."

"A what?"

"You know. Probation. Like when you get out of jail. Where they monitor you and stuff to make sure you aren't going to hold up a 7-Eleven or something."

Okay, now I'm totally confused. "Angelique, are you in trouble with the law?"

She snorts. "Not real probation. The work kind. You know, for when you're not doing your job and they want to fire you, but they have to document your ineptitude first so they won't get sued."

"Angelique, I'm not going to fire you."

"Oh." That deflates her indignation.

"It's someone else. I've got to fire one of the other staff members, only I don't want to do it. I don't even know how to do it."

"Well, I've been fired a ton of times, so I can help you out there."

"Really?" I know Angelique's had a hard life. After all, she came to us from a welfare-to-work program. But she's a jewel, really, beneath her brash exterior. And although she's not always the most competent administrative assistant, she's certainly the kindest and the toughest. A tricky combination that not many people can pull off.

Angelique slides into her desk chair, and I perch on the corner of her desk. "Okay, then, if you're the voice of experience, give me the scoop. Tell me what to do because, frankly, I'd rather eat dirt than fire Earlene."

"You're gonna fire Earlene?" Angelique scowls. "I can't believe they'd make you do that."

"Well, with the decline in offerings, she's in the most vulnerable position. Jed's safe, and Lester can do the heavy lifting." What I don't say is that Earlene's main talent is some light dusting while she watches *Days of Our Lives* on the television in the youth lounge. "I already know it's awful. I just need to know how to make it as painless as possible—for both of us."

"How could it not be painful?" Angelique says with a snort. "I mean, she's been here forever."

"I know." My shoulders slump with defeat, but then the faintest glimmer of an idea causes me to straighten them again. As the idea slowly develops in my mind, my vertebrae slide to attention one by one until I've got the spine of a drill sergeant.

"I've got it," I say, snapping my fingers. "I can't believe I didn't think of this before."

"This ought to be good," Angelique says with a smile.

"It's so easy I can't believe it took me this long to think of it."

"Well?"

"I can't fire her if I don't see her today, can I?"

"Nooo," Angelique says in a slow drawl. "But in case it's escaped your attention, you are, in fact, here."

I jump up off the corner of her desk. "Not for long. A

pastoral emergency has suddenly come up."

"What pastoral emergency?" Angelique asks, but I'm already moving toward my office to get my purse.

"I have no idea, but I'll think of something."

"What if Peyton Driscoll calls? What should I tell him?"

That one stops me in my tracks. What should she tell him? I stand there for a long moment, praying for inspiration.

And for once it strikes at the very moment I need it. "Tell him I'm out making a pastoral call."

Chapter 9

Every preacher girl needs a sugar daddy, and Harry Snedegar is mine. Now, I know that sounds bad, but I don't mean it in the literal sense. There are no sexual favors involved here, although I suspect we both have the littlest bit of a crush on each other. Harry, though, is some forty-five years my senior, and since I'm not into the whole Anna-Nicole-Smith-marry-a-senior-citizen scenario, we have maintained our relationship as a mutual admiration society. Harry's been in Boca Raton since I was promoted to senior minister, so this will be the first time I've seen him since he got back.

I need to stretch out my time away from the church, so I decide to make a day of running errands. The local Cokesbury store to pick up some adult Sunday-school curriculum. The Parent-Teacher Store in Green Hills for posters of the Ten Commandments and the books of the

Bible. Stops at Kroger, CVS Pharmacy, the public library, a deli, and David-Kidd Booksellers. Finally, when I've procrastinated as long as I can, I call Harry's house on my cell phone. His wife, Joann, answers, and she sounds as pleased to hear from me as I am to talk to her. She doesn't seem to mind that I have a crush on her husband and vice versa. But, then, he's so charming and loving that I imagine half the female population of Nashville is as infatuated with him as I am.

When I pull into the driveway of his gracious, columned mansion on Franklin Road, I can see Harry around the side of the house on the tennis court. His tennis whites don't disguise his paunch or his shaky backhand. He's batting the ball back and forth with a lovely, young blond woman.

I park near the house and walk across the side lawn to the court. Harry's serving, and he has the motion of a mechanical windup toy—jerky and underpowered. Clearly his ability to make money and his ability to serve a tennis ball are in no way connected.

"Ace!" he shouts with good-natured glee when his opponent fails to return his snail's pace serve.

"Nice placement," the woman says, hitting the strings of her racket with the heel of her hand to applaud his efforts. Of course, I guess you'd find it hard to serve over the net, too, if you were trying to do it from a wheelchair like Harry.

"Hi, Betsy!" His blond partner turns out to be his daughter Antonia. Like so many children of my parishioners, she doesn't attend Church of the Shepherd. But she's always pleasant to me and never antagonistic like some of the other offspring who fear I'll wrangle a huge bequest for the church out of their parents in their dotage.

"Hi, Toni." I return her greeting with a smile, which is always a nice way to begin a pastoral visit. Some of them start with more of a grimace or a wince of pain.

"Hello, Reverend." Harry grins and lays his racket across his lap, using his massive upper body to propel himself off the court toward me. He's a big bear of a man—or at least half of a big bear of a man. He was the whole enchilada until a drunk driver took out his Jag on I-440 five years ago.

"Hey, Harry." We meet at the edge of the court, and I reach down to hug his neck. I will always wonder what it would be like to be hugged by Harry Snedegar from a standing position. I bet it would be a lot like being hugged by the aforementioned bear.

The thing I liked immediately about Harry when I met him was that there isn't a drop of self-pity in him. Evidently there was a whole river of it once upon a time, right after his accident happened. I've heard tales from other church members about the rages, the drinking, the language. And then one day, as Harry tells it, Jesus showed up at his front door and told him to get over himself.

Okay, it wasn't really Jesus. It was Dr. Black, but Harry says he was as good as the real thing. That day Harry pulled himself out of the Slough of Despond—or let God pull him out. So Harry has a pretty high opinion

101

of the clergy, which he was kind enough to extend to me without hesitation upon my arrival at Church of the Shepherd. I've known him less than a year, but I feel as if I've known him all my life.

"Did you show Toni any mercy?" I ask with a smile.

"None whatsoever. My fatherly feelings evaporate the minute I roll onto the court."

I don't believe that load of bravado. Neither does Toni, who squeezes his shoulder as she joins us.

"Nobody buys the macho act, Dad. You might as well give it up." She greets me and asks, "How does a glass of lemonade sound, Betsy?"

"Great." Joann has become a connoisseur of lemonade since the day Harry threw the entire contents of their liquor cabinet into the trash. Dr. Black helped him. Rumor has it that hundreds of dollars of Jack Daniel's alone was destroyed that day in under twenty minutes.

"I'll be back in a minute," Toni says and disappears into the house.

"Come on," Harry says. "Let's go sit by that self-indulgent pool I spent too much money on."

Sitting by the pool with Harry is one of my favorite things about being a minister at Church of the Shepherd. It's like nipping over to Tahiti on a moment's notice. Lush, green foliage. Fountains and tiki torches. The only thing missing is the sound of the waves against the shore, and I'm sure Harry would provide that via the cleverly concealed Bose speakers if you asked him.

"So what brings you here today, Reverend? Throwing in the senior-minister towel already?"

"I need some advice." Which is pretty much stating the obvious since I tend to show up on Harry's doorstep when I'm in need of counsel.

"Is the problem animal, vegetable, or mineral?"

I smile. "None of the above. Or maybe all three." I pause, trying to decide where to start. "A man named Arthur Corday came to see me."

Harry's eyebrows rise in the same arch as the fountain in his pool. "Arthur, hmm? Was he wearing his blue seersucker or his gray?"

I laugh. "Does it matter?"

"Absolutely." Harry tries to look all sagelike, but there's a definite twinkle in his eyes. "Blue means that he's not ready to make a deal yet. He's still in the exploratory stages. Gray means he wants to talk turkey."

I should mention that Harry owns the largest real estate development company in town. Even larger than the one Arthur Corday represents. Harry finally retired after his accident, but he still owns the company, and he's still got his finger on the pulse of Nashville commerce.

"Corday's company wants to make an offer on the church property. And he was wearing his blue suit," I say. "Is that good or bad?"

"Too soon to tell. What did he offer?"

I name the figure that Arthur wrote in the margin of my sermon notes. Harry whistles. "Maybe I had him pegged wrong," he says. "Because that sounds like a gray seersucker amount to me."

"So it's a good offer?"

"Yes. Very fair. I'm suspicious."

"You are?"

"In all the years I've known Arthur Corday, I've never once known him to do anything but lowball the other guy. That's a mighty nice number for an opening salvo."

"But you think he's definitely serious?"

Harry's quiet long enough that I start to get a little nervous. Finally he says, "I don't see how he could be anything but serious, naming a figure like that. That's what makes me wonder. Why make such a high offer to a church? Especially a cash-strapped, dying one?"

Well, there it is in black and white. The very thing that has been bothering me, despite my enthusiasm. Arthur Corday's offer is a little too good to be true, and I've discovered by hard experience that things that are too good to be true generally aren't. True, that is. Or good, either, for that matter.

Toni emerges from the house with a tray in her hands. "Hey, you two. Can you take a break from talking shop long enough to indulge?"

"Sure, honey." Harry smiles fondly at his middle daughter. "Pour 'em up."

Toni obliges, then excuses herself. "I've got to pick up the kids at preschool." She kisses her father, and he beams at her with fatherly pride. Then she's gone, leaving us alone again.

"So the finances are doing poorly, hmm?" Harry says after a long drink of his lemonade. He pauses and closes his eyes to enjoy the sour sweetness. I, too, observe a moment of ritual silence in thanksgiving for Joann's lemonade.

"Peyton says I have to fire Earlene."

Harry frowns.

"I'm not asking you to bail me out," I say quickly before he misinterprets the reason for my visit. "Me or the church."

Harry reaches over and pats my hand. "I know, Betsy."

"It wouldn't help in the long run even if you did."

"I know that, too."

"So what do I do?"

"I think you'd better have another chat with Arthur Corday."

"The Judge won't like it."

"Well, The Judge isn't the senior pastor. You are."

I can express my doubts to Harry. That's why I drove out here. I fiddle with the damp edges of the drink napkin beneath my glass. "Maybe I'd do better to just sit tight until they hire the permanent senior pastor."

"You'd still have to fire Earlene."

"I could take a pay cut."

"You could. But that wouldn't solve the problem any more than my writing you a blank check."

And there it is in a nutshell. Because the truth in this situation is that no one person can save a church. If someone does play Rescue Ranger, even for the short

105

term, the church ceases to be God's and ends up belonging to that individual.

"I have to fire her, don't I?"

"I'm afraid so, Betsy." He reaches for the pitcher and tops off my glass. "And it probably won't be the last time. Not if the finances don't improve."

I think of Angelique. Of Jed. Of all of us who depend upon Church of the Shepherd for our daily bread. "Any advice?"

"Do it at the end of the workday. And don't apologize."

"But I am sorry for having to fire her. Shouldn't I tell her that?"

"Your pity won't make it any easier on Earlene. Don't say something just to make yourself feel better." Harry's expression is as serious as I've ever seen it.

Now where have I heard that before?

"She needs someone to resent, Betsy, and you're going to be the target."

"I don't want to be the target."

"But that's part of the job. Part of being the chief and having all those Indians."

"I guess I knew that in theory; it's just that practice isn't turning out to be quite what I thought it would be."

Harry pats the arm of his wheelchair. "Most things don't turn out to be what you think they're going to be, Betsy. That's what makes life interesting."

"Yeah, well, I just wish my life wasn't quite so *interesting* at the moment."

"I have a cure for that."

"You do?" Finally, some relief.

"Sure. More lemonade."

I'm happy to comply. The rest of the visit passes in chitchat, the exchange of pleasantries, catching Harry up on the news of my engagement. That's okay. I've found out the most important thing I needed to know: I can't take Arthur Corday at face value.

Plus, by now it's too late for me to go back to Church of the Shepherd and fire Earlene because she'll have gone home for the day.

My conversation with Harry is fresh on my mind when Arthur Corday calls me at home the next day. It's Saturday, and my sermon still isn't finished even though I spent last night sitting at home while David prepped his funeral eulogy for today. Arthur wants to know if I'd like to drive down to Williamson County with him this morning to look at potential building sites for the new and improved Church of the Shepherd.

"It might help you convince the committee to consider selling if you can talk about real possibilities for the future."

"Sounds great," I say, glad that it's an impromptu expedition even if it will take up half of one of my few days off. This way I don't have to include The Judge, and when he asks why he didn't get an invite, I can truthfully say there just wasn't time.

"Excellent," Corday says. "The Judge and I will be by to pick you up in twenty minutes."

"You invited The Judge?" Rats.

"The quickest way to win over an adversary," Corday says, "is to make him think he's a decision maker."

That sounds Machiavellian enough to actually work.

Twenty minutes later I'm ensconced in the back of Corday's big black Lincoln Town Car. He and The Judge talk about mutual cronies all the way down I-65, so for twenty minutes I'm hearing about Otto Cotter's delinquent grandson and the redundantly named Eddie Edwards's wayward wife. I'm always tickled how older men usually turn out to be far bigger gossips than the women of their generation. When the two men start to compare the achievements of their grandchildren, I clear my throat and perform the daring act of interrupting their hen party.

"So, what kind of sites do you have in mind for us, Arthur?"

The Judge's shoulders tense, as if he'd forgotten why we're all riding merrily along in Corday's Lincoln on a Saturday morning.

"Some good possibilities, Reverend Blessing. No property is perfect, but I think we have some strong contenders today."

Are we scouting property or going to a horse race? Plus, the whole "no property is perfect" thing is a big red flag for me. That's like the salesgirl at the mall who says that the expensive jeans are "really flattering." She just doesn't clarify whether she means they're really flattering to you or to the previous customer who weighed twenty pounds less and wasn't carrying your saddlebags.

"I don't want to go too far south of Franklin," I say.

"Not a problem," Corday says and flicks on his turn signal to exit on Cool Springs Boulevard near the Galleria. "In fact, this one practically touches the Brentwood city limits," he says, referring to the suburb that lies between Nashville proper and Franklin fourteen miles to the south. Brentwood owes its existence to the white flight of the seventies. The attractive thing about that location is the Cool Springs Galleria and its big-box shopping environs. Still, I can't imagine that we could afford property here in a million years.

"How big is this site?" I ask, but Corday evidently doesn't hear me. He and The Judge pick back up with the litanies of their grandchildren's achievements. It's another five minutes before Corday turns off Wilson Pike and onto a side street. The surrounding area is a sea of McMansions, and I practically salivate at the thought of all the young families under each of those roofs. The median income in this postal code has to be close to $175,000 a year. If even half of these people tithe . . . well, welcome to the Promised Land, Church of the Shepherd.

Corday's car rolls to a stop beside a fairly small piece of undeveloped land. It's not on a major road, and the ground looks a bit marshy to me.

"Now, this site is on the cozy side," he acknowledges as we climb out of the car. "But it's close in, and you're surrounded by neighborhoods." He then names the asking price, and I would just as soon he punched me in the stomach. It's most of what he's offered for Church of the Shepherd. I guess if we wanted to hold services in a tent for the next twenty years, we could swing it.

"We can't afford it," The Judge pronounces, but I'm just perverse enough not to reveal that I agree with him.

"It can't hurt to look," I say and take off across the three-acre parcel.

"It's too small," The Judge says, hot on my heels.

"We may not want to duplicate the size of the current sanctuary at first," I say. "That might come later."

"It's not on a major street," he replies. "We'll be buried in a neighborhood."

"A neighborhood full of kids," I counter.

"We still can't afford it."

Well, he's got me there.

"Perhaps something farther south." Corday catches up with us in time to hear the last part of our exchange. So I concede this one, but I haven't given up hope just because the first possibility didn't pan out. And later I don't give up hope when the second possibility turns out to be an old chicken farm that hasn't been fully decontaminated. The third property Corday shows us is in an old strip mall in Franklin between Hobby Lobby and the Dollar Store.

The Judge is practically gloating. "Seems like staying put is the best option after all," he says with more than a note of triumph in his voice.

"I do have one more option," Corday says, but I can tell that even he's growing weary.

"I'd like to see it," I say, and The Judge scowls. Well, he should know by now that I'm stubborn. Or passive-aggressive, depending on whom you ask.

Arthur takes us to the last option. It's the farthest south, a pretty long haul from Nashville proper, but it's also perfect. Ten acres of gently rolling pasture with subdivisions springing up all around like daffodils in the spring sunshine. As we pace off the length and breadth of the property, I imagine school buses crawling by in a slow line like enormous yellow ants.

"It's too far out," The Judge says. But I don't agree.

"It's perfect," I say.

"Folks will never drive this far."

"The ones who—" I stop myself. Because what I almost said was, "The ones who live out here will." And the truth of what I'm trying to do hits home with fresh power. This move would save the church, but at more of a sacrifice than just Booger. I think of Edna and Bernice, Ralph and Peyton. How long would they continue to make the drive before they realized "their" church wasn't their church anymore?

And with that thought, fear rips through me as if lightning struck out of the clear blue sky. Who am I even to be out here in the middle of Williamson County scouting property like some big-steeple preacher? I'm just Betsy, a cheap and temporary fix to Church of the Shepherd's leadership crisis. This whole trip is nothing but a wild-goose chase powered by my need to feel important. Isn't it?

And then I think of Angelique. And all the other people who work at Church of the Shepherd. Sooner or later, if something drastic isn't done, we will all lose our jobs. I can probably find another one, as can Jed, who's been the head custodian for so long that some other church will snap him up. But Angelique and some of the others aren't such good candidates for employment outside the forgiving walls of a church. What will happen to them?

It hits me, in this moment, that there's no win-win scenario here. Something and more than a few some-ones are going to have to give. And part of my respon-sibility is to decide which someones are going to be doing the involuntary giving.

Is this what God wants? This new start in the sub-urbs? I was pretty sure until we got out here. Now it seems like no option will make everyone happy—with the future or with me.

Chapter 10

If there's one thing I'm an expert at, it's do-overs. Saint Benedict said, "Always we begin again," and I have made that my personal mantra. I made it through church yesterday—I wrote my sermon at approxi-mately 11:30 p.m. Saturday—and we're back to Monday, one week exactly since the fateful engage-ment party.

So when David calls halfway through the morning, I'm prepared to offer him (and me) a fresh start. Sure, things have been rocky the past seven days, but I truly believe that if we can find a little time alone together, everything will be all right.

"Let's try again for dinner," David says over the phone line that has become our main Love Connection since the engagement party. "It'll be my treat. You name the place."

I hate it when a guy does that whole "You pick and I'll pay" routine. Because if you go for something expensive and upscale, he thinks you might be a gold digger. Although, in David's case, I'm not sure he has enough gold to warrant much digging. But if you select a modest restaurant, one too low on the dining chain, then you won't feel it's a truly romantic evening. Gazing into each other's eyes over Jamaican chicken from the affordable Calypso Café just doesn't work as well as the intimacy-inducing candlelight at the Park Café.

So, what's a girl to do? Well, it seems pretty obvious.

"No, you pick," I say. Hah! Now he can be the one to wrestle with the thorny restaurant dilemma. Only for guys, it's usually pretty thornless.

"Okay. I'll see you at Noshville at six."

Double rats. Noshville's a yummy deli, especially when you have a cold coming on and need some matzo-ball soup, but it's very loud and not terribly romantic.

"Okay. See you at six." I'm too beaten down by dealing with both Cecilia's wedding plans and the potential Great Migration of the church. I may not be sick in body, but I'm getting pretty run down at heart. Maybe that matzo-ball soup isn't such a bad idea after all.

I'm starting to feel that I conduct most of my life in a variety of restaurants and coffee shops around

Nashville. Maybe that's just the reality of the modern woman. I mean, I'd love to say to David, "Just show up at my place, and I'll have an amazing dinner on the table," but the only hot meals that grace my home these days are either warmed up in the microwave or come in carry-out containers.

All my angst and exhaustion, though, recede into the background when the hostess seats David and me in a booth at Noshville. This time I'm fairly sure there won't be various parishioners and family members pouring out of a back room to surprise me. Just quality time with David, a remedy even more effective than soup. A real, actual first date.

We haven't even opened our menus when David reaches over the table and takes my hand. We both have to stretch our arms a bit because the table's a little high, but his touch reassures me in a way that all the phone calls in the world can't do.

"I've missed you," he says in a low voice, stroking my thumb with his and giving me a meaningful look with his big brown eyes. And I'm Putty with a capital *P.*

"I've missed you, too." We exchange goofy grins, and I'm sure that if a diabetic is within ten feet, he or she is plummeting into sugar shock by now.

"How are you doing?" He continues to stroke my thumb with his, and at this rate I'm going to slither underneath the table in another thirty seconds.

"Well, to tell the truth—" I really need his counsel about the whole Arthur-Corday-sell-the-church thing, and there just hasn't been a good time to bring it up.

"Hey, folks. How are you this evening?" The waitress appears beside our table with a smile and two glasses of water. "What can I get you?"

Too bad you can't order quality time with your new fiancé off a restaurant menu. I bet it would be a very popular item.

"I'll have a bowl of the matzo-ball soup and a Diet Coke," I say. David orders a grilled-cheese sandwich and a glass of milk. I guess we're both in need of some comfort food.

"Got it," the waitress says with a wink and walks away. I turn my attention back to David.

"How are *you* doing?" I ask. Frankly, now that I've gotten a few minutes to study him, I don't think he looks very good.

"I'm okay." But it's clear that he's not.

"Are you feeling all right?" I ask.

"Yeah, yeah. I'm fine."

At that moment the waitress returns and slips a bowl of Noshville's signature pickles under our noses. I enjoy munching on them while waiting for my meal, but David suddenly turns a shade of green not dissimilar to the pickles.

"David?"

"Sorry, Betz. I'd better—"

But before he can finish his sentence, he leaps out of the booth and heads for the rest room. I get up to follow him, but he waves me off. Hard as it is, I slide back into the booth. I've known David a long time, and one thing I learned early on is that when he's sick, he wants to be left alone. This goes against my every instinct, but I've learned to control myself. While I might want someone hovering over me, offering me Jell-O and Gatorade and taking my temperature on the quarter hour, David becomes a hermit when he doesn't feel well.

So I wait alone in the booth, my stomach a knot of worry, but I know there's nothing I can do at the moment. Eventually the waitress brings our food, and I ask her if I can get carry-out containers and pay the check. When David emerges from the rest room, I can drive him home.

"Sure thing, hon. Hope he'll be okay. That brunette he was in here with yesterday got sick, too, while they were eating. I meant to ask him if she was okay."

Brunette? What brunette? And why is he eating at Noshville with some unnamed brunette on a Sunday?

Before I can grill the waitress for more information, David appears over her shoulder.

"Betz, I'm sorry, but I think I'd better go."

"I'll drive you," I say. Now I'm not only concerned for his well-being, but I'm also dying of curiosity. You will have noticed by now that I am not a very pure or pious person. Worry for others and self-interest coexist quite happily inside my head.

"You can't leave your car here." David squeezes my shoulder. "I can make it home. I'll give you a call when I get there."

"Are you sure?" David lives down in Franklin, not far from where I was looking at property with Arthur Corday and The Judge, and it's a pretty good distance in the back of a Lincoln Town Car, much less if you're sick to your stomach and all alone.

"I'll be okay. Promise."

"Well, okay." I squeeze his hand where it rests on my shoulder. "But I don't mind."

"I'll talk to you later." He's going green around the gills again, so I shoo him out the door, sign the credit-card slip, and transfer our food to a couple of carry-out containers.

The waitress comes back by to pick up the credit-card tray. "He'll be okay, hon," she says, trying to be helpful.

"Can I ask you a question?" Even as my mind screams *NO! NO!* I can't resist the temptation to pump her for information. "Can you describe the brunette he was here with yesterday?"

She looks thoughtful for a moment. "Maybe I shouldn't have said anything. I'm sure it was nothing."

"Was she tall? Thin? Lots of teeth?"

The waitress grimaces. "Yeah. A real Cindy Crawford type."

"Laughs like a horse?"

Her eyes widen, and she chuckles but with a rueful undertone. "I'm afraid so."

My stomach cramps, and I'm glad I never got the chance to put any soup into it. Because David was here yesterday with Jennifer, his former fiancée—and he didn't say a word to me about it. And as afraid as I am to ask him about their rendezvous, I'm even more afraid of the answer.

I don't know why I thought that Cecilia's going back to New York would mean she was out of my hair. Clearly I didn't make allowances for e-mail, voice mail, and fax, because she's showering me with all of the above this week. In a few short days, it's gotten to where I'm afraid to turn on my computer or look at the little Message Waiting display on my phone. Once more, thank heavens for caller ID.

David's been out of commission, too, ever since the other night at Noshville, so he's in no position to help mediate between our mothers, who have apparently decided to make wedding planning a competitive sport. My mother may have made nice with Cecilia at the engagement party, but when she found out about the chipped china and the DIY wedding invitations, she went ballistic. Also, David's been in no condition for me to interrogate him about the Reappearance of Jennifer, as I've come to call this distressing new development, so I've just been left to stew in my own juices.

On top of all this, I've been dodging both Peyton and Earlene this whole week, and quite frankly, I'm exhausted.

On Thursday I find myself alone at Target registering for wedding gifts. Only I'm not truly alone because Cecilia's on the other end of my cell phone providing helpful consultations on the merits of various coffee makers and DustBusters.

"You'll want to register for some dish soap," she

advises as I make my way through the housewares department, aisle by torturous aisle. I'm trying to juggle my cell phone, the little price-gun thing they give you to pick out your stuff, and my purse, which weighs approximately three hundred pounds.

"Dish soap?" She's kidding, right?

"You know. Palmolive. Ivory. Whatever kind you like, although I recommend the store brand for the best value."

I guess that's the mark of the truly cheap—using your wedding to rack up some free cleaning supplies.

"I don't know—"

"I need you to. For the magazine." Cecilia's never shy about playing that trump card. If I lodge a protest about something, she tells me that it has to be her way "for the magazine." How am I supposed to argue with that? Plus, I'm still waiting for her to reimburse me for the china and the wedding invitations. Financially speaking, I can't afford to make her any more irritated with me than she already is.

"Okay. A 12.6-ounce container of store-brand dish-washing detergent. Check."

"What have we forgotten?" she asks, but I know by now it's a rhetorical question. She's been ordering me up and down the aisles like a seasoned drill sergeant, and we're not even in the same time zone.

"Maybe that's enough—"

"Oh, I remember. Dish scrubbers."

Dish scrubbers? She's got to be kidding. Well, in my dream world, she would be. But here in the Target on

White Bridge Road, via Cingular's closest cell tower, she's dead-on serious.

"Right. Two packs of assorted cellulose sponges at $1.99 each. Check."

And then, blessedly, the call waiting on my cell phone beeps. I pull the phone away from my ear long enough to check the caller ID. It's my mother. Great. Out of the frying pan—$5.99 for the smallest one in the store—and into the fire.

"Cecilia? Can you hang on a sec? My mom's on the other line."

For a long moment, there's silence. Then a slight harrumph. "I'll go back over the list," she warns, "and see what else we've forgotten."

You know, it would have been easier to just ask the store for the complete list of their inventory and enter that as my bridal registry. I hit the Pound key on my phone and switch to the other line.

"Hi, Mom."

"Hi, honey. What are you up to?"

I deliberate as to how honest I should be. But I know if she finds out later that I let Cecilia walk me through registering for my wedding, even if it was at Target, I'll never hear the end of it.

"I'm at Target, actually. Picking out some things."

"Do you mean you're registering?" If I could use her voice, I wouldn't need to register for an icemaker.

"Yeah. Cecilia's on the other line. She's been walking me through it—for magazine purposes," I say, emphasizing the magic *m* word to temper my mom's likely reaction to this news.

"Oh." A world of hurt birthed into being by that one little half sound, half syllable.

"But maybe you could help me," I say, improvising with the guilt and agility of a seasoned professional. Professional daughter, that is. "I'm not sure about some of these choices."

And so, within five minutes, I'm standing in front of the dinnerware collections, debating the merits of plain white stoneware versus faux Fiesta dinnerware with both my future mother-in-law and my mother, even though neither of them happens to be within eight hundred miles of me at the moment. Let's hear it for modern wedding planning. All of the guilt and none of the fudging, courtesy of modern technology.

"Go for what's on closeout," Cecilia advises, but when I switch over to run that by my mom, she balks.

"It'll all be gone by the time people pick out your wedding gifts. No, you'd better go with one of the new patterns, or you're going to wind up with sixteen plates and no cups or saucers."

And so it goes, until my finger's sore from pressing the Pound key on my phone. My feet are starting to hurt, and I swear my eyes are so bleary I'm seeing double.

"Mom, I don't need highball glasses," I say. "It's not like we're going to be throwing a lot of cocktail parties."

"You never know," she says. "Better safe than sorry."

"I won't be sorry. I just want to get this over with."

"Then add them to the list."

My phone beeps. Cecilia's hung up and is calling again to get my attention.

"Just a minute, Mom."

I switch over to answer the incoming call.

"Sorry, Cecilia. My mom and I were just trying to decide about the barware."

"Forget the barware," Cecilia says. "Have you found any dustcloths?"

"I don't think—"

The phone beeps again. Looks as if my mom has figured out Cecilia's trick, because she's hung up and redialed too.

"Just a second, Cecilia."

I click back over. "Mom, can you give me—"

"Don't let her talk you out of the barware," she says. I can tell Mom is pursing her lips even though she's several states away.

"I'm not going to let anyone talk me—"

Beep. Cecilia again.

"Hang on, Mom."

I hit the Pound key. "Cecilia—"

"Don't let her talk you into the pricey stuff—"

"I won't—"

Beep.

I switch back to the other line. "For heaven's sake, can you just leave me alone for five seconds?"

There's a long pause. "Um . . . Betsy? Is that you?"

"Edna?" Rats, rats, and more rats. Of all the people to snap at. Or to have her think I'm snapping at her.

"Yes. It's Edna. Angelique said I could reach you at this number." Her tremulous voice doesn't sound like her at all.

"What can I do for you?" I'm more worried about why her voice sounds funny than about whether she'll turn back to the Dark Side if I'm rude to her.

"Well, I think I may have hurt myself."

My pulse picks up. Has she done something to her shoulder again? "Are you at home? Are you bleeding?"

"Yes, I'm home, but there's no blood. It's just that, well, I've been here awhile, thinking I'd be able to get up, but I don't seem to be feeling any better."

You know, we all laugh at those "I've fallen and I can't get up" television commercials, but when it happens in real life, it's pretty frightening.

"Where's Alice?" Edna's housekeeper and maid-of-all-work is one of God's angels here on earth.

"She's off this week. Went to visit her sister."

"Are you on the floor?"

"Yes, in the kitchen."

Why couldn't she have fallen on a carpeted surface instead of a hard tile floor? "How long have you been there?"

At this point other shoppers are starting to listen in on my conversation. Some of them look concerned. Others just look intrigued by the gory details.

"Oh dear. I'm not sure. What's today?"

What's today?

My blood turns to ice. "It's Thursday."

"Then I've just been here since yesterday."

And that puts everything in perspective, all this stupid wedding stuff and the whole impossible task of trying to run interference between Cecilia and my mother.

"Edna, just stay still. I'm calling for an ambulance right now. Is your front door unlocked? Is there a key hidden outside somewhere?" Unfortunately, I've had enough experience in these situations to think about whether the paramedics can get in without having to break the front door down.

"There's no need for an ambulance," Edna says with more than a touch of asperity. Under pressure, she reverts to form, but I can't really blame her. "I just need you to come over and help me get up off the floor."

Considering the last time Edna called for my help several weeks ago to hook her bra when she injured her shoulder, getting her off the floor should be a cakewalk. Except that with someone whose bones are like tooth-picks, you don't want to take any chances.

"I'll be there as soon as I can, but you still need an ambulance."

Edna sniffs. "If you insist. There's a key under the pot of geraniums on the front porch."

Thank goodness for that. Given Edna's massive mahogany front door, breaking in could wind up being an expensive proposition.

"Stay as still as you can," I say. "I'll be there in three minutes." Thankfully, Edna's Belle Meade mansion isn't far from the Target where I'm standing.

"Thank you, Betsy."

We hang up, and as I walk toward the front of the

store, I call 911. By the time I've finished speaking with the dispatcher, the call waiting on my cell phone has beeped six times. Three each for my mom and for Cecilia. With a sigh that combines exasperation and worry, I toss the price gun onto the customer-service counter and race for my car.

Chapter 11

I'm always astounded by how people who once struck fear into your heart can look so vulnerable when they're laid up in a hospital bed. I've been with Edna since the paramedics loaded her into the ambulance early this afternoon, and I waited while she had surgery. Now it's growing dark, and I'm strung out on too many cups of Starbucks from the kiosk in the lobby. Another church member might not have needed me to stay. Anyone else would have been surrounded by friends and family. But Edna is pretty short on both. Since her physician-husband retired, he pretty much lives on a golf course in Florida. In fact, she wouldn't even let me call him.

"What's the point? He'll talk doctorspeak to my orthopedist, they'll decide I'm going to be fine, and then he'll go right back to his seven iron."

So that's how I came to be the person sitting at her bedside, refilling her cup of ice water, and trying to figure out which buttons raise and lower the head of the bed—all things that would be difficult to manage even if Edna didn't have one arm in a sling along with a broken hip.

"You don't need to stay with me," she says, shaking a finger at me for emphasis. I'd be more convinced I could leave, however, if I hadn't seen her weeping when the paramedics transferred her from her kitchen floor onto the gurney. When it comes to pain, we all suffer it. It's the great equalizer of the human race. Rich or poor. Male or female. We are all one when it hurts. Today Edna's as human as anyone.

"I think I'll stay awhile longer. I don't have anything pressing." Well, nothing except for a sermon to write, a runaway wedding, and a fiancé who may be seeing his old flame on the side. Other than that, I'm golden.

"If you insist." Edna presses her lips together in faint disapproval, but I can tell by the way the rest of her face softens that she's secretly pleased. A hospital room is a scary place to be alone.

A nurse comes in to do the usual nurse-type things— temperature, blood pressure, et cetera—and then we're left alone again.

"So, how are your wedding plans going?" Edna asks.

I look at my watch. "How about a little television?" I say with false brightness. "Anything good on tonight?"

Edna snorts. "Please. If I want to hear the screeching that passes for entertainment these days, I can go listen to the howler monkeys at the zoo. Don't try to change the subject. I want to hear about the wedding."

What is it about wedding plans that turns perfectly normal people into emotional vampires? It's as if they feed on your angst and indecision. Or else they use it as an opportunity for recreational criticism.

"The plans are going fine," I say demurely. "Would you like some fresh water? I can go to the nurses' station for more ice."

Edna's eyes have the slightest gleam of self-satisfaction. "Not going so well, then. I'm not surprised."

"You're not?"

"That's what comes of marrying a Lutheran. You should have found a nice boy from your own denomination."

"I don't think it's a doctrinal problem."

"Then what kind of problem is it?"

I can't stop the grimace. "More like a maternal one."

"His mother?" Edna sniffs and then fiddles with the plain white sheet covering her. "I remember her from the engagement party."

Cecilia would be pretty hard to forget, but I keep that thought to myself.

Edna continues to pluck at the sheet. "What's the problem? The bridal registry? The invitations? The dress?"

"Yes," I say, agreeing to all of the above.

"In my experience," Edna says with all the solemnity of The Judge at his most pompous, "the one unbreakable rule is this: never compromise on the dress."

"Really?" I try not to smile. Here I thought she was going to give me some big secret to being a happy bride, and all I get is, "Don't compromise on the dress"?

"You laugh, young lady, but it's true. If you're not happy in the dress you're wearing, you won't be happy in the marriage."

"Are you sure?" I say before I have a chance to consider whether I should ask the question. And when I see the shadow that passes over her face, I wish I'd considered my words more carefully.

"I know it from hard experience, Reverend Blessing. Very hard experience."

I think of her husband striding up to the putting green of some Florida golf course instead of sitting here by her side. "But I thought you wanted to model your gown for the mother-daughter banquet."

Edna sniffs. "That was Bernice's idea. Of course, I can still fit into my wedding dress, so I have to model, don't I? So many women can't."

This has to be one of the more bizarre conversations I've had in a hospital room, and believe me, I've had some doozies.

"But you didn't like your dress."

"My mother-in-law picked it out," she warns me darkly, her eyes narrowed. "Never let your mother-in-law pick out your dress. It will doom the marriage." She sounds like an oracle from ancient Greek mythology. That or she's starting to get loopy from the pain medication.

"I think budget constraints will dictate my choice of dress far more than my mother-in-law will." Which reminds me that I meant to stop by Goodwill again today to check for any abandoned wedding gowns.

Edna's eyes are drooping, so I reach for my purse. "I think I'd better go and let you rest."

"Mmm." Edna's acknowledgment is half agreement,

half snore. In a few more seconds, she's sleeping softly. I tiptoe out of the room and wave good-bye to the nurses as I make my way down the hall.

Whether it was drug-induced wisdom or not, Edna has a point. I should choose a dress that makes me happy. Everything else about this wedding is going to be a compromise, but this one thing ought to be just for me. I can do it. I can stand up to my mother and Cecilia on this one issue. As David says, we should let the rest of it go. In twenty years none of that other stuff—invitations, flowers, canapés for the reception—will matter. Or even be remembered.

What will remain are pictures of David and me on our wedding day, arm in arm and beaming with happiness.

At least I hope that's what the photographs will show.

I continue to avoid both Earlene and Peyton on Friday by spending the morning with Edna at the hospital and the afternoon visiting bridal shops. I've taken Edna's advice to heart and decided that on this one issue, the choice of my dress, I will not compromise.

The salesclerks, however, don't seem to be of the same opinion as Edna. They're all about compromise. No, I take that back. They're all about total domination of prospective brides.

You would think autocratic, demeaning behavior would work against their self-interest. Do all brides really collapse like wet tissue when presented with some of the hideous creations that masquerade as wedding gowns? Apparently so, when the salespeople make

Milosevic look like a cream puff. At least, that's what I'm learning as I work my way through the bridal salons listed in the Yellow Pages.

That's how I find myself standing on a raised dais in front of a three-way mirror staring in horror at my reflection. Truly, I had thought that the dresses at Dearly Beloved Discount Bridal represented the bottom of the barrel, particularly the Little Bo Peep confection. But here at Tulips, Roses, and Trimmings, I've discovered a new low in wedding couture. Or lack thereof.

The first tip-off should have been the name of the store, which sounds more appropriate for a florist than a place to buy a wedding gown. My second clue ought to have been the inch-thick glasses on the saleswoman. If she can see her hand in front of her face, I'm a monkey's uncle. But that hasn't stopped her from declaring every dress I've tried to be, "Perfection, my dear. Absolute perfection. Shall we pin it for the seamstress?"

She even said that about the two dresses that were too tight to zip up the back.

I wish LaRonda were here. I wish it so desperately that I almost pick up my cell phone to call South Africa. But frugality and technical incompetence stifle my plans. No, this one I'm going to have to figure out on my own. Or I could call Angelique at the church before she leaves for the day. Now there's an excellent idea.

"Church of the Shepherd," she answers in a distracted tone.

"Hey, Angelique. It's me."

"Betsy? When are you coming back to the office? The Judge has been here looking for you. And Peyton's left half a dozen messages."

"I think you just answered your own question."

"You can't hide forever."

"Maybe not, but I'm not ready to fire Earlene quite yet."

"So where are you?"

I look down at the miles of satin and tulle hanging from my hips. "Would you believe I'm contemplating whether ribbon roses make my butt look big?" I mean, I know that the back of the dress needs to be interesting, since that's what the congregation will be observing for the balance of the ceremony, but these roses are the size of dinner plates. I definitely do not need my derrière looking like a serving platter while I'm reciting my vows.

"I can't believe you're dress shopping without me," Angelique says. "Have you learned nothing?"

"Apparently not."

The visually challenged saleswoman taps her nose, trying, I think, to indicate that this dress is, once again, The One.

"Angelique, what am I going to do?"

"You'll have to be more specific than that."

"About all of it. The dress. The wedding. Firing Earlene."

"Running away from your problems won't get them solved."

"Yeah. I know."

131

"You have to face up to things."

My shoulders slump. "I know."

"You're the senior minister now. And the bride. You should be in the driver's seat."

Yes, I should. But somehow things don't seem to be working out that way.

"It's time to come home, Lassie," Angelique continues.

"Arf," I say into the phone, and the saleswoman looks at me like I've lost my mind.

"See you in a few."

Careful to lift up the skirt of the dress, I step down off the dais. There's so much beading on the train that the thing weighs nearly as much as I do.

"Shall I ring it up?" the saleswoman asks.

"No. No, I don't think so."

She nods icily. "I can understand your dilemma. Perhaps you can lose some weight and come back to try it on again."

Zing! What's the deal? Does this woman moonlight as a CIA assassin? I'm dying to say, "Well, I can lose weight, but you're forever stuck with your personality." I don't, though. Years of ministerial training have taught me to swallow those kinds of words. And maybe that's the right thing, but at the moment I wish it weren't.

So, feeling about three inches tall, I divest myself of the bridal confection and don my street clothes. By the time I emerge from the dressing room, Attila the Saleswoman has found another victim, a cute young blonde, who I'm sure will fit into anything in the store.

Tail between my legs, I slink to my car and head for the church.

"Thanks for stopping by, Earlene."

Yes, I've finally given up trying to run away from my problems. And I've followed Harry's advice. It's not only the end of the workday, but Friday to boot.

Earlene sits across from me, my desk providing a barrier between us. Dr. Black made sure that his desk chair sat up higher than the two chairs on the other side. He said that when it came to confrontations in the pastor's study, you should build in every possible advantage. My desk chair, however, is a relic someone dug up at the secondhand office-furniture store. The only thing that sits lower than the chair is the carpet.

"Earlene, we need to talk." I can hardly bring myself to look into her dark brown eyes. Heavy wrinkles, the legacy of years of smoking, combine with her soulful eyes to give her the appearance of a basset hound.

She nods soberly. "Look, if it's about all those days I missed when the boys were sick—"

"No. No, it's not that."

Earlene leans back in the chair, relieved. "Thank goodness. I was afraid you were going to fire me."

My cheeks flush like wildfire. Why couldn't Peyton be the one to do this?

"Actually, Earlene . . ." I trail off because I don't know how to say this. But as Harry told me, there's no glory in being a wishy-washy executioner. If you're going to separate someone's head from her neck, the least you can do is deliver the blow cleanly.

"It's not about the boys, Earlene. Are they feeling better?"

"Yep. Think we've got that strep thing licked now."

My throat's so tight, it's hard to speak. I'd spent a lot of time dreaming of the advantages of being a senior minister. Now I wish I'd spent more time considering the pitfalls.

"It's about the budget. About the church's finances."

Earlene sits up straight again. "Yes?"

"Giving is down. We have to make cuts, Earlene." I take a deep breath, and my words come out in a rush. "We have to let someone go. We have to let *you* go."

Have you ever watched someone's face as her heart breaks? I have, too many times to count. When a woman discovers that her husband is cheating on her. When a father finds out that his son is addicted to drugs. And it never gets any easier. Earlene's face crumples, her head drops, and she begins to sob.

Instantly, I'm out of my chair, moving around the corner of the desk, grabbing for the ever-present box of tissues I keep for times like these.

"I'm really sorry," I say even though Harry told me not to apologize. I pluck some tissues from the box and tuck them into her hand.

Earlene doesn't answer; she just continues to sob. Finally, she looks up at me, her wrinkled, tear-stained face awash in misery. "How will I feed the boys?"

The thought of her two little grandsons is my

undoing. I burst into tears too. "I don't know, Earlene. I wish I did, but I don't."

And so for the next fifteen minutes, we just cry. I cry for Earlene, but I also cry out of frustration with the wedding plans. I cry for Edna's loneliness in the hospital as well as for my fear that David is seeing Jennifer again and doesn't have the nerve to tell me. I cry because the saleswoman was so dismissive of me and because The Judge won't cooperate with the idea of selling the church. And then I cry when I think of Booger and all the others who will lose their connection with Church of the Shepherd if we move.

At some point I lean over and put my arm around Earlene. She tucks her head into my shoulder and continues to weep.

"It's going to be okay," I say, lying through my teeth, because I have no idea how it's going to be. "We'll find you another job. We'll figure something out."

And there it is—the difference between being the CEO of a big company and the senior minister of a church. Firing Earlene may be best for Church of the Shepherd, a sound and sensible business decision, but caring for her and helping her in the aftermath is what's best for the kingdom of God.

"You'll help me?" she asks, sniffing.

"Sure. Absolutely. I'll write you a letter of reference," I say. "And we can work on your résumé."

Earlene dabs at her eyes. "What's a résumé?"

I choke back a laugh and blot my own eyes with a wad of tissues.

"It's a place to start, Earlene." We smile through our tears, and I squeeze her hand. "First thing Monday, okay?"

"Okay."

We hug before she leaves my office, and I know I haven't done this like Harry told me to. But I also don't know any other path I could have followed.

Chapter 12

On Monday morning I'm hard at work on Sunday's sermon—because I'm so tired of not getting it done until the last minute—when my phone rings.

"David's on line two," Angelique says in a teasing voice.

"Thanks." At the sound of his name, my heart thumps in a manner reminiscent of a junior-high girl with her first boyfriend. But I also hesitate for a second before punching the button. In all the whirlwind of Edna's accident and dealing with Earlene and just getting through another Sunday's services, I haven't seen him since last Monday night at Noshville. And I certainly haven't had a chance to put my suspicions about him and Jennifer to rest. More than anything, I want to reconnect with him. Since the engagement party two weeks ago, I feel as if I've talked to him less than at any point in our eight years of friendship.

I take a deep breath and push the button.

"Hey, David." I hope I sound calm and collected, and not like I actually feel—desperate and panicked.

"Hey, Betz. You doing okay?"

"I'm fine. How are you? Feeling any better?" I checked up on him a couple of times via e-mail and phone tag, but I'm still worried.

"Yeah. The doctor said it was just an intestinal bug."

"But you're okay now? I would have been happy to bring you some soup or something."

"I know. I appreciate it. But you were better off staying away."

Because he's such a bear when he's sick—or because someone else was there nursing him?

A great wave of shame washes over me, because what has David really done to deserve this type of suspicion? Okay, so he had a meal with his ex-fiancée. Just because he didn't mention it doesn't mean anything. There's probably some perfectly innocent explanation. *Probably.* Sigh. I'd prefer *absolutely.*

"But you're definitely feeling better?" I ask.

"One hundred percent. I can't believe I haven't seen you in a week. Can we do dinner tonight?"

"Sure." The enthusiasm in his voice warms the cockles of my heart.

"Good. I'll be at your place at six." The relief in his voice renews my hope in us as a couple. Because guys don't use that tone when they're making a duty date. Really, I can be so suspicious sometimes. I'm sure he'll tell me all about seeing Jennifer when we meet up tonight. It's probably such a minor thing that he forgot to mention it.

Again with the *probably.* And the sigh.

I never did much like probabilities.

I've barely hung up the phone with David when Angelique knocks on the door to my office.

"Come in."

Today her pierced nose sports an impressive faux ruby. I'd love to ask her how you get the fastening on the other end of the post, but I'm afraid enough of the answer that I don't.

"What's that?" I ask. She's holding a large FedEx box.

"Dunno, but it's for you. From Cecilia."

Now I feel like I'm the one with food poisoning.

"Okay. Just put it in the corner there."

Angelique cuts her eyes at me. "You're not going to open it?"

"Sure I will. Later."

Angelique drums her impressively long and pointed fingernails on the top of the box, and I look up from trying to get my head back into my sermon notes.

"What?"

"Oh, come on, Betsy. You've got to open it."

"Nope. I don't."

"Aren't you curious?"

"Not in the least." But I am, and Angelique knows it. So she walks over to my desk and plops the enormous box on top of my piles of Bible commentaries, Greek lexicons, and legal pads.

"Humor me," she orders.

My eyes meet hers, and I know I won't win this battle.

"It will just make me mad," I warn her. "I'll be in a bad mood the rest of the day."

"I'm willing to take that risk," she says with a smile.

"Fine." I plop down my pen beside the box and reach for the pull tab. "But if this turns me into a raving lunatic and I never finish my sermon, you have to preach on Sunday."

Angelique laughs. "Deal."

I rip the end of the box open. It's crammed full of bubble wrap, so I grab the end of it and start pulling. Angelique slides the box toward her, and then, in a *whoosh* of plastic, a large, flat bundle lands on my desk.

"What is it?" Angelique asks.

"I'm not sure." I peel back the bubble wrap and then several layers of tissue paper. What new travesty will Cecilia perpetrate today? Discount tablecloths monogrammed with someone else's initials?

The last layer of tissue falls away, and I see what it is.

"It's a . . ." Angelique's voice trails off.

"Yes. It's definitely . . ." My entire vocabulary seems to have deserted me as well.

I brush my fingers on my skirt to make sure there aren't any ink smudges, and then I gingerly lift the item from its bed of tissue paper. As I pick it up, I step away from the desk so that the yards and yards of silk shantung unfurl like a sail.

"Is that what I think it is?" Angelique whispers in awe.

No words can pass my lips. I just nod, throat too tight for speech. Because what I'm holding in my two hot little hands is the most beautiful wedding dress I've ever seen.

"Look. There's a note." Angelique hands me a folded piece of paper. It's a page torn off one of those daily calendars. I recognize Cecilia's handwriting.

"From a Vera Wang sample sale," the words say. "Alter as needed."

Tears spring to my eyes, tears of relief and gratitude. For the first time since the night of the engagement party, I think everything might possibly turn out all right.

"Is it who I think it is?" Angelique asks. She may have multiple body piercings, but the woman knows her designers. She pores over every issue of *InStyle* magazine as if it were Holy Writ.

"She says it's Vera."

We both observe a ritual moment of respectful silence.

"I guess Lizzy Devereaux isn't going to be the only woman modeling Vera Wang at the mother-daughter banquet," Angelique says.

A little thrill shoots through me. If Edna's right, and your wedding dress determines the success of your marriage, then David and I will be wed until, well, until always.

"I can't believe this," I say, although the dress is real enough.

"Will it fit?"

"There's only one way to find out."

I catch the dress up in my arms and, carrying it before

me like a sacrificial offering, head out of my office. Angelique follows me through the reception area to the sanctuary and beyond to the bridal dressing room at the rear of the church. Once there, my fingers tremble as I slip out of my "office casual" black pants and pink sweater.

"Step in, and I'll help you pull it up," Angelique says.

"Here goes nothing," I mutter under my breath. Careful not to tear the material, I put my feet into the little doughnut hole in the midst of the ocean of skirt. Together we work it up until it's in place, and Angelique begins to do up the million little buttons down the back. Instead of ruffles, the strapless neckline and voluminous skirt feature row upon row of pleats. The effect is luxurious, tailored, and elegant. In short, the antithesis of Cecilia's taste to date.

"Suck it in, Scarlett," Angelique says when she gets to the buttons around my waist. And I do. Because after you try on enough wedding dresses, you start to get good at this. "It's going to be tight. You'll need to have it let out in the bust."

I look down at my cleavage where the strapless cut of the gown reveals my feminine assets in all their glory. Hah! Take that, Jennifer.

Everywhere else, though, the dress fits like a dream. So, okay, maybe this *Budget Bride* magazine thing will pay off after all. I feel so light with happiness, I could float off like a helium balloon if there wasn't an arched Gothic ceiling over my head.

"Look." Angelique spins me to look in the full-length

mirror that has reflected countless Church of the Shepherd brides.

"Oh."

Ministers aren't often speechless. Especially me. But at the moment I can't find any words to express what I'm feeling.

It's perfect. From the asymmetrical pleats on the bodice to the tiny vertical pleats at the hem.

"Look at the back," Angelique urges me, so I turn a little bit to take advantage of the three-way mirror.

I didn't know that I could actually squeak with pleasure, but I do.

"Look at it, Angelique. It's like a work of art."

The back of the dress looks kind of art deco—like the Chrysler Building in New York, but in a feminine, flattering way. An inverted V starts at my waist and breaks the rows of horizontal pleats with the same tiny vertical ones on the hem.

"Girlfriend, your mother-in-law hit the jackpot."

"Amen."

I twist and even try to twirl in an attempt to admire the dress from every angle.

"Can you believe it, Angelique?" For once the flush in my cheeks is from pleasure, not embarrassment.

"I guess her administrative assistant didn't buy this one on eBay."

"I guess not."

I can't stop admiring myself. "I think I'll just stay here all day," I say as I continue to preen.

Angelique shakes her head. "No ma'am. That

sermon's not going to write itself."

"I don't know why not. Doesn't it know I have better things to do, like stand here and admire myself?"

Angelique tackles the buttons once again, and I reluctantly submit my back to her nimble fingers. Today, a brief glimpse of heaven is all I need to make me feel invincible once more.

"It's going to be okay, isn't it?" I ask.

I can't see Angelique's smile since she's standing behind me, but I hear it in her voice.

"With a dress like this, how could it be anything else?"

How indeed?

As it turns out, I might as well have spent the morning modeling my dress instead of wrapping it up as tenderly as a mother swaddles a newborn and stowing it underneath my desk. I'm looking up the Greek word for *heaven* in a lexicon when Angelique taps on my half-open door once again.

"Someone here to see you."

Now, I'm pretty sure I don't have any appointments this morning, and people who drop in on their pastors rarely do so for pleasant reasons.

"Who is it?"

Before she can answer, a man appears over her shoulder.

"Reverend Blessing?" he asks, and I wish my office had a hidden door or an escape hatch because I can tell from the sound of his voice that he's a salesman. I stand up and walk over so I can shake his hand. Angelique disappears back to the reception area.

"I'm Betsy Blessing."

"Kevin. Kevin Kimmel. I'm with the Faithful Remnant, the premiere pew cushion company in Nashville." He taps the emblem emblazoned on his red polo shirt. He's a linebacker type, and the open collar of the shirt strains to circle his neck.

Rule for Women Ministers No. 4: Don't trust anyone who comes into your office carrying a sample case.

"What can I do for you, Mr. Kimmel?" I don't offer him a seat. I'm not that stupid.

"Call me Kevin, ma'am."

The aforementioned sample case is hanging from his left paw. As if noticing my gaze, he lifts it up and gives it a little jiggle.

"I heard from Arthur Corday that you might be in the market for some new cushions when the church relocates, and I wanted to be the first one to offer my services."

He steps around me just as he maneuvered past Angelique and hoists his case onto my desk. Truly, it's been an interesting day for my sermon notes. First a wedding gown and now this.

"Well, it's a bit premature—" But I don't get any further than that.

"That's what most people think, Reverend. But I'm here to tell you that it's never too soon to decide whether you want faux velvet or pseudobrocade."

"Pseudobrocade?" He's got to be kidding. Or I'm

being whatever is the church equivalent of *Punk'd*. Now that could be interesting. Maybe Ashton Kutcher will appear at any moment.

"I really don't think—" Again, Kevin doesn't seem to register any of the intended discouragement in my tone. Instead, he flicks open the latches of his sample case and takes off the lid. Before I can object, he's spread five or six kinds of fabric over my desk. Then he pops open yet another compartment, and several long streams of foam rubber pop like snakes out of a trick jar.

I jump and Kevin Kimmel looks pleased with himself. "Gets 'em every time," he chuckles and then proceeds to wrap a piece of burgundy velvet around one of the foam strips.

"Now this, Reverend Blessing, is the Cadillac of pew cushions." He walks behind my desk and plops it down in my chair. "Here. Give it a try."

He's got to be kidding.

"I don't think—" I try again, but I don't get any further than before. Because Kevin the Pew Cushion Guy has grabbed my arm and is guiding me around the corner of my desk.

"You'll never look at church upholstery the same way again," he says with creepy enthusiasm. Clearly, the only way to get rid of him is to comply, so I sit down in my chair. The strip of foam is only about five inches wide, and it feels more like a serious wedgie than a comfortable place to nod off while listening to a sermon.

"Well, it's certainly—"

Again I have no chance to finish my sentence. But this time it's not the assertive Mr. Kimmel who interrupts me. It's someone new entirely.

"Your secretary said I could come on back." A tall, cadaverous man in a leisure suit—weren't those all burned when the seventies ended?—looms in the doorway. I see Angelique's warped sense of humor in sending him into my office. She's probably sitting at her desk chortling at my predicament.

"Sorry, I seem to be interrupting," the cadaver says.

And then I realize what it must look like—me squirming in my chair and Kevin Kimmel leaning over me to pat the end of the cushion as if to demonstrate its resiliency.

"Really, you're not—"

Kevin clears his throat. "We're kind of in the middle of something."

Great. Couldn't he have said something a little less, I don't know, incriminating? I pop up out of the chair, my head narrowly missing Kevin's chin.

"Please come in." I escape back to the other side of the desk and vow to myself that by the end of the day, I'm going to push the darn thing against the wall. Who knew that something as innocuous as the arrangement of office furniture could be a veritable minefield of disaster?

"I'm Bill Bond," the cadaver says. "Of Bond Paper."

I almost laugh, except Mr. Bond's sour expression reveals no hint of humor. Having learned early on in my ministry to laugh at the irony of my own last name, I sometimes wrongly assume that other people share my sense of the ridiculous.

"What can I do for you, Mr. Bond?" I'm so delighted to have a buffer between me and Kevin Kimmel that I sound perkier than I intend.

"Well, Arthur Corday mentioned your upcoming relocation," he says, "and we at Bond Paper have found that when a church moves, it's the perfect opportunity to redesign and reprint the Sunday-morning worship bulletins."

First pew cushions, now worship bulletins. Who will Arthur sic on me next?

"Gentlemen," I begin, "I really think—"

And then a third man appears at my office door. Thankfully, though, he's not a salesman. It's Booger.

"Come on in." I wave my hand in invitation.

Booger looks around uncertainly. "I can come back."

"No, no. Now's fine."

The two salesmen exchange glances as Booger enters the office in all his fragrant glory. Maybe it's low of me to use Booger's presence to evict these guys, but frankly, given a choice, I'd pick hanging out with Booger over dealing with them any day. And if Arthur Corday thinks that a few salesmen dangling shiny baubles in front of me will influence the sale of Church of the Shepherd, he has sharply underestimated what it will take to motivate me. Now, if he wants to send along a Jimmy Choo representative . . .

"Gentleman, this is Booger Jones, one of my parishioners."

147

I have to give these two guys their props, because they each extend a hand and greet Booger.

Booger's growing more uncomfortable, so I move to pull my office door open a little wider and hope that Kevin Kimmel and Bill Bond will take the hint.

"Gentlemen, if you have some brochures you want to leave for me, I'll be glad to look them over once I've finished my sermon for Sunday."

"Of course. Of course." Mr. Bond reaches into his briefcase for a thick folder. "I'll just leave our catalog."

"As will I," Kevin says, pulling his pamphlet from yet another concealed compartment in his sample case. I swear that thing is like one of those cars at the circus where the door opens and clown after clown pours out.

"Thanks." I take the materials while privately vowing to put them in the round file as quickly as possible. I wonder whether I should be offended that Corday's strategy of reminding me how much shopping I'd get to do if we moved has at least got me thinking. So much of the interior of Church of the Shepherd is fifty years out of date, if not more. The prospect of redoing everything from the carpeting to the communion ware definitely holds a strong appeal.

But I can't be played quite that easily. I exchange a cordial "Have a good day" with the sales guys, and then it's just me and Booger alone in the office. I'm feeling pretty self-satisfied at shucking off Mr. Kimmel and Mr. Bond until I take a good look and see the sorrow in Booger's eyes.

The pain there brings me sharply back to reality.

Chapter 13

Still too flustered by the pew salesman's foam demonstration to return to my regular spot, I lower myself into the nearest chair. "You arrived in the nick of time, Booger." I'm ready to laugh about the whole incident, but he isn't. His Santa Claus face is as sober as I've ever seen it. "Hey, Booger, are you okay?"

"I was hoping you'd changed your mind." He plops down into the chair next to me.

Guilt forms yet another tangle in the ongoing series of knots in my stomach. "It won't be my decision alone, Booger. The administrative committee will have to decide whether to accept the offer."

"But you can sway them."

Part of me is flattered he thinks I have that much influence. The other part of me, the more self-serving side, resents his request the tiniest little bit. I mean, Church of the Shepherd is a group effort. We have to look at the big picture, not just how individual pieces will be affected.

"I wish I had a crystal ball," I say to Booger. "All I can tell you is I promise to do what I think is right."

The light in his eyes dims, and my guilt rises in proportion.

"I know you have to do what you think is best, Preacher. I just wish I could change your thinking."

"I know it's not going to be easy, Booger, but we'll get through it. I'm still your minister." I pat his hand on the arm of the chair next to mine, but the action feels condescending. I mask my discomfort by giving his hand a further squeeze. "Look, I think there's more of those sausage biscuits in the freezer. What do you say we have a midmorning snack?"

"I can't afford to turn down free food," Booger replies, but his eyes don't meet mine.

"All the more reason for a feast." We stand up, and I lead the way out of my office. Booger follows. I can only hope that if the church does move, Booger will keep following. Privately, I vow to do whatever it takes to make sure that he remains a part of the church. If I have to swing by downtown and pick him up every Sunday in the future, I can do that. I'll have to. Otherwise, I might not be able to live with myself.

The pew-cushion guy and the bulletin man aren't the last salespeople to grace my office. Before I escape at three o'clock to visit Edna at the hospital, I've warded off the marketing advances of a man who sells and installs pipe organs, an HVAC specialist, and two potential architects. I'm expecting a parade of builders brandishing fruit baskets when I show up at the office tomorrow. So it's with relief and gratitude that I drive back out to St. Thomas Hospital.

Nashville, like lots of other cities, has different names for the same street, so although I never make a single turn, I travel Broadway, West End Avenue, and Harding Road to get to the hospital. The only thing more confusing for visitors to our fair metropolis is that Old

Hickory Boulevard actually circles the city. An address on that street could be anywhere. Since my life is often as random as Nashville's streets, I've always felt right at home.

When I get to Edna's room, she's propped up in bed watching the end of *General Hospital*.

"Shh!" She puts a finger to her lips and hisses at me before I can manage to utter a syllable. "They're about to take Carly's sons away."

I know better than to come between a woman and her soap opera, so I settle into the visitor's chair and hold my tongue for the next ten minutes. In classic soap-opera tradition, the episode ends with a cliff-hanger—a tearful young woman weeps while some man wrestles her young sons out the door. Since I've always been an *All My Children* person myself, I can't work up much enthusiasm for this woman's plight. But give me Erica Kane with a child at risk, and that's an entirely different story.

The closing credits roll as the theme music plays, and Edna presses the Off button on her remote. "Now then," she says, tucking the remote beside her, "we can have a nice visit."

Turns out that Edna's idea of a "nice visit" is listing all the sins and inadequacies of the hospital staff.

"At four this morning, of all things, a male nurse came by asking if I'd like a suppository for my pain." She couldn't be any more appalled than if the nurse had asked for a peek at her bloomers.

Edna sniffs. "Not a man's profession—and never will be."

I keep quiet on that one.

"The Judge was by earlier," she says.

"That was nice of him to pay you a visit."

"Humph. The only reason he came here was to try and influence my vote on the administrative committee."

"About selling the church?"

"Of course. Old coot. As if he could do that." She smiles at me fondly, or at least what counts with Edna as fondness. To me it looks more like she's decided to refrain from eating me but will instead be content to gnaw on my leg a little. "Although The Judge did make some good points," she adds.

"I appreciate your support," I hurry to say before she can recount his arguments. "I know it's a big decision, but we need to be open to the possibilities. Arthur Corday took The Judge and me to look at some new sites, and one of them had definite possibilities."

"What kind of possibilities?"

"Well, it's a bit farther south than I'd hoped, but it's a large parcel—ten acres—with subdivisions going up all around it. It's on a major thoroughfare, so we wouldn't be buried in a neighborhood."

"How far south?"

"On the other side of Franklin."

"Franklin?" Edna purses her lips to keep her opinions from spilling out. I know she thinks we're brand-new best friends, and she's trying, bless her heart. I just hope it doesn't kill her in the process.

"I guess we'd adjust," she says, determined to say

something positive, and my persistent twinge of guilt flares again. "When will the vote be? The Judge may try to push for a decision before I get out of here."

I hadn't thought of that. Without Edna on my team, I don't stand a chance of coming out on top with the administrative committee.

"I'll stall as long as I can. Besides, with the mother-daughter banquet next week, we'll all have lots of other things to keep us occupied."

That's true enough. Between the women putting on the bridal fashion show and the men preparing and serving the meal, the event will consume all the energy in the church for the next ten days. And that reminds me I haven't told Edna about the dress, so I proceed to do so.

"It's perfect," I say after describing it in detail. "And if what you said is true—that a wedding dress determines the success of a marriage—then David and I should be set for life."

"That's nice, dear." Her smile sags, but she props it back up again. "I do hope you'll be happy, Betsy." *"More than I have been."* The unspoken words, tremulous and grieving, hang between us.

And in that moment, between all her fussing and criticizing, Edna Tompkins shows herself to be a real human being. That in and of itself is enough to give a preacher hope. But Edna's history is also a cautionary tale. One I would probably do well not to forget.

I'm pulling out of the hospital parking garage when my

cell phone rings. I glance at the number and almost hook a U-turn back into the garage where my phone won't get any reception.

I have to answer it. It's my mother.

"Hello, dear."

How can the woman make an innocuous greeting sound like the prelude to the Last Judgment?

"Hi, Mom. What's up?"

"I just wanted to let you know what time to pick me up."

"Pick you up?"

"Next Tuesday. I thought I should come in early."

"Early for what?" Panic pools in my stomach. What have I forgotten?

"For the mother-daughter banquet, Betsy. You didn't think I'd miss that? And the extra good news is that I've found you a dress."

"A dress?" My voice is a hollow echo.

"It's perfect. Yards and yards of lace. And the cutest bow on the derrière. Cap sleeves. Seed pearls. Everything you could possibly want."

I wasn't aware I ever wanted anything in particular in a wedding dress except not to look like a meringue. Or the Stay-Puff marshmallow man.

"Actually, Mom, I already have a dress."

There's dead silence on the other end. Then, after a long pause, a single, hurt-filled, "Oh."

"It just arrived today, but it's really lovely. I think you'll like it a lot."

"Where did it come from?"

I swerve to miss an oncoming car—crazy Nashville driver—and try to frame my words carefully. Very carefully.

"Actually, Cecilia found it at a sample sale. It's Vera Wang, Mom," I say, placing great emphasis on the designer's name.

"Vera Wang? I thought this was a budget wedding."

"Honestly, Mom, you'll love it. And while you're here, we can go shopping for your dress."

"I already bought my dress," she says, sniffing. "To match the wedding dress I picked for you."

What can I say to that? "Well, bring it with you so I can see it. In fact, if you want to model in the fashion show, I bet I could arrange it."

I know from hard experience how to work my mother, and appealing to her vanity is a surefire method.

"Model? Me?"

I can picture Mom with her hand pressed against her chest, as if she's just learned she's won the Oscar for Best Performance by a Mother in a Manipulative Role.

"Sure. We can stroll down the runway together."

Of course, I use the term 'runway' loosely. It will more likely be the ancient risers left over from the days when Church of the Shepherd had enough kids to have a children's choir.

"By the way, honey, when's your bridal shower? I was hoping you'd have it at the same time as the banquet so I wouldn't have to come back twice."

Bridal shower? Oh no. I'd rather eat dirt-flavored

wedding cake—with a side of worms. I've been to enough of them to easily envision the worst: me wearing a veil made from wrapping paper and being forced to fashion a bouquet from the bows and ribbons to carry for "practice" at the wedding rehearsal. Petits fours. Oohing and aahing. Punch in tiny crystal cups. None of that stuff has ever come naturally to me.

"I don't know whether I'm having one," I say to my mom. "Who usually does that sort of thing?"

"The maid of honor should have that scheduled by now." There's a pause. "You do have a maid of honor, don't you?"

I'm sure that's one of the things on the to-do list that Cecilia keeps faxing me, but I think it's somewhere on my desk beneath my *Harper's Bible Dictionary* and a tattered copy of *My Utmost for His Highest.*

"Well, no. I haven't asked anyone. Not yet."

"I assume you haven't asked your sister because she's on bed rest. What about LaRonda?"

"LaRonda's in South Africa."

A wave of sadness hits me, sweeping my emotional feet out from under me and carrying me out to sea. How can I possibly get married without LaRonda here to bully, coax, and cajole me through the process?

"Why don't we talk about the shower when you get here?" I say. "Cecilia's coming for the banquet; maybe she can help us figure something out."

My mother's little sniff says it all, and she lets the subject drop. We talk a few more minutes, and I swear that I've written down her flight number and arrival time. This bit is particularly tricky since I have to cross my fingers around my bulky engagement ring while trying to drive and hold the cell phone to my ear. It's impossible to explain to my mother that I can go online to the airline Web site and find the information when I actually need it.

Yes, I confess. I live most of my days in reactionary mode, scrambling to meet the demands of the moment. Don't ask me to plan more than thirty minutes in advance—except for getting ready for my date with David tonight. For that, I've specifically planned an extra hour's head start. I mean, he can only propose once, so tonight it's going to be just the two of us. We have two months to date until the wedding.

At long last, I'm going to be romanced the way I've always dreamed of.

Indeed, God is good.

When David arrives at my front door, I'm freshly showered, plucked, shaved, and perfumed, compliments of the health-and-beauty section of CVS.

"Hi, honey." He steps across the threshold and kisses me in a way that makes up for the disappointments of the past two weeks.

"Hi." I manage to keep from swooning by clutching his shoulders.

And then I notice two things. One, he's wearing faded jeans and his favorite Dave Matthews Band T-shirt. And, two, he's carrying a large brown bag with "P.F. Chang's" emblazoned on the side.

"I brought dinner," he says, as proud as a kid bringing home a lopsided ashtray to give to his mom on Mother's Day.

"Oh. Oh, okay. I didn't realize you were going to pick something up." *I will not be disappointed. I will not be disappointed.*

"Yep. I even remembered your favorite. Spinach with garlic. You can have the whole container."

Ha! Only if I want to give him a reason not to come near me all night. I do adore the spinach from P.F. Chang's, but the garlic is enough to drive away an entire vampire nation. Not to mention a new fiancé.

"We can eat out on the patio," I suggest, determined to make the most of our time together even if we won't be dining out.

"Sounds great. I'm beat." And he does look tired. As if he hasn't fully recovered from his recent illness.

"What's happening with the fire marshal and the new hood for the kitchen?" I ask as we pass through my small living room and into the postage stamp of a kitchen.

David starts to unpack the containers of food, and I pull plates out of the cupboard.

"Well, I may have found a funding source for the hood. The fire marshal still won't approve the sanctuary until it's taken care of, though, so we're going to have to delay the building dedication. Again."

Honestly, I'm sorry I asked because the more upbeat David who appeared at my door quickly deflates.

"At least there's hope for the money," I say, trying to

comfort him. But David is not a "Please comfort me" type of guy. Before, when we were just friends, I would have listened to his frustrations, commiserated, and moved on. But now that I have more of an emotional stake in his well-being, I don't really know what to say. Should I do as I've always done? Or is my role different now that we're significant others?

"Can we talk about something else?" David asks with a rueful smile, rescuing me from my dilemma. But even as I let the subject drop, I know it's an issue we'll have to come to terms with sooner or later. I've seen too many clergy couples split up because they either didn't talk about their work at home or they couldn't stop talking about it. Surely there's some happy middle ground David and I can discover.

"How are the wedding plans going?" David asks me as he spoons a heaping helping of garlic spinach onto what I assume is my plate.

"Speaking of things under the heading of 'Can we please not talk about it?'"

His brow furrows with concern. I love it when it does that. It's so cute.

"Is it that bad? Do I need to rein in my mom?"

I keep myself from asking him whether that's actually possible for anyone to do. The fact that David is willing to intervene means a lot to me.

"It's just a bit tricky navigating the maternal tides." And then I remember my beautiful wedding dress, and I smile. "I do have some good news, though. Your mother sent me the most fabulous wedding gown I've ever seen." Remembering the dress makes me beam from ear to ear. "Prepare to be bowled over, Reverend Swenson, when you see your bride coming down the aisle."

To my concern, a shadow, not a smile, passes over David's face. He puts down the container he's holding and takes me in his arms. Okay, now this part of the old-married-couple scenario I could definitely come to appreciate, although I don't know why his mother sending me the perfect dress should make him so serious.

"Are you sure you like it, Betsy? Because if you don't—"

"No, no. I love it. It's amazing, David. She got it at a Vera Wang sample sale."

He peers down at me from his superior height, studying me intently with his big brown eyes. "You're sure you like it? You're not just saying that because you don't want to tell my mom the truth?"

Now he asks that question? Why couldn't he have caught on during the whole wedding invitation thing? Or prior to the mismatched china fiasco? But I'm so pleased with my dress that I can't hold a grudge. "Honestly, David, it's the most beautiful dress I've ever seen."

"I know it's not easy, Betz, juggling our mothers. And I'm sorry you're bearing the brunt of it. It's just that . . ." He trails off.

"It's just that what?"

He sets his hands on my shoulders and looks me straight in the eyes. "It's just that I don't want to wait any longer than necessary to be married to you."

And from the way he kisses me, I totally believe him. Despite my trampled dreams of courtship, I feel the same way. Having David with me every moment, and I do mean *every* moment, is not something I want to delay any longer than necessary either. It's one of the reasons I'm willing to put up with this whole *Budget Bride* thing.

Maybe it's time to let go of this whole romantic courtship notion. Maybe romancing and moonlight and roses just aren't in the cards for us. Can I make my peace with that? Can I accept that my official first date with my future husband consists of takeout Chinese food eaten on my tiny patio? More important, if I eat the mountain of garlic spinach David has heaped on my plate, will he be up for canoodling on the couch after dinner?

I can't answer such deep existential questions on an empty stomach. "Come on," I say, slipping out of his embrace and picking up the plates. "Let's enjoy our dinner."

Chapter 14

Well, it's not a restaurant-type date at La Paz. It's not even a quick bite of comfort food at Noshville. But as David and I settle in around the little café table on my patio, the late April evening couldn't be more pleasant, and David's making me laugh like no one else can. Mr. Rosenburg's azaleas next door give off a pungent, sagelike aroma, and the wind chimes I picked up at the flea market sing in the breeze. So why won't the gnawing in my stomach finally ease up?

I try to appease it, even going so far as to give in to the garlic spinach. I offer my anxious insides orange-peel chicken and beef with broccoli to no avail. I hope David won't notice that I'm stuffing my face like a Vanderbilt lineman at the training table, so of course he does.

"Nice appetite," he says. "Not like—" He stops suddenly and quickly scoops a robust amount of brown rice into his mouth, an impressive feat considering he accomplishes it with chopsticks.

"Not like who?" I smile when I ask the question, like I'm teasing him. But now the tiny gnawing in my stomach becomes more like significant chomping.

"Hmm?"

David can try to pull that classic male gambit where the guy pretends not to hear the question he doesn't want to answer, but I'm not falling for it.

"Like who?" I ask again.

He pauses, wipes his mouth with his napkin, and then takes a long drink of his iced tea. When he's done, he opens and closes his mouth a couple of times, like a fish stranded on the bank, before clearing his throat and taking my hand.

"Look, Betz, I need to tell you something, but I don't want you to freak out."

"Freak out? Why would I freak out?" I remain calm, although right now I wouldn't mind an oxygen mask dropping out of the sky like they do when you lose cabin pressure on a plane.

"It's just that, well, I don't want you to misunderstand what I'm about to say."

"Yes?" I ask with an equanimity I don't feel.

David looks me in the eye and says, "Jennifer has been in town the past week, and I had to talk to her."

"You had to talk to her?" Somehow I achieve the perfect tone of polite, yet vague, interest. As if David has unearthed a fascinating but ultimately negligible piece of Bible trivia. Not as if he's seeing his old fiancée behind my back.

"I needed to talk to her about something, and she was going to be in town. So we had lunch."

I'm surprised by how much his confession hurts, even though it contains no information that I wasn't already aware of.

"What did you need to talk to her about?" I'm all innocence on the outside even as my insides seethe with jealousy.

David leans back in his chair. This would not be a bad thing except that he also lets go of my hand.

"Just some unfinished business. I wanted to get it cleared up before the wedding."

"Was it anything serious?" I ask. And then more boldly, "David, is there anything I need to know?"

Okay, my voice breaks a little bit on that last word, and he's a smart enough guy to pick up on that. He springs up out of chair and comes around the table to pull me to my feet.

"I swear, Betz, we're totally over. It was nothing."

"What kind of nothing?"

His face freezes, and my stomach sinks.

"I can't, Betz. It's something private. Between me and her."

And there it is. The truth of being a thirty-year-old bride-to-be with a thirty-two-year-old fiancé. Neither of us is a blank slate. We both have histories, David more than me, quite frankly, and maybe it's not the best thing for our relationship to divulge every detail of our pasts. Would knowing what David still needed to resolve with Jennifer truly make me feel any better?

"Okay." I swallow the tears that threaten. "I can respect that." I don't add that I can also obsess, worry, and fret because that's not the kind of unflattering revelation you particularly want to share with your new fiancé. Sometimes being a grownup blows.

"Thanks, honey." He kisses me, a quick peck on the lips. "How about we walk down to Baskin-Robbins before I have to head back to the church?"

"You can't stay?" Well, at least this time we actually consumed an entire meal in each other's presence.

"The building committee is meeting to discuss our options for raising the rest of the money for the hood."

I'm at least smart enough to take what I can get. "Okay. I'm glad we could at least have dinner."

And I soon discover that there's also a lot to be said for strolling down to Hillsboro Village hand in hand with David. I like the way his fingers thread through mine and how he squeezes my hand and winks at me in the twilight when we see a little girl jumping rope on her front sidewalk. Her blond hair bounces with each hop, and she grins at us as we pass.

A bit later we're making the return trip, ice cream dripping down our cones and our fingers, when David asks me how things are going at Church of the Shepherd.

I hesitate before I answer. I don't want to spoil our time together. I have a feeling David's going to be as enthusiastic about Corday's offer and the prospect of relocating to the suburbs as The Judge is. David's church is just across the river from downtown, and they struggle with a lot of the same problems we do. He's always been adamant, though, about the importance of a church adapting to its changing environment.

"Things are pretty good. Exciting, in fact." I paste a big smile on my face as I tell him about Corday's offer and my hopes for relocating the church.

Finally I say, "I wish you'd been with me when we went to look at property. I could have used your opinion. Arthur Corday and The Judge pretty much cancel each other out."

"So you're definitely going to push for the sale?"

If I were a dog, the hairs on my back would be standing on end. As it is, I settle for sounding really defensive.

"It's the right thing, David. An opportunity like this may never come along again. Harry Snedegar says that Corday's offered a good price."

"You talked to Harry? What else did he say?"

Well, why did he have to go and ask that? "He said that there might be more to this offer than meets the eye," I answer honestly.

"He's right, you know. The timing seems strange. Why is Corday pushing so hard for the sale?"

"The developers he represents are in a hurry. I don't see that it matters. Their motives don't change the fact that Church of the Shepherd is dying on the vine."

"It just seems like there should be another answer besides selling out."

"I wish there were. Church of the Shepherd's going to die, David, if I don't do something."

"Why are you pushing so hard for such a major change? I thought you wanted a place to lie low when you came back to Nashville."

He's right. That was what I wanted when I came back here licking my wounds from my first church. Being summarily fired can make a half-dead, downtown church look pretty appealing. I thought that all I would have to do at Church of the Shepherd was show up on Sundays, make sure the Sunday-school classes met, and perform an occasional funeral or baptism. I never dreamed I'd end up as the senior minister, interim or otherwise. I also never dreamed I'd have the chance to make this kind of difference to the church's future. Frankly, it's the kind of opportunity you dream about in divinity school.

"Are you sure your interest in relocating isn't a reaction?" David crunches a bite from his cone.

"A reaction?"

"Well, don't get mad, Betz, but you're starting to sound like a woman with something to prove. Church of the Shepherd's struggling, but selling out isn't the only answer. Couldn't you explore other less drastic options for growing the church first?"

"Corday says the offer's good for only thirty days."

"No wonder Harry's suspicious."

My frustration grows with each lick of my ice-cream cone. I know David's trying to help, but his questioning my judgment does not feel very supportive.

"Maybe we should just drop the subject." The words come out a lot grumpier than I intended.

My ice cream's melting so fast that it's dripping over my fingers and onto my shirt. Why didn't I think to grab some of those tiny napkins at Baskin-Robbins? Once again I'm left to clean up a mess without the proper materials to do the job.

"Okay," David says. "We don't have to talk about it. Just be careful, Betz. You're wading into some pretty deep waters here."

"I'm a big girl who knows how to swim."

He stops, turns me toward him, and squeezes my shoulders. "Don't be angry. I'm just looking out for my best girl."

I didn't know I could melt more quickly than the ice cream. At least we end the date properly—with one whopper of a kiss.

By the night of the mother-daughter banquet, the only thing getting me through each day is the thought of wearing that beautiful Vera Wang dress when I walk down the runway. I hang the gown from my closet door, the train fully draped and extended, so that it's the first thing I see when I wake up in the morning and the last thing I see when I go to bed at night.

My mom arrives the night before the banquet, which gives her ample time to not only admire the dress but also to harangue me into addressing envelopes for the invitations.

"If you're going to use those awful things from your computer," she says, sniffing the air as if the very odor of the paper offends her, "the least you can do is make sure they're hand addressed."

There's no use telling her that Microsoft Word comes with several lovely calligraphy fonts. So on the day of the banquet, I'm bleary-eyed from staying up until 2:00 a.m., and my writing hand has cramped into a permanent pen-holding position. Which I guess will come in handy for the wedding, because we can just slide the stem part of the bouquet right in there, and I won't have to worry about dropping it.

My mom and I arrive an hour early at the church for the banquet. The men have been in the industrial-size kitchen all day, and as we pass by, I smell the appealing aroma of the meal they're preparing. On top of a bridal fashion show, the ladies chose a tropical theme this year. I peek inside the fellowship hall to find that it's been transformed into a South Seas paradise. Or at least a cheap plastic version of one. Inflatable palm trees flank the stage, and there's a plastic lei at every table setting. Tissue-paper parrots and pineapples, the kind you open around in a circle like unfolding an accordion, dot the tabletops. Even the iced-tea glasses are wearing little hula skirts. Piñatas of various tropical fish are hanging from the ceiling. If I'm not mistaken, these decorations were left over from last year's Vacation Bible School, which was cleverly called Hit the Beach with Jesus. Looks like my wedding's not the only event on a budget.

"Is this someone's idea of a joke?" my mom asks. She's gone as white as my wedding dress.

"I don't think so. No."

We're both quiet for a long moment. Then we hear a strident "Hello!" and turn to see David and his mom walking toward us.

"Hello, Cecilia," I say with as much warmth as I can muster. I even kiss the air near her cheek. Then she and my mother greet each other, although the greeting is more like two lionesses sizing each other up for the looming battle—superiority in the pride. Over the past ten days, my disagreement with David about Arthur Corday's offer has melted away like our ice cream did that night. That may be in large part due to the fact that we've both been so busy we haven't seen each other.

"Hey, David." The mothers are distracted by each other's scent long enough for me to give him a quick kiss hello, but that's all there's time for before they turn their attention back to us.

"David, you know you can't stay, don't you?" my mom says in a playful, teasing voice. She even swats him lightly on the arm. "You can't see our girl in her dress before the wedding."

David takes my mother's faux flirting with good grace. "I know. I'm just playing chauffeur, and then I'm on my way."

Why is it that so many of the rituals surrounding weddings are designed to keep the bride and groom separated? Is it so they'll be so desperate to spend time with each other that they'll agree to anything?

"Isn't it a shame about there not being a bridal shower?" my mom says to Cecilia, who pauses for a long moment before answering.

"Oh, didn't I tell you?" she says. "We've taken care of that."

"Wonderful," my mother says. "I so hated for Betsy not to have one."

"Well, actually she's already had it."

My mother spins on one high heel, and her eyes shoot daggers at me. "You had a bridal shower and I wasn't invited?" Big crocodile tears pool in her eyes. "I see."

"No. Wait," I sputter, looking helplessly at David for support. "I haven't had a shower. I promise."

Cecilia twists the stack of gold bangles on her wrist. "Well, you have, in a manner of speaking. We just didn't need you there to pull it off."

Okay. Will someone please explain to me how you can have a bridal shower without a bride?

"Mom? What's going on?" David asks as he squeezes my hand. I'm grateful for his presence.

"We sort of, oh, how would you say it? We sort of

staged a bridal shower in New York. For the purposes of the magazine. It was really just a photo op. Not real presents or guests or anything."

David frowns. "How can you put Betsy's bridal shower in the magazine if she wasn't even there?"

Cecilia flashes her toothy smile, oozing confidence to cover her faux pas. "We just sort of Photoshopped her in."

"Photoshopped?" my mother asks. "What does that mean?"

Cecilia waves a dismissive hand. "Just a little computer magic. I knew Betsy would be far too busy to fly up to New York, and this way she wasn't inconvenienced."

I'm so stunned that I literally can't speak.

"Mom—," David says sternly, but Cecilia puts a finger to his lips. Ew. That would creep me out. David, to his credit, calmly but firmly grasps his mother's wrist and moves her hand away from his face. "Mom, this is going too far."

Cecilia's crocodile tears are far more impressive than my mother's. I've got to give her props and snaps for that.

"I didn't mean to hurt anyone's feelings. I just thought it would be the quickest way to take care of it. I'm under such pressure at the magazine. Circulation's down, and we've got to cut costs."

Cecilia's so obviously distraught that I can't even properly enjoy the irony of a budget-based magazine having to cut costs.

"It's okay, Cecilia. Really," I say. I'm not sure where that graciousness comes from, but when David shoots me a grateful look, I'm glad that I can take the high road. At least if they're going to Photoshop me into my bridal shower, they can remove some of those budding crow's-feet and maybe trim a little off the end of my nose.

My mother looks at me as if I've just flipped my skirt up over my head. "But—"

"It is fine. Really," I repeat. I'm determined to remain focused on the outcome here, not the process. David and I just want to be together, and it's going to take sacrifices like these to make that happen quickly. Also, I'm kind of relieved to have avoided any close contact with a bridal shower.

David has offered Cecilia his handkerchief, and she blows her nose into it with gusto. My mother is slightly mollified by Cecilia's remorse.

"Well, as long as Betsy doesn't mind," she says.

"Betsy!" Bernice Kenton is headed toward me from the opposite end of the fellowship hall, and she's clearly a woman on a mission. "We've been waiting for you," she says, gasping for breath between words when she joins our little group. "All the other models are arriving. Come with me, and we'll see about your hair and makeup."

"Okay, Bernice. I'm all yours."

"Jeremy needs to set up the shots," Cecilia says, referring to her photographer-sidekick.

"I'm headed back to church," David says, giving me

a quick kiss good-bye. "Will you be okay?"

"Yes. I'll be fine." I don't have any choice at this point but to believe that. He gives me another quick kiss and heads toward the exit, looking back over his shoulder just before he slips out the door.

"My mom's modeling too," I say to Bernice when I turn back to the ladies gathered around me, and my mother beams.

"Oh, that's nice," Bernice says with a smile. "We'd better get her hair and makeup done as well."

Implying that my mother is anything less than impeccably made-up and coiffed at any moment is tantamount to a death wish. Even if you know she's headed for Angelique's transformative powers with a curling iron and a tube of mascara. Bernice must realize that my mother's taken offense at her words because she takes her arm and draws her close, like two friends ready to swap juicy bits of gossip.

"Not that you need it, Mrs. Blessing," Bernice says. "But sometimes those stage lights, well, let's just say that they forgive nothing."

Bernice ought to know. She was an actress on Broadway before she snagged Darwin Kenton, a wealthy Nashville businessman who happened to see her in a matinée of *Sweet Charity* on a trip to New York. Bernice left behind the bright lights of the Big Apple decades ago, but she hasn't lost her penchant for drama.

However, when it comes to drama, my mom doesn't play understudy to anyone—even a former Broadway star.

"Yes, we do need our touch-ups, don't we?" She feigns applying cover-up underneath her eyes. "Especially as we get older."

Zing. On top of the usual frustration with my mother, I feel sorry for Bernice, who really didn't mean to be unkind.

"You both look gorgeous," I say, "but we don't want to hurt Angelique's feelings, so we should let her do her job." I recruited her personally since I knew she'd make me look fabulous. She's done it before when I needed semiprofessional help in the beauty department. Plus, I was afraid of whomever Cecilia might find to do the job.

Bernice and my mother visibly relax, so I take the opportunity to herd them toward the dressing area. I'm not even bothered by their cattiness because I have Vera waiting for me in the dressing room, and I'm going to look absolutely gorgeous in a national magazine. That's in addition to marrying the man I love and bringing new hope to my congregation.

Now if I can just keep from falling off the runway and bring The Judge around to my way of thinking. Per usual, the devil is in the details.

Chapter 15

The ritual of the mother-daughter banquet must certainly date back to Roman times. I can envision the first-century equivalent of the ladies auxiliary setting up long tables in the catacombs and dishing up their version of poppy-seed chicken casserole. I can even picture the apostle Peter waiting tables. Okay, well, maybe not Peter, but definitely some of the lesser-known disciples. Like Thaddaeus and Bartholomew.

At Church of the Shepherd, the mother-daughter banquet dates only from the 1950s. And while the church has steadily declined in the past twenty years as succeeding generations of daughters moved to the suburbs, they always return for this particular event. And they bring with them granddaughters and great-granddaughters so that Church of the Shepherd rings with the sounds of little girls' shrieks and maternal chatter.

The women of the ladies auxiliary are in their element. Margaret Devereaux is the most in her element of all. Because if a return to the glory days means a full sanctuary to the men, to the women it means a packed fellowship hall. Margaret sweeps around the room adjusting an inflatable palm tree here and a hula-skirted iced-tea glass there.

The incongruous tropical decorations notwithstanding (I'm still not sure what they have to do with a bridal fashion show), the ladies have done a nice job of decorating for the festivities. The fellowship hall exhibits more vigorous signs of life than at any point in my tenure here. I was the first one in the makeup chair, so I wander into the kitchen to see how things are going with the men while my mom and the rest of the ladies get powdered, buffed, and varnished.

The Judge has taken charge of the kitchen, but in a

hands-on fashion—not the purely dictatorial role I would have expected.

"Get those rolls in the oven," he orders Fred Mason, the chair of the membership committee, even as he flips mounds of greens in a humongous bowl. Judging from the deft flicks of his wrists with the tongs, it's not the first time The Judge has tossed a salad.

Booger's here too, among the cadre of kitchen soldiers, and he pauses to give me a wink and a smile. "The Judge runs a tight ship," he says, but there's no resentment in his voice. I can tell by the smile on his face that he's having a great time. For once he's just another pair of hands in the kitchen, not Booger the Homeless Guy.

Fred passes me with a tray of rolls bound for one of the four industrial-size ovens. "The Judge was a cook in the navy," he says. "In case you didn't notice."

The Judge a navy cook? It's hard to reconcile my mental images of him seated on the bench in his black robe, banging his gavel, with the traditional picture of a musclebound Popeye slinging hash.

"The Judge helped cook the dinner?"

"Reverend Blessing, The Judge *is* the cook. He even made the rolls from scratch."

I had no idea The Judge had culinary leanings. Since I've been at the church, I've made it a point never to enter the kitchen when a big meal was being prepared.

Rule for Women Ministers No. 5: Never let the congregation know you can cook. Because if you do, you will shortly be preparing lasagna for the legions instead of preaching, teaching, and making hospital visits. It also works in your favor not to let them know you can sew, or you'll end up making Bible-times robes for the children's Christmas pageant.

"The Judge made the rolls from scratch?" I repeat. "Are you sure it wasn't his wife?"

Fred smiles. "You've never seen his kitchen, have you?"

"Uh, no." I'm a bit embarrassed to admit that I've yet to call on a leading parishioner like The Judge, but I'm not generally someone who volunteers for combat.

Fred opens the oven door and slides the rolls inside. "I guess it's a nice change from presiding over family court."

"Family court?" I would have pegged The Judge for the federal bench at a minimum.

"He and Harry Snedegar used to be drinking buddies, but after Harry's accident, The Judge retired and started cooking again," Fred confides.

I don't know what to say. I had no idea. And that's what often happens in churches. Just like that, you see a whole new side to one of your church members and you have to do a complete reassessment of the person.

But I don't want to do a complete reassessment of The Judge.

"I didn't know Harry and The Judge were close."

"They're not—now. Like most drinking buddies, they discovered that booze was their only bond."

I catch a glimpse of myself in the glass of the oven door when Fred snaps it shut. The steam from the range is starting to make the wispy curls on the sides of my face wilt, and this insight into the inner life of The Judge is not something I want to deal with right now. So I mumble an excuse about needing to get my gown on and hastily exit the kitchen.

Leading with your insecurities is never an attractive habit, so I try to refrain from making it as plain as the freckles on my face that I've always lacked confidence in my physical appearance. But tonight, at long last, is my night to shine. For once the spotlight will be on me, and I plan to enjoy every moment of it. I am a mature, poised woman who knows that beauty comes from within.

Also, the Vera Wang gown doesn't hurt.

It seems as if other women always have little beauty tricks up their sleeves when desperate times call for them. Shades of eye shadow in their makeup bags that transform them into the second coming of Heidi Klum. Or smart new outfits that take an inch off their waistlines and two inches off their hips. But I've never figured out these little feminine secrets. With me, what you see is pretty much what you get. Tonight, though, there's hope for my having an Official Moment of Aesthetic Glory.

The other ladies look beautiful in their wedding dresses, and if this particular experience is bought at the price of the women sitting in the audience who couldn't dream of fitting into their bridal gowns, well, then I guess I'll dedicate this moment to them, since I'm sure

I'll be one of them someday. There's barely enough room in the hallway outside the children's Sunday-school classrooms for all of the hoop skirts, crinolines, trains, and veils. We're all giggling like schoolgirls, and the older the woman is, the more she's giggling.

Bernice Kenton leads off the show in her tea-length dress with a smart matching pillbox hat and veil. She looks like Grace Kelly. Bernice even has short white gloves and a little white Bible to carry. Her vintage look would be chic even if she were to walk down the aisle today.

"Remember, ladies," she advises us as she turns back to deliver her final instructions, "you have to sell it!" She flashes a blinding smile that's as white as her gloves and struts past the curtain onto the stage of the fellowship hall. Enthusiastic applause greets her arrival.

Not only is Bernice the leadoff hitter as it were, she's also emceeing the show. The sound system blares out "The Prince of Denmark's March" —also known as the theme song to *Masterpiece Theatre*—and there's more applause as Bernice struts the runway. A few moments later we can hear her voice out in the hallway as she takes the podium.

"Good evening, mothers and daughters, and welcome to Weddings of Yesteryear—A Celebration of Bridal Memories. We begin our evening," she continues, "with a trip back in time to the sixties. And here is our first model, Mrs. Robert Devereaux."

I haven't seen Margaret since I left the makeup chair, so I'm surprised when she brushes past me to enter the

179

stage where it connects with the Sunday-school hallway. I would have expected to see her in a tailored gown with clean, crisp lines—very Tricia Nixon. Instead, she's draped in a gauze-and-lace number with a peasant neckline and tiered skirt that wouldn't have been out of place at Woodstock. All she needs is a leather thong around her forehead and some Birkenstocks on her feet. She must notice the surprise on my face, because she lifts her nose a little higher in the air and shoots me a challenging glare.

"Even I, Reverend Blessing, was not immune to the social forces of the day." She glides past me, the loose sleeves of her gown billowing out behind her. Well, I guess her dress gives some clue as to why she's always hightailing it over to Our Lady of the Mink. Evidently she's making up for past lapses in good taste.

Beverly McHenry, wife of Mac, the ponytailed chair of the deacons, slides past me in exactly what I would expect—a confection from the late seventies that's a cross between Victorian lace and prairie calico. I remember that my sister, Melissa, owned at least three of that particular kind of dress when we were little. Beverly has a cameo pinned to a wide ribbon around her throat, and her hair is plaited in one long braid down her back. She, in fact, does have Birkenstocks on her feet, but they're some of the new fashionable ones, white with rhinestone buckles, in honor of the occasion. She prepares to step out onto the stage, and the music shifts to the theme from *Love Story*.

I'm practically quaking in my Payless undyed, dyeto-match strappy sandals with the four-inch heels. I'll need all the height I can get to reach David for the all-important kiss at the end of the ceremony, but for now, these things are instruments of pure torture. Not to mention a disaster waiting to happen on the runway. Why is women's ceremonial clothing always uncomfortable and high risk? Men may complain about bow ties, but they don't have their lungs squeezed in a corset-cum-vise or their arches stretched beyond human proportions by high heels.

There's a shift in the music, and the next model slips through the door and onto the runway to the strains of "Endless Love." This particular member of the ladies auxiliary is decked out in eighties shoulder pads and a nipped-in waist that would make Krystle Carrington of *Dynasty* fame weep with envy. The point of her hat drapes down her forehead, the dotted loop of a veil concealing her face.

I can hear Bernice chattering away as each model takes her turn on the runway, and the applause is polite, if a bit restrained. Of course, considering that the audience is made up of women who are excluded from modeling today, I guess that shouldn't be surprising.

Finally, we make it to the nineties. Claire Kenton Morgan and Elizabeth Devereaux Mitchell move past me and make their way onto the stage. Now there are definite oohs and aahs from the audience as they get their first glimpses of designer gowns. My confidence wilts a bit because I know I can't compete with two women who wear sizes that have the zero in front of the number instead of behind it.

Of course, my mom picks that exact moment to be "supportive." Or at least her version of it.

"You look almost beautiful, honey," she says as she squeezes my hand and then reaches up to wipe what she perceives as a stray bit of lipstick from the corner of my mouth. Frankly, I'm just glad she's not spitting on her handkerchief and wiping my face.

"Thanks, Mom." I hide the sarcasm in my words by giving her a big smile.

And suddenly it's our turn. My mom ducks through the doorway and onto the runway. I can't see anything because of the curtains in the wings that block my view of the stage and the audience. But I can hear Bernice as she describes my mom's version of the mother-of-the-bride look. No tailored jackets with a floor-length skirt for Saint Linda. No, she's got a slinky beige gown with a slit up the side that's made tolerably modest by the addition of a see-through wrap of nude chiffon. Tiny crystals sparkle from her neckline to her hem. Of course, my mom and I know that the true purpose of this dress has nothing to do with being the mother of the bride and everything to do with showing my dad what he gave up when he left her for Tracy.

The audience cheers for my mom, so I assume she's done some saucy little spin at the end of the runway. The other brides who've completed their sashaying are behind me in the hallway, whispering and muffling giggles. And then it's my turn.

"I can't," I protest, suddenly flooded with stage

182

fright, as Claire and Elizabeth herd me through the doorway.

"Smile," Claire hisses as she gives me a semigentle shove.

And then I'm out there, at the top of the runway, the spotlights blinding me. I feel a tug on the back of my dress and resist the urge to spin around to see what I've caught it on.

"Just fluffing your train, dear," my mom says. A brief *whoosh* of air puffs out my dress, and then she moves back to stand next to Bernice.

"And here is our very own Reverend Betsy Blessing," Bernice says into the microphone, "in none other than Vera Wang."

The roar of applause and the cheers are what I've always dreamed of hearing after one of my sermons.

"Walk," my mom orders me under her breath. "And smile!"

I paste a happy expression on my face, because I'm having some sort of weird, out-of-body experience. A part of me is thrilled to be in this moment, my ears filled with the approving cacophony of the womenfolk of Church of the Shepherd. But another part of me is curiously detached. Is this all there is? I mean, I'm no different in this moment than when I stand up on the chancel on Sundays, except that right now I'm wearing a designer dress and a face full of makeup. Maybe it's the very public statement that I've finally snagged a man that's drawing all this applause. With that thought, I realize the reason for that disconnected part of me.

183

While I'm fabulously happy to be with David, it doesn't seem like my having a romantic relationship should qualify me for this sort of adoration. Not when doing my job on a day-to-day basis evidently hasn't.

All these disturbing thoughts continue to swirl in my brain as I move down the runway. The PA system blares "The Wedding March," so this is definitely a full-on preview of what my big day will be like. And I wonder, Is this how the brides I've married all these years have felt? As if something is missing? Or is it me? Am I just not cut out to enjoy the experience like a normal woman?

Matching me step for step, Jeremy snaps pictures from his position on the floor alongside the runway. I hear him saying, "Yeah, baby. Yeah, baby," and I have to suppress a giggle, since it sounds more like he's encouraging an actress in a porn flick than a preacher-turned-model.

Some part of me hears Bernice describing my dress in detail—satin, pleats, cathedral-length train. I can even hear a few oohs and aahs. And then I reach the end of the runway, strike a pose, and make eye contact with Booger, who's hovering at a table in the front row with a dessert in each hand. His smile stretches from ear to ear, and I think it's the first time I've ever seen him truly, genuinely happy.

"Beautiful," he mouths to me, and I wink at him. A fabulous sense of well-being floods through me from my veil to my strappy sandals. Maybe for this night I need to let go of analyzing everything and just enjoy this ritual for what it is—a celebration of what should be among the happiest moments of a woman's life. I decide to let go of all the disappointments and what-ifs and my worries about all the women in the audience who couldn't be onstage. I will simply enjoy the moment on their behalf, for all of us who feel we don't quite measure up to the mythical image of modern womanhood.

I strike my own saucy pose and then execute a graceful turn. Impulsively, I stop and look back over my shoulder. Then I take the stand-in bouquet of silk flowers I was given to carry and toss it in a hook shot worthy of Kareem Abdul-Jabbar.

The audience goes wild. In fact, their shrieks are more than I expected. I look back over my shoulder again, and this time a genuine grin breaks out on my face when I see that Booger has dropped his desserts and caught the bouquet.

I glide back to the top of the runway with my head high and applause ringing in my ears. My mom's in tears, and I'm practically weeping myself. If wearing this dress at a church fashion show is this good, just think what it's going to be like when I'm actually walking down the aisle.

Chapter 16

Flush with power from my smashing appearance at the mother-daughter banquet, I spent the weekend mustering my courage and plotting my strategy for the showdown over the sale of the church property. The Judge has managed to avoid getting this matter in front of the administrative committee, so I've decided to force the issue by pushing for a vote now, on Monday, rather than waiting until Arthur Corday's deadline. Fortunately, Edna was very amenable to having the meeting in her hospital room. Said she wouldn't miss it for anything.

The administrative committee is assembled at various points around the room. The Judge occupies the only visitor's chair. I'm leaning against the sink. Peyton and Mac are leaning against the windowsill. Ralph Pennybacker, the treasurer, hunches over the adjustable bedside table. He's got his infamous accordion file at his feet and a two-inch-thick stack of spreadsheets fanned out across the top of the table. Bernice, in her role as secretary, sits at the foot of Edna's bed, stenographer's notebook open in her lap.

Edna is propped up against a bank of pillows, wearing a silk bed jacket and a sling. Since her injured shoulder is on one side and her broken hip on the other, she was transferred to the rehab hospital to convalesce. She nods regally at each one of us, like a queen holding court.

"I'll call the meeting to order," Peyton says.

To tell you the truth, I'm more nervous about this meeting than I was about strutting the runway at the mother-daughter banquet. When you're a woman minister and you know you're right about something, the trick is to push your agenda while still seeming properly feminine. So although I'm totally committed to convincing the committee to approve the sale, I'm also aware how I will have to present myself to achieve my goal. I'm more than happy to use qualifying adjectives when I speak, to end declarative statements with a questioning tone, and otherwise to make myself as non-threatening as possible. I did not, in fact, learn these techniques on the job. No, I acquired a working knowledge of this strategy from years of watching my mother manipulate my father.

"I know we've all needed some time to think and pray about this decision," I begin, deliberately making eye contact with each person in the room, "but we can't delay too long. The deadline is approaching."

"I still don't think it's in the best interests of the church," The Judge declares, crossing his arms and letting his jowls quiver. "I'll acknowledge that we have our problems to solve, but running away is the wrong choice."

I nod sagely and don't try to disagree with him. "Peyton?" I ask, turning my attention to the chair of the congregation.

"I still don't like it, Betsy. Why the hurry?"

"I think Mr. Corday explained that. These particular investors want to move quickly. They want to announce their project very soon." Although I pressed Corday to tell me what would be replacing Church of the Shepherd, he said he couldn't reveal that information. And obviously once the property passes from our hands, we have no say in what takes its place. Given the price of the property, it will have to be condos or a parking structure to recoup the investment. "Do you have other objections?"

Peyton frowns. "Not specifically. But I think we're putting the cart before the horse."

"I understand why you feel that way," I say, acknowledging his feelings, which is the first thing they teach you in Theological Foundations of Pastoral Care and Counseling. "Anyone else?"

I did a mental voting poll prior to the meeting, and I figure that Edna, Mac, and Bernice will vote to approve the sale. The Judge and Peyton are dead set against. So Ralph, the money guy, is the one I need to bring over from the Dark Side if I'm going to win the vote.

With that in mind, I make my arguments primarily financial ones. "Ralph was kind enough to run the numbers," I say. "At our current rate of income versus expenses, we will be tapping into the principal of our endowment within a few months."

The Judge frowns even more fiercely, Peyton sticks his hands in the pockets of his golf pants, and Bernice scribbles notes as fast as her hand will move.

"I'm afraid it's not really about a choice," I say. "We can sell the property now at a very good price, relocate, and have hope for a good future for Church of the Shepherd." I stop, clear my throat, and then continue. "Or we can refuse the offer and watch this church die a little more each day." I called Harry to talk with him again, just to make sure my take on the sale of the property was correct, and he said I was right. A better offer wasn't likely to come along anytime soon.

"Are we sure the offer is a good one?" Edna asks.

"Yes. Harry Snedegar said it was an excellent price." I omit Harry's additional comment about wondering why Arthur Corday was offering such advantageous terms for the property.

The invocation of Harry's name causes Ralph to nod. My heart leaps in proportion to the movement of his head.

"Betsy's right about the numbers," he says, "but the move will come at a significant cost to many of our members. A good number of them won't come to Williamson County with us."

"That's true," I say. "But we also have to acknowledge that as the church continues to decline, people will leave for that reason as well."

Ralph keeps nodding. "People also don't give money to a lost cause." He takes off his glasses, wipes them with a handkerchief from his pocket, and then slides them back in place. "I'm afraid Betsy may be right about our decision. Much as I'd rather not do it, it may be the right thing to sell Church of the Shepherd."

My heart leaps with hope. Have I brought Ralph over to my side?

"We might as well go ahead and vote," Peyton says. "I don't think anyone's mind is going to be changed by what we say today. Do I have a motion?"

"I move that we accept Arthur Corday's offer," Edna says.

"I second it," Ralph says. My heart leaps with joy at his show of support.

"Any discussion?" Peyton asks as a matter of form. No one says anything. "Then all in favor?"

Three hands go up—Edna, Mac, and Bernice.

Wait a minute. What happened to Ralph? I shoot him a questioning glance.

"All opposed?" Peyton asks. He raises his hand as does The Judge—and Ralph. Wait a minute. You can't vote against a motion you just seconded. Isn't that against *Robert's Rules of Order*?

"I'm sorry, Betsy," Ralph says. "I know you're right, but I've been at Church of the Shepherd since I was an infant. I guess I'd rather bury the church than sell it."

Peyton frowns. "That makes the vote a three-to-three tie." He looks at me. "Our constitution says that in the event of a deadlock on the administrative committee, the senior minister casts the deciding vote."

It's up to me to decide the future of Church of the Shepherd. I think I may throw up.

All eyes are on me, but not in that approving mother-daughter banquet kind of way. No, this is more like how people look at someone who's about to save the world—or shoot Bambi.

"Betsy?" Peyton asks, prompting me, but my throat freezes with sudden panic. The mantle of senior-minister responsibility suddenly feels more like a straitjacket. Or a shroud. Perhaps a noose.

"I . . . I . . ." Ay-yi-yi. I look at Peyton, The Judge, then Ralph.

I ask Ralph, "Are you sure you won't reconsider your vote?"

He shakes his head, and my stomach drops to the tile beneath my feet. *Deep breaths,* I remind myself. *Deep breaths.*

I push away from the sink and clear my throat. It's now or never. If I'm ever going to take my professional future by the horns, this is the moment.

"Then I vote aye," I say.

"The ayes have it," Peyton says, stating the obvious.

Edna's smiling. Bernice continues to scribble furiously on her steno pad, but the corners of her mouth are definitely turned up. Mac clasps his hands and rubs his palms together in a twisting motion. "Now we'll have some money to give to outreach. I've got several worthy projects in mind."

Money for outreach? We never discussed that. And it's going to take every penny we get from the sale to buy land and make a dent in the cost of the new building. But I'm not going to correct him now, not while the committee's still officially in session and he could change his vote.

"I'm sure we'll sort all that out very soon," I say, walking that ethical tightrope with the lumbering grace of an elephant.

"Then I guess we're adjourned," Peyton says tightly.

"No, wait." He holds up a hand to stop Ralph, who's started gathering up his spreadsheets. "As long as we're in session, I'll go ahead and submit my resignation as chair of the congregation."

"Resignation?" Mac says, voicing our common surprise.

Peyton looks around the room. "I won't stand in the way of what has to be done, but I won't be a part of it either. So I'm resigning, effective immediately." He sticks his hand out to me, and instinctively I shake it. "Best of luck, Betsy. You're going to need it."

"Peyton, I never meant for—"

"No, but big decisions have big consequences, Betsy. You're doing what you feel is right, and so am I."

I don't know what to say. I guess I thought that even the folks who weren't excited about the move would come around once the decision was made.

"Peyton, I hope you'll change your mind," I say. The others in the room nod their heads in agreement.

"I appreciate that, Betsy, but I won't." He moves toward the door. "It's been a pleasure, folks, but I'll excuse myself so you can conduct the rest of your business." By that, he means replacing him as chair of the congregation. "Mac, I'm appointing you the acting chair."

"Sure, Peyton." But Mac looks distinctly uncomfortable at the prospect of taking over the leadership of the church.

And just like that, Peyton walks out the door, and I'm gasping for air like a fish out of water.

"Well, I guess we need to elect a new chair," Mac says.

I look at him, the question in my eyes.

He shakes his head. "Sorry, Betsy, but I'm not the man for that job."

I look at Ralph, who also declines with a shake of his

head. "I'm strictly the money man."

"Edna?" I ask with a growing sense of desperation, but since we're conducting this meeting in her hospital room, I'm pretty sure of her answer.

"I don't think so, Betsy. Much as I'd like to."

The fact that I would even consider asking Edna to chair the congregation clearly indicates my mounting desperation.

"Bernice?"

"I'm sorry, Betsy. I'll stick to being secretary."

There's only one person left in the room.

"Judge?" I ask, feeling like a woman awaiting a death-penalty verdict.

"Thank you, Reverend. I accept the position."

Mix two parts dread with one part pure fear and you'd have a close approximation of the cocktail brewing in my stomach.

Ralph looks relieved. "Then I move we elect The Judge as the new chair of the congregation."

There's a long pause while we all wait for a second to Ralph's motion. None is forthcoming. The silence grows longer and more uncomfortable. At that moment the door to the room swings open and an orderly bearing a lunch tray tries to squeeze past me.

"Afternoon, folks," he says with a friendly smile, oblivious to the tension in the room. When no one responds, he shrugs his shoulders, puts down the tray, mumbles something about too many visitors being a violation of the rules, and makes his exit.

And in the wake of his departure, I know what I have

to do. "I second the motion."

"All in favor?" Mac asks, his shoulders slumping with relief. My seconding the motion gives Mac, Edna, and Bernice permission to say aye, which they do.

"Then it's unanimous," Mac says. He mocks wiping his hand across a perspiring brow. "That's a relief. Congratulations, Judge. That's the longest I've ever been, or ever hope to be, in a position of power."

Well, my victory was thrilling while it lasted. Because I'm pretty sure the first thing The Judge will do is take another vote on the sale of the property. Unless I do some quick maneuvering.

He opens his mouth to speak, but I jump in first. "I think that according to the bylaws, we can't conduct any more business until we appoint someone to replace The Judge as chair of the elders. Besides, I'm sure Edna's exhausted. We should let her have her room back."

The Judge raises his eyebrows in a knowing gesture. "Which we will do with all haste."

To some people his words might sound reassuring, but I recognize them for the challenge they are. My window of opportunity to push through the sale of the building is going to be very small. Particularly when the person authorized to sign the contracts won't be a willing participant in the matter.

"It may take a few days to find someone to lead the elders," I say.

"You leave that to me, Miss Blessing," The Judge says.

I feel like a participant on *The Amazing Race*, ready to fly from the room at breakneck speed. The next few days are going to be a footrace, both literally and figuratively.

Luckily, I have Arthur Corday's number on speed dial on my cell phone.

The good news for me is that The Judge will have a hard time finding anyone who will agree to serve as chair of the elders. You wouldn't think it would be that difficult. All the elders usually do is have meetings, study some innocuous Christian how-to book, and pray for the homebound members. The problem is that they're supposed to provide spiritual guidance and leadership, while the deacons look after the more mundane tasks. It's been my experience as a minister that very few people feel equipped to take on the role of elder. And whenever a church conflict erupts, everyone looks to the elders to mediate and solve the problem. Well, if you've ever been in the middle of a church fight, you know the extent of the casualties. It's not pretty.

Arthur Corday has the sale papers in my office first thing the next morning. I try to read through the legalese of the voluminous pages of the contract, but it's hopeless. I'd do better if it were written in Hebrew or Greek. Soon after nine o'clock Hart Haddington, the church's attorney, arrives. So far in my tenure at Church of the Shepherd, I haven't had occasion to spend much time with Hart, but this morning looks to be a lengthy session. Angelique will be hovering, offering us frequent coffee refills, because Hart was recently declared one of the most eligible bachelors in Nashville.

"I must say that I'm surprised the church is willing to sell the property," he says as he reads through the opening paragraphs.

"We believe it's a wonderful opportunity. We'll be looking for land around Franklin, and then we'll build a new building. It will give us a chance to attract a whole new influx of members."

"Mmm."

His noncommittal answer makes me antsy. *Please, please don't let him find anything fishy,* I half pray, half wish.

Hart makes funny little noises as he reads, sort of like a pig rooting around in the dirt for an unexpected treat. I swallow a smile and try to busy myself with the article for the church newsletter Angelique's been hounding me to finish. Between the wedding plans and trying to maneuver around The Judge, I'm just the tiniest bit behind. Well, to tell the truth, I'm panic-and-scream behind, but I'm trying not to dwell on that fact.

Angelique peeks in around my half-open office door. "Can I get y'all anything?" She's checking out Hart Haddington in a major way, but he's oblivious. Plus, can't she hear him making those weird little noises?

"No, Ange. I think we're fine."

"You sure?"

Hart's lost in his own little legal world, so I shoo her away with my hand and a teasing grin that tells her I'm onto her. She flashes back a saucy smile and shrugs her shoulders in a way that says, "You can't blame a girl for trying."

I finally give up accomplishing anything and play solitaire on my computer while Hart finishes reading the contract.

"Everything seems pretty much in order," he says. "There's just this one clause that concerns me."

"What clause is that?" As if I could tell one clause from another. For all I know, there's a section where we've all pledged our firstborn sons to Cumberland Realty.

"It's this one here. It says that if a historic landmark designation is applied to the property within sixty days of signing, then the contract becomes null and void."

"Historic landmark? Why would that matter?"

"It restricts what can be done to the building."

"Does that mean the developers couldn't tear down the church if there was a landmark designation?"

"Yes. The building is historic, but the church never wanted to limit itself by applying for the designation. Once you do that, it opens a whole can of worms if you want to expand."

"So it's not anything to worry about?"

"I guess if some of the preservationists got wind of Corday's plans to redevelop the property, they might try to pursue it. You'd just have to cross that bridge when you came to it."

"But other than that, you don't see anything wrong with the contract?"

"No. They're being more than fair. Surprisingly fair, actually."

Okay, that's yet another person who's mentioned how generous Arthur Corday and his cohorts are being. I swallow and force myself to ask the question that I really don't want to ask. "Do you think we should go through with the sale?"

Hart lays the papers on my desk. He has on his serious lawyer face. "Betsy, every contract has risks. There's no such thing as a sure thing. But if the administrative committee thinks this is the best course for the church's future, then I don't see any reason not to move forward."

I'm so relieved that I want to jump up and hug Hart Haddington, but I don't think that's what you're supposed to do with three-hundred-dollar-an-hour legal counsel. So I settle for standing up, walking around my desk, and shaking his hand with my firmest grip.

"Thanks, Hart. I appreciate how quickly you got to this. I'll take these to The Judge right away for his signature."

"No problem." He squeezes my hand before he lets it go, and then he winks at me, which I absolutely know is not what expensive legal counsel is supposed to do.

"Um . . . well . . . thanks again." I can't look him in the eye. Because even though I'm an engaged woman, I feel a little tug of attraction. No wonder Angelique keeps finding excuses to come in here, even if he does make funny noises when he reads.

"Anytime." He smiles again, picks up his briefcase,

and leaves the office with a confident stride.

I, on the other hand, collapse into my chair. If that little twinge is telling me anything, it's saying that I need to spend more time with my fiancé.

Chapter 17

I thought I would feel more elated as I watched The Judge sign the contracts for the sale of Church of the Shepherd, but I found the whole experience rather flat. I dropped the papers off at his house last night, but he didn't show up at Church of the Shepherd first thing this morning as I expected. So I end up having to track him down at the Riverfront Café and retrieve the papers from him in front of his coffee cronies, which works to my advantage from a functional point of view but really antagonizes The Judge.

I can tell he's unhappy because he's being so nice to me.

"Teresa!" he calls to the bouffant-haired waitress straight out of the fifties. "A cup of coffee for Reverend Blessing."

Since he's calling me "Reverend" for a change, I know I'm in big trouble.

"Hard as I tried, I couldn't find a reason not to sign them," he says, pen poised just above the signature line. "Is there anything else I should know?"

Hart's mention of the historic-landmark clause springs to mind, but I'm not falling for that old counseling trick of one last leading question. I guess they teach it in law school, too. Or in judge's training. It's amazing how asking that simple question can get somebody to spill the beans like crazy.

"Not a thing, sir."

Once he turns his gaze back to the papers, I risk taking a good look at him. And then I wish I hadn't. Because I see a wave of deep sorrow rolling across his face. The wave apparently keeps rolling across the table and crashes over me, because I'm suddenly swamped by guilt. I've been trying not to give in to the very real pain that this sale will cause. Instead, I've been focusing on the joy it will bring to folks who don't have a church home yet. But when someone like The Judge, who bullies other people mercilessly, flinches in front of me, I can't remain unaffected.

"I'm sorry," I mumble.

He doesn't look up. Instead, he presses the point of his pen to the paper and signs his name in a thick, unreadable scrawl without acknowledging my words.

Teresa offers to refill my cup, but all I want to do is escape. "No, thanks," I say.

She smiles and then pats me on the back. "It's okay, honey. We all know you're just doing what you have to do."

What? Even Teresa the Waitress knows the in-house business of Church of the Shepherd? We might as well take out an ad in the *Tennessean*.

"Thanks," I say and pray that someone in The Judge's posse will comment on the weather or deliver a character assassination of some local politician.

200

No such luck.

"So where's the new property?" Fred Mason, the membership chair and designated roll baker, asks. "If we were going to make this move, shouldn't it have been twenty years ago?"

"We've got our eye on a very nice site in southern Williamson County," I say primly. Sure, I could agree with his assessment of the timing, but that's not going to make either me or The Judge feel any better at the moment.

"It will be a shame to watch them tear down that beautiful building," Fred says.

Then it hits me. I don't know why it hasn't really struck home before, but my head is now filled with images of cranes with wrecking balls demolishing the beautiful golden stone steeple of Church of the Shepherd. The vat of coffee in my stomach threatens to make a return appearance. But I have to be strong. Heaven knows that the Israelites thought slavery in Egypt looked pretty good once they'd suffered a little deprivation—and depravation—in the desert. Moses had to stay strong to keep them from turning around and marching right back into captivity.

"Yes, it will be difficult," I say, "but the church isn't a building. It's the people."

"What about the people who won't follow us to Franklin?" Reverend Squires asks.

Okay, who are these guys? The chorus from a Greek tragedy? I don't need them chanting a litany of the difficult parts of this decision.

"We trust that God will help everyone through this process," I say, pawning off the hardest question on the Big Kahuna, who isn't likely to appear suddenly as a pillar of fire or a giant cloud and undercut my authority. I'm always disdainful of folks who conveniently match up their own agendas with God's will, but I do think it's true that in the life of any congregation, people come and go, and the best we can do is trust God's grace to provide for them.

I gulp down the last of my coffee, scoop up the papers, and say my good-byes as quickly as possible. Then I flee the Riverfront Café and head for Arthur Corday's office.

All the complications and details of selling the church building consume my days and most of my evenings over the next four weeks, which turns my resolution to retrieve control of my wedding into a joke. I try to adopt David's attitude of "Go along to get along" when it comes to picking tables for the reception (round or rectangular?) and a pen for folks to sign the guest book (jeweled or feather?). Frankly, it all seems pretty trivial—color of the netting and ribbon for the little bags of rice: white or silver?—so I just admire my wedding dress each morning when I wake up and then again before I go to sleep. It's become my own personal ritual, and I'm more devout than a Benedictine monk saying the offices.

I had hoped to feel connected to some part of the wedding plans. At least some part other than staying up until

202

the wee hours addressing invitations by hand—or baking cupcakes for the pyramid stack that will serve as our wedding cake. (No, I'm not kidding.) At least I don't have to hand-write place cards for the reception. Since we're using paper tablecloths, Cecilia got the bright idea to buy a big wad of those "Hi! My Name Is . . ." stickers from Wal-Mart and affix them to the tablecloths. She also said this would keep people from switching their assigned places. By this point I'm too tired to ask why in the world it would matter if people switched their seats. Having that control seems to make Cecilia a little easier to work with, so I let it go.

Other things—things I thought I would really enjoy—have turned out to be more burdens than pleasures. Like the final fittings for my dress, believe it or not. I've been carefully monitoring my points on Weight Watchers, but my bustline doesn't seem to be cooperating with my efforts. It keeps expanding! The seamstress is ruthlessly determined to make the dress fit me exactly. I haven't been poked and prodded this much since my last doctor's exam.

Filling out the rest of the wedding party was no picnic either. With LaRonda out of the country, Angelique's declining with an emphatic no, and my sister not an option, I give in to Cecilia's pleas to make Claire Kenton Morgan and Elizabeth Devereaux Mitchell my bridesmaids. Apparently she picked them because they're the right sizes to fit into the dresses she scored at a bridal seconds' sale. I guess one of them will actually have to be the maid of honor; maybe they can draw straws. David finally got around to asking his room-mate from college to be his best man. A couple of his guy friends from divinity school are going to serve as groomsmen.

Cecilia got the wild idea to dispense with any fresh flowers at all for the ceremony—unless, of course, they could be salvaged from someone else's wedding and reused—but I put my foot down. I'm going to have a pretty bouquet if it kills me. Which it may, because we compromised on Cecilia's ordering the flowers from a wholesaler if I would put the bouquets together for myself and my two pencil-thin bridesmaids instead of paying a florist.

Who knew it was so hard to arrange a few roses? They make it look so easy in those DIY bridal maga-zines. I've been practicing on cheap flowers from the grocery store, but so far all I've managed to produce is some wan-looking clumps of foliage. And apparently I'm supposed to have bridesmaids gifts, even though I barely know these two women. So, as instructed by Cecilia, I'm spraying pieces of an old jigsaw puzzle with glitter paint and then gluing them to a wooden pic-ture frame. These travesties are apparently meant to represent my gratitude for preceding me up the aisle. Frankly, I think they look like something I made for my mom the summer my parents sent me to sleep-away camp so they could fight without my overhearing them.

Another thing I thought I'd enjoy would be buying a wedding present for David. But what do you get a man who doesn't really value material possessions? He needs only so many Dave Matthews Band T-shirts or Coldplay albums. I know he'd really like a new hood for the kitchen stove at his church, but that's a little out of my price range.

I've seen him only sporadically as the weeks pass, and none of our meetings feel like a real date. Just a few stolen moments snuggling on my couch or brown-bagging lunch in one of our offices.

"I know it's hard, Betz," David said last night when he dropped by my apartment for a brief hour after his last evening meeting. "But it's going to be over soon. And then we'll be together all the time."

That thought is the only thing that's kept me from losing my mind these past weeks.

Here's how two ministers from different denominations negotiated their wedding's liturgy via instant messaging. Please note: this is a particularly tricky process when one party—me—comes from a "free church" tradition where we freely borrow from different denominational liturgies, and the other party—David—thinks that God penned the service authorized by the Lutheran Church.

Me: I don't want to be given away. It smacks of patriarchy, and women are no longer to be counted like property, as if we're sheep or goats you can trade for a bushel of grain.

David: Will you at least agree to be "presented" by your parents?

Me: What am I? A debutante? Okay, fine, I'll be

"presented" by my parents. But you have to convince my dad to say "Her mother and I" when the minister asks, "Who brings this woman to be married to this man?" He hasn't allowed anyone to refer to them both in the same sentence for the past fifteen years.

David: I'll take care of your dad. What about the Declaration of Intent?

Me: I like the one used in the United Church of Christ service.

David: C'mon, Betz. Since we're doing this thing at your church, the least you can do is let me use some of my church's liturgy.

Me: Fine. We can do the Lutheran Declaration of Intent if we use the Presbyterian liturgy for the Exchange of Rings.

David: What about vows? Whose vows are we going to use?

At this point I briefly considered suggesting that we write our own. After all, we're both highly trained professionals with graduate degrees in our field. We ought to be able to pull that off. But late one night, in between addressing invitations and baking cupcakes to be frozen for use on the big day, I curled up on the couch and tried to write some vows for us. You know what? They were awful. Like a Hallmark card dipped in maple sugar and rolled in Fun Dip.

The hardest part of trying to craft my own vows was that my relationship with David rests, in large part, on our shared dry sense of humor, which can be an acquired taste and which also doesn't translate well in a worship setting such as a church wedding. I don't think it would really work to change the traditional wording to, "If anyone knows of any reason why these two should not be wed, please keep it to yourselves, and for heaven's sake, don't go saying 'I told you so' if for some reason this doesn't work out."

After several days of intense negotiation, though, we resolved the ceremony itself. Then we had to select the officiating minister. When you're a preacher, choosing someone to officiate at your wedding is somewhat akin to a surgeon trying to decide whom she can trust to perform a risky operation on a loved one. If LaRonda were here, she'd be the one we'd choose hands down to perform the ceremony. But since she's not even in the same hemisphere as we are at the moment, we had to choose between David's bishop—an authoritarian cranky pants who thinks women should be barefoot, pregnant, and in the kitchen of a modest three-bedroom ranch-style home—and the nice-but-sonorous Reverend Squires.

David finally conceded the choice of officiating minister when I pointed out that there's no guarantee we can keep his bishop from inserting the word *obey* into the service, as in *love, honor, and* . . . And I told him that if the *o* word is used, I will turn around and march back down the aisle to live the rest of my days in glorious spinsterhood. Even a conflict avoider like me has her limits.

David's amusement at my threats demonstrated that he didn't actually believe them, but he did make the concession to my choice of minister. Now I just have to make sure that we get a Starbucks quad venti latte down Reverend Squires prior to the ceremony to pep him up a little.

I've had too many lattes myself lately, and again I'm wide awake at 3:00 a.m. If I'm not worrying about the future of the church, I'm fretting over wedding stuff. Frankly, I'd much rather be sleeping. At this rate I'll be able to use the bags under my eyes to pack for my honeymoon.

So maybe it's not so strange when I pick up the phone and, after several fruitless attempts, figure out how to dial South Africa. Well, not the whole country. Just the school where LaRonda works. Surely it's daytime there since it's half a world away.

A very nice woman answers the phone, and between our two distinctive accents—South African and southern American—it takes us a minute to work out that I want her to call LaRonda to the phone. I feel guilty thinking that I might have dragged her out of class or something else important, but when LaRonda comes on the line, she doesn't sound peeved, just concerned.

"Betsy? Is everything okay?"

"Yes, it's fine. Sorry if I scared you."

"What time is it there?"

"Oh, about three, I guess."

LaRonda chuckles. "I'm pretty sure that's a.m., not p.m."

"Yeah."

"Did you want me to sing you a lullaby?" I can just see LaRonda's beautifully arched eyebrow rising even higher, but there's a smile in her voice.

"I guess I'm having some bridal jitters."

Until I say it out loud, I realize I haven't wanted to admit it, even to myself. I've cloaked my anxieties about my upcoming marriage in angst over the wedding plans.

"You're having second thoughts?"

"Yes. No. I don't know. Not really, but—"

"You know that's normal, right?"

"So absolute panic is nothing unusual?"

This time she doesn't laugh. "What's bothering you, Betz?"

I think about this for a minute. "I don't know. I thought it was the wedding plans, which David's mother has hijacked for the most part. But now I'm thinking maybe it's something else."

"Like?"

"Like I guess this doesn't feel how I thought it would."

LaRonda sighs. "I know what you mean."

And then I remember our last phone call and her distress over fitting in at the school. "Are things better there?"

"I guess so."

Now it's my turn to smile. "You guess?"

"It's not what I thought it would be."

"Tell me about it." And I mean that as both commiseration and a question.

"I guess I've learned a lot about what's really important. That's not a very comfortable experience, but I'm glad now that I came. I see things so differently."

"Like how?"

"Well, material things, for one. In the States, we have so much stuff, but it doesn't make up for things we don't have. Like community. Caring for one another. Being with the people we love."

As usual, LaRonda's wisdom hits home. "I need to remember that when I get frustrated with Cecilia. I know all of the trappings for the wedding aren't the important thing. I just want to spend the rest of my life with David. That's what matters."

"Then just keep focused on that," LaRonda says. "How bad can it get?"

I stifle my bark of laughter. If she only knew. "Well, whatever happens, I'll have the people I love around me on my wedding day. With one important exception."

"I wish I could be there, Betz, but I'm committed here. Next time you decide to get engaged and married, would you give me a little more notice?"

I know she's a half a world away, but LaRonda on the other end of the phone gives me a familiar feeling of comfort.

"Betz, I need to go. My next class is about to start. Look, focus on David and just let the rest of it go. And make sure you take lots of pictures, because I'm going to want to relive every little detail."

"Even the packing peanuts?"

"What?"

"Nothing. Thanks, Ronnie. I don't know what I'd do without you."

"Same to you. Take care, Betz. Just follow your heart."

"Okay. Good-bye. Keep those e-mails coming."

"Will do."

When I set the phone down on my bedside table, I feel considerably more relaxed than I did a few minutes ago. LaRonda's right. I just need to keep focused on the marriage and surrender the wedding.

With one last look at the dress hanging from my closet door, I burrow beneath the covers and allow myself to slide into sleep.

Chapter 18

And then suddenly, before I know it, the wedding is tomorrow. The wedding is tomorrow! How did that happen? It can't be time for the rehearsal dinner already. But it is.

As I put on a new linen sheath I bought at Ann Taylor for the occasion (some things about this wedding are not going to be budget!), I tamp down any lingering misgivings about this whole wedding planning process with the same rigor I use to get my hips into the dress. If I can just hold in my stomach, I can get through all of this. But that thought depresses me, because shouldn't your wedding be more than something you just "get through"?

211

I've officiated at enough ceremonies to know that not many brides and grooms get the opportunity to enjoy the process. I've tried to be realistic in my expectations, but instead of excited anticipation, I feel a strong under-current of sorrow. It feels like one of those soap-opera weddings that you know isn't going to actually happen because the bride's dead husband is going to walk in during the middle of the ceremony or because the groom will reveal that he's actually a woman. You can tell those nonstarter weddings because the wedding dress is always a little off. I mean, it's passable, but you can tell just by the gown on a soap opera if they're going to go through with the wedding.

That thought's kind of reassuring, actually, because if you can tell whether the wedding's going to happen by the gown—a variation on Edna's a-happy-marriage-depends-on-the-dress theory—then I'm in terrific shape with my fabulous Vera Wang. So I try to be outcome-based, as the management books say, and focus on the end result. In twenty-four hours I'll be married to David. While wearing Vera Wang. Life is good.

Plus, David's coming to pick me up for the rehearsal dinner, so we'll have at least ten minutes together in the car. The groom's family is in charge of this event, and Cecilia opted for having the dinner at the church because there's no fee for using the building. I've been afraid to ask who will be catering because I don't want to be told that we're having Kentucky Fried Chicken. The theme is A Midwinter's Eve, which is totally weird when it's eighty-five degrees outside, but I have chosen to overlook that as well for the sake of family peace.

When David picks me up, he's almost monosyllabic in the car, which doesn't bode well for the evening. Turns out that the person he thought might underwrite the new hood for the kitchen range at St. Helga's decided to fund a pet cemetery instead, so David's not in a very chatty mood. I endeavor to be content with just being in his presence, and he does reach over to hold my hand whenever he doesn't need to shift gears. His ancient Volvo lurches down Twenty-first Avenue, around the corner near Vanderbilt where it turns into Broadway, and then on toward Church of the Shepherd. Again, disappointment haunts me. I would have thought we'd have more scintillating conversation on the way to our rehearsal dinner than speculating on ways to take out the fire marshal.

Unfortunately, our rapport doesn't improve the closer we get to the church. David's shoulders are hunched with tension, and I'm wondering if the fire marshal alone is enough to account for the stress radiating from him.

"Are you okay?" I ask.

"Yeah. Sure."

I clear my throat and collect my courage. "Look, David, I'm a little concerned. We've hardly seen each other in weeks. It just seems like things are moving so fast."

We're approaching the light in front of Beaman Toyota just as it changes from green to yellow. David slams on the brakes, and I snap against the shoulder belt. He flings out an arm to protect me, but the force of the car's sudden stop makes it more like a blow than a protective gesture.

"Ouch!"

"Sorry, Betz. You okay?"

I don't really know how to answer that question. "Yeah. Yeah, I'm okay."

Only am I really? I've been downplaying my instincts since the night of the engagement party, and they're all screaming for me to put the brakes on this wedding with even more vigor than David just did. But that thought is too awful to contemplate, so I shove it aside once again. I am determined to marry David and be fab-ulously happy. Or else. For the thousandth time I tell myself that it will all be better once the wedding is over. I know as well as anyone that the ceremony is really little more than a glorified photo op. It's a trial to be endured, and then the real fun will begin. Life with David. Every day. Waking up next to him, his face the last thing I see before I go to sleep at night. Anything— even Cecilia being in charge of the wedding plans—is worth that.

Isn't it?

The light changes again, and we move forward toward the inevitable.

As it turns out, my future mother-in-law is the one doing the catering, not KFC. Or at least Cecilia is the one boiling fettucine and opening jars of alfredo sauce. And here's her budget twist on the traditional rehearsal dinner: the guests get to help cook the meal.

That's why the entire wedding party is in the huge kitchen of Church of the Shepherd when David and I arrive. Some are grating parmesan cheese, and others are spreading garlic butter on long loaves of Italian bread. Turns out that in keeping with the theme of the dinner (once again with the winter wedding motif), all the food will be white. Cecilia's got the menu posted on the bulletin board just outside the kitchen door. In addition to the chicken fettuccine with alfredo sauce, we're having garlic bread; a salad of jicama, onion, and white beans; and white cake with white icing for dessert. There's sparkling water to drink. Oh, and milk, of course. I haven't seen a meal like this since I was six and my best friend, Katie Greenway, refused to eat any food with a shade of color to it. She subsisted for nearly a year on Wonder Bread and cottage cheese. The memory makes me queasy.

As soon as Jeremy spots David and me, he starts clicking away with his camera. His flash goes off in our faces over and over until I can't see anything but little green spots dancing in front of my eyes.

"Hi, honey." My mom comes over to give me a hug, but she's stiff as a poker when I put my arms around her. "This woman is insane!" she hisses in my ear. Then she turns to David's mom.

"Cecilia! The happy couple's here!" Butter would melt immediately in her mouth, she's acting so warm and gracious, even though her smile appears to be frozen on her face.

"There you are!" Cecilia comes swinging around the large island in the center of the kitchen, a bundle of something in each hand. "I had these made just for you."

She thrusts one cloth into my arms and a matching one into David's. I unroll it to discover a white butcher-style apron with the word *Bride* embroidered on the front in girlie script. David, meanwhile, unfurls his black apron, which bears the matching designation *Groom* in bold and manly silver block lettering. Oh no. These are worse than those dorky veil-and-top-hat Mickey Mouse ears that honeymooners wear at Disney World.

"C'mon. Put them on." Cecilia claps her hands at us as if she's our first-grade teacher—or a Broadway director. "This dinner's not going to make itself."

I see my dad across the kitchen, dutifully slicing jicama. He shoots me a pained smile across the room. My bridesmaids—Claire and Elizabeth—are cutting and plating pieces of cake. Fred Mason has apparently been pressed into service for the evening to bake the rolls just as he did at the mother-daughter banquet, and Reverend Squires is standing in front of the range stirring a cauldron of pasta.

"Betsy?" Cecilia calls from the safety of the other side of the island. "Would you help your father with the jicama? I don't know how your mother's telling him to slice that, but he's almost lost a finger three times."

I refrain from replying that he's lucky he hasn't lost an even more important appendage if he and my mom

216

are in the same kitchen with sharp knives. I look around for Tracy, Dad's second wife. For the past two months, since the night of the engagement party, I've had to listen to my mother rant and rave about Tracy coming to the wedding. My mom wanted me to exclude her, but I refused. There has to come a point when you quit being the go-between for your divorced parents, and I decided that point was going to be my wedding. So my goal for the evening is to keep my family from killing one another.

"Hey, Dad. Where are Tracy and the boys?"

While I didn't want to exclude Tracy, I did entertain the possibility of excluding my half brothers Matt and Corey, otherwise known as Thing One and Thing Two. Although I love the twins, I recognize that they could reduce a drill sergeant to tears. There's no telling what they might do at a wedding. They're not malicious. Let's just say they have a low threshold for boredom.

"The boys kept trying to juggle the jicama," Dad said. "So Tracy took them to get a Coke."

Good plan. Let's allow two hormonally challenged adolescents to mainline a large dose of sugar and caffeine and see if that improves their behavior.

"Can I give you a hand, then?" It's rare these days for me and my dad to spend time even semi-alone. Well, to be honest, we've never spent much time alone, semi- or otherwise. When it comes to quality time, the ninety seconds it will take for him to walk me down the aisle may very well turn out to be our personal best.

"I wish you would take this over," he says, handing

me the knife. "Your mother said to slice this really thin, but so far the only thing I've managed to get the right size is the piece I took out of my thumb."

"Here. I'll do it."

It does not escape my notice that this is how it's always been between me and my parents. I like to call it the Betsy Sandwich. They're the bread, and I'm the filling—the only thing keeping them together as well as holding them a safe distance apart.

"Betsy!" Tracy makes her usual dramatic entrance into the kitchen. She's so tan she's practically mahogany, and the only thing darker than her skin is her roots. The rest of her hair is a sunny blond, which goes well with the inordinate amount of gold jewelry she always wears. Tracy's only five years older than I am, and frankly, I don't bear her excessive ill will over my parents' divorce. Once my mom wasn't throwing dishes at my dad anymore, we spent considerably less on dinnerware.

"Hi, Tracy."

She embraces me in what she perceives to be the Continental manner, but instead of kissing the air near my cheeks, she actually leaves a hot pink smear on each side of my face.

"How's the blushing bride holding up?"

"Great," I say, my standby, frozen smile plastered on my face. That's one thing I definitely get from my mother.

Tracy winks in a conspiratorial manner. "Don't let *her* get to you," she says.

I refrain from asking Tracy which "her" she might be referring to—my mother or my future mother-in-law.

"Betsy! We need that jicama!" Cecilia calls right on cue, so I have to turn back to the cutting board. My mother, who was flirting with Reverend Squires over by the stove in a tired attempt to make my father jealous, has spied me fraternizing with the enemy, so she makes a beeline across the kitchen.

"Here, darling, let me do that." My mom doesn't acknowledge Tracy as she squeezes in between me and my dad. Tracy frowns, my dad tries to move back but is trapped by the ninety-degree angle of the corner, and I want nothing more than to flee screaming into the night.

At that moment Matt and Corey come bounding back into the room like a couple of monster Labrador retriever puppies. They're doing their usual pushing-and-shoving routine as they try to pour whatever liquid is left in their Coke cans over each other's heads.

"Boys!" my dad says in an attempt at a reprimand, but I know from experience it's useless. The only way you can get their attention is to hose them down with cold water.

Matt sees me, and a smile breaks out across his sunny face. The boys have naturally curly blond locks, a color Tracy pays her hairdresser a fortune to give her.

"Dude! It's the Betz-Meister!" says Thing One. And they exchange identical looks of gleeful inspiration.

"Get her!" Thing Two yells.

The twins are only initiating their usual ritual of greeting me. It normally involves noogies and a headlock or two, followed by some merciless tickling. But tonight I'm just not up for it.

"No, guys," I warn and hold the jicama knife in front of me. "I've got a weapon."

"Just once, Roger, could you keep those . . . those . . . monsters under control?" my mom snaps.

"Monsters?" Tracy's voice shoots up an octave. "Who are you calling monsters?"

Where is David when I need him? I glance around the kitchen frantically. It's one thing to play out the usual family drama in the privacy of my apartment, but it's another thing entirely in the middle of my rehearsal dinner.

"Look, everyone—" But before I can finish, several things happen. Cecilia, who has been frosting the cupcakes for the "cake tower" for tomorrow's reception, puts the last smear of frosting on the final cupcake and places it triumphantly atop the precarious pyramid. She's assured me repeatedly the thing will be structurally sound, but I'm not certain I believe that some well-positioned toothpicks are enough to anchor it together. Plus, aren't those cupcakes going to be stale by this time tomorrow?

"Ta da!" Cecilia trills. She waves her hand with a dramatic flourish. "The wedding cake of your dreams for less than fifty dollars!"

"Cool," the twins say in unison. Jeremy clicks away, getting the cupcake tower from every angle. The timer dings, and Fred bends over to take the rolls out of the oven.

"The pasta's boiling over!" Reverend Squires calls out. He's wearing those bulky, padded oven gloves for handling hot dishes and trying to get the pot off the burner, but the frail retiree is no match for the ten-gallon monstrosity. "Can someone help me with this?"

"We can do it," the twins say in unison.

"Wait!" my mother cries.

"David!" I screech, since he's closer to the stove than I am, but even though he moves quickly, he's not in time. The twins reach for the side of the pot opposite the reverend.

"Ow!" they howl, letting go as quickly as they grabbed it, and the sudden change in balance tips the pot forward.

"Move!" David orders, pulling Reverend Squires out of the way. He lets go of his side of the pot, and the whole mess upends onto the floor. Hot water splashes everywhere, and we all jump to get out of its way. A flood of fettuccine streams across the tile.

"Watch your step," David calls, but it's too late. My dad steps toward the twins, but all it takes is one foot in the slippery pasta, and he goes flying as if he stepped on the proverbial banana peel.

"Dad!" I try to step toward him, but Mom and Tracy both beat me to it.

"Boys!" Mom and Tracy scream in a unison as good as the twins could ever employ.

My dad's on the floor, clutching his back in pain, and he tries to roll onto his side. At least he landed out of range of the hot pasta.

"I'll help," David says, trying to move my mother and Tracy aside so he can get my father to his feet.

"The dinner!" Cecilia wails. "What are we going to do about the dinner?"

"Who cares about the dinner?" my mom screeches, flinging her hand out in a dramatic gesture. Only the drama's just beginning, because she accidentally back-hands the top cupcake on the tower. In a shot worthy of a Wimbledon champion, she sends the cupcake flying, frosting side first, toward Tracy. The smack it makes when it hits Tracy's carefully made-up cheek reverberates through the kitchen.

Tracy shrieks, and in between the lumps of white frosting covering her face, I see her eyes narrow ominously.

I try to grab her, but I'm not quick enough.

"You witch!" she screams at my mom and dives for the cupcake tower.

"No!" Cecilia tries to come between my stepmother and her weapon of choice, but to no avail.

"David!" I cry. "Do something!" But he's got his hands full trying to keep my father out of the watery pasta mess. Reverend Squires has gone white around the edges. *Please, dear Lord, don't let him be having a heart attack.*

Fred slams the oven door shut and goes to help David with my father. The bridesmaids have ducked for cover behind the kitchen island. That leaves me to throw myself into the line of fire.

"Tracy, put the cupcake down," I order, but she's having none of it.

"This," she snaps at my mom, "is for trying to get Betsy to keep me out of the wedding."

Did I mention that Tracy was a standout college softball pitcher? The cupcake goes sailing straight for my mother and lands—*splat!*—in the middle of her face.

"Why . . . why . . . you . . ." Mom wipes the frosting out of her eyes with gloppy fingers. If this were an episode of *I Love Lucy*, I'd be laughing hysterically—but it isn't. It's my rehearsal dinner, the night before the biggest day of my life, and I can't believe my family is doing this. Plus, Jeremy's continuing to snap away, calling out instructions the way he did beside the runway at the mother-daughter banquet.

"Let her have it," he encourages Tracy. Then he calls to my mom, "Are you going to let her get away with that?"

Mom doesn't really need any encouragement to let loose on Tracy. She's been waiting for this opportunity for fifteen years, and not even the dignity of my wedding is enough to turn the tide of her anger. She picks up not one but two cupcakes and advances on my stepmother.

"Mom!" I lunge for her to grab her wrists, but she's too quick for me. Tracy's backing away. In fact, she backs right into Cecilia.

"This," my mom hisses between clenched teeth, "is for those nights at the Ramada Inn while I waited for him to come home."

My mom may not have lettered in softball, but apparently she's not without some hand-eye coordination.

She slings a cupcake, and it smashes against Tracy's temple.

"And this," my mom continues, "is for all the lipstick stains I washed off the collars of his shirts." The second cupcake shoots out of her hand and smacks Tracy on the other side of the head.

Mom grabs a third cupcake off the pile. "And this," she says, drawing back her arm, "is for every day I've had to live with the humiliation of my husband leaving me for his *pregnant* mistress."

My frozen smile has apparently infected the rest of my body because the only thing that seems to still be moving is my pounding heart. Tracy, though, does not suffer from my current immobilization. This time, when my mom launches a cupcake, Tracy ducks.

Leaving Cecilia to take the missile square in the face.

"Argh!" she yells.

"Linda!" My dad's still writhing in pain on the floor, but he's not oblivious to what's going on around him. "Stop it right now."

Jeremy's still clicking away, and David's still half bent over my father, trying to get him to his feet. I finally find my voice, but it takes a minute to get any words to come out because of the tears clogging my throat.

"Stop it, all of you!"

"Food fight!" the twins yell, and suddenly cupcakes are flying everywhere.

"Boys! Stop it!" my dad keeps yelling, and Reverend Squires has slumped to the floor. The bridesmaids are crawling toward the kitchen door, but Matt and Corey spy them trying to make their escape.

"No!" I grab for the boys, and if there's one good thing about carrying around an extra fifteen pounds, it's that I can still take the pair of them down when I'm determined.

And that's the moment, of course, when The Judge walks into the kitchen, followed by Arthur Corday.

"Miss Blessing," he barks, "what in the world is going on here?"

I'm holding down the boys, who are attempting to scramble out of my reach so they can get to the cupcakes, so it takes me a minute to answer him.

"Just a little family squabble, sir," I say, from the floor where I'm literally sitting on the twins. "But it's over now. Isn't it, boys?"

David finally manages to get my father to his feet, and I get off the boys and stand up. My mom has found a dishtowel to wipe the frosting out of her eyes, and Tracy falls against my dad's shoulder, sobbing noisily. Cecilia's ranting at David, the bridesmaids make a dash for it past The Judge and Arthur Corday, and Reverend Squires appears to be deep in prayer. Either that or we've actually killed him.

The Judge's eyes narrow. "This is hardly conduct becoming a senior minister, Miss Blessing."

Well, that's probably true. But it's conduct entirely becoming my family.

David finds another dishtowel for his mom, who icily scrubs gooey frosting from her face.

"I cannot believe this," she says, biting out each word like a shard of broken glass. "I have never seen anything like this in my life."

David shoots me a dark look—me!—and puts an arm around his mom's shoulders. "It's okay. It's over now."

Cecilia looks around the kitchen, and she's so crestfallen at the disaster my family created that I'm racked with guilt.

"Look, we can fix it," I say, making it up as I go along. "We've got tons of Minute Rice in the cabinet to replace the fettuccine. And if we're creative enough restacking the cupcakes—"

"The jicama's still there," Dad says, trying to be helpful, but Tracy just wails more loudly.

My mom's managed to get all the frosting off her face, but her mascara's running down her cheeks, diluted by her tears. She turns to me. "I'm sorry, Betsy. I didn't mean . . ." Her voice trails off as it usually does when she's almost apologizing but never quite getting to the all-important words of regret.

I hold up a hand to forestall the usual barrage of defensive excuses. "No, Mom. Not now."

"But, Betsy . . ." And once again we're back to where we started all those years ago when Dad walked out the door. She's the mother and I'm the daughter, but only until a crisis hits, and then suddenly I'm the one cleaning up the mess. Although I've never had to do that quite so literally before.

"There's a rest room across the hall," I say to my mom in a low voice. "Why don't you go get cleaned up." Then I turn my back on her. The ache in my chest feels like an elephant is sitting there. I walk over to help Reverend Squires, grateful it's my heart that feels as if it's being squeezed by a vise, and not his. By now he's maneuvered back to his feet, and there's even a small smile playing at the corners of his lips.

"Well, Betsy," he says, "you certainly know how to throw a rehearsal dinner. Or would that be throw *things* at a rehearsal dinner?" And then he winks at me.

But even his kind attempt to make me feel better can't steer me around the iceberg of despair that's looming in front of me. I mean, I knew the wedding was going to be tacky. I knew Cecilia would push me to my limits, and I knew that my family would misbehave in some fashion. But in all my wildest dreams, I never imagined that my rehearsal dinner could rival the *Titanic* in the disaster department. At this point I don't think things could possibly get any worse.

Chapter 19

As it turned out, David was really great about the whole rehearsal dinner fiasco once he got his mom cleaned up and a Cosmopolitan down her throat. He even convinced her that she could use Jeremy's photos if she tweaked the captions to make the food fight look like a spontaneous outbreak of bonhomie instead of the volcanic explosion of anger and recrimination that it actually was.

Still, the rehearsal dinner left a bitter taste in

everyone's mouth, and it wasn't just the not-quite-ripe jicama. The only thing that kept me from a total meltdown last night was the presence of The Judge and Arthur Corday. Eventually we got the kitchen cleaned up, fed everyone some semblance of a meal, and got through the actual rehearsal under Reverend Squires's direction. For a mild-mannered scholarly type, he did a pretty good job corralling my mom and Cecilia, who had widely differing viewpoints on how and in what order everyone should proceed down the aisle. Of course, since his hearing isn't what it used to be, he might just not have heard all the suggestions and complaints.

This morning, though, in the cold light of my wedding day—"cold" being a metaphorical term since this is Nashville in June—I'm awash in misgivings. As I shower (extra conditioner in my hair), apply antiperspirant (extra-dry on the armpits), and swallow a couple of Tylenol (extra-strength for my headache), I can't do anything but entertain the misgivings that have taken up residence in my brain. To tell the truth, I'm not just entertaining them; I'm serving them a gourmet meal, soup to nuts. But just when I think I may drown in doubt, the phone rings.

The invention of caller ID is to me one of the greatest blessings of modern living. Although I can't simply choose not to answer the phone if it's a parishioner, I can at least experience a few seconds of anticipatory joy when I see the illuminated number of one of my nearest and dearest.

This time, though, the little LCD screen shows not only an area code but a country code as well. And since I know only one person living abroad, that can mean just one thing—LaRonda! Hooray!

"Betsy's Bridal Boutique and Taco Shack," I say, swallowing back a laugh.

For a long moment, there's silence. Then, "I am sorry," a voice with a lilting South African accent says. "I must have the wrong number. I am attempting to reach the Reverend Betsy Blessing."

"No, no, I'm sorry," I say, blundering my way out of my faux pas. "This is she." My skin tingles with embarrassment.

"This is the Reverend Charles Mkambe," the man with the lovely voice says. "I am calling on behalf of Reverend LaRonda Mason."

A cold chill sweeps over me. "Is anything wrong? Is she okay?"

"Reverend Mason is fine," he says. "But she could not be near a phone today. So she asked that I call to tell you she is thinking of you and praying for you on this, your special day."

Did you ever have one of those moments where you knew something really special was happening, but you were also kind of disappointed with it? That's how I feel as I hear this very nice man relay LaRonda's message to me. It's like getting something you really need for Christmas instead of getting what you really want. Like when I was sixteen and my mother gave me a hope chest instead of a stereo.

"It's very nice of you to call," I say automatically, and I mean the words, but I'm also struggling to mask my disappointment. If ever I needed to talk to my best friend, today would be the day. Maybe she could help me sort out what matters and what doesn't in this fiasco of a wedding. I thought I knew. I thought David and I had made the right decision, to focus on the marriage itself instead of on the trappings of a ceremony.

"Reverend Mason said to ask you if you are very sure," Reverend Mkambe says. "She said not to go through with anything if you have doubts."

What? No, no, no.

"Please tell Reverend Mason that I have no doubts whatsoever," I say, lying through my teeth. That lie's such an enormous whopper, I don't even bother to cross my fingers behind my back. "But thank you so much for calling. Tell Reverend Mason—" My voice breaks, and I have to swallow and start over. "Tell Reverend Mason that I miss her. And to hurry home."

"I will tell her. Best wishes to you, Reverend Blessing, on your marriage. I hope you will be very happy."

Well, that makes two of us.

"Thank you. Thank you again for calling."

There's a click on the other end of the line, and I hit the Cancel button on my phone to disconnect the call. I'm still holding the phone in my hand when it rings again.

"Hello?" I say, putting the receiver to my ear by instinct before I have a chance to glance at the caller-ID window.

"Betsy, it's Cecilia. Where are you? You should be at the church." Her voice is pitched half an octave higher than usual.

"But it's only ten o'clock. The wedding isn't for four hours." I was planning to meet my mother at the church at noon for hair and makeup. Angelique has promised to work her magic once again.

"Didn't I tell you? Jeremy has to reshoot your bridal portrait. And there seems to be a little problem with the air conditioning in the sanctuary."

Now anyone who has ever been on a church-property committee can tell you that when it comes to the sanctuary, there's no such thing as a "little" problem with the air conditioning.

"What do you mean 'a little problem'?"

"It's very warm in here," Cecilia answers. I can picture her pacing up and down the burgundy carpet in the center aisle. "Plus, there's a . . . um . . . a gentleman here who calls himself Booger who keeps following me around."

"Jed should be around somewhere," I say. "He's the chief custodian. He can see what's wrong."

"I looked, but I can't find him anywhere," Cecilia says, and I can hear her forcing the words through gritted teeth.

"Try calling his pager. The number's taped next to the phone in the sacristy. Or have Booger go look for him."

"I'll try his pager." She doesn't even acknowledge my suggestion that she engage Booger's help. "But I'd really prefer it if you came down here yourself."

231

Does the woman not realize that I can't even change the toner in the copier? What can I do about an ailing, two-ton HVAC unit?

"Besides," Cecilia adds, "this other man is making me very nervous. Is he safe?"

I decide not to tell her the truth—that the safety factor of Booger depends on the alcohol level in his blood-stream. In any event, the minister in me has to respond to the very real distress in her voice.

"Okay, okay," I say. "I'll be there in a half hour." There goes my leisurely breakfast with a second cup of coffee. And for once I was actually going to get some prayer time. I had carefully planned in some meditation and reflection, hoping some close association with the Divine would get me centered for the craziness of the day. I guess God's going to have to be a mobile prayer partner yet again.

"Well, don't take too long. The packing peanuts are starting to wilt."

Until this moment I had managed to block out the reality of the packing peanuts. But no longer.

"Okay, make it twenty minutes. But I've got to stop and get a latte, or I'll never make it through the day."

"Don't forget your veil," she warns me.

"Got it," I say, snapping it up from the top of my dresser.

"Or your heels," she adds.

Ah yes. Where are those instruments of torture anyway? "Already packed."

That's two fibs in the course of one morning. I

wonder how many more I will add to my total before the day is over. I start sifting through the detritus around the edges of my bedroom in search of my shoes.

"Good. And would you pick me up a mocha Frappuccino?"

"No problem." A properly caffeinated wedding party is a more cooperative wedding party, I always say. "See you soon."

I disconnect before she can give me any further instructions. And before anyone else can call, I stuff the rest of my wedding paraphernalia, including my shoes, into my big tote bag and grab the dress from the closet door. It's like carrying a bulky bag of the previously mentioned packing peanuts, but I manage to wrestle it through the bedroom door.

Four more hours, I chant to myself. Four more hours—and then it will all be over.

Even a venti latte, though, can't prepare me for what I find when I step inside the tall mahogany doors of Church of the Shepherd. At first my line of sight is somewhat hindered by the mound of satin and tulle I'm carrying. But then I realize that all the white filling my vision isn't just my dress.

Where do I even begin to describe what she's done to the sanctuary? I take a few steps down the aisle, and some stray packing peanuts crunch beneath my feet. The warm, sticky air doesn't fit with the faux icicles suspended from the fishing line that's been strung back and forth overhead. At the end of each pew, a jaunty snowman in a spray of silver-painted leaves holds a little sign that reads "Mazel Tov on Your Bat Mitzvah." I'm guessing that inscription will be Photoshopped out of the wedding pictures as easily as I was edited into the wedding shower. Up front, across the steps leading to the chancel area, is a silver arch threaded with what looks like Christmas tree tinsel. Atop the arch, two fake turtledoves perch in what I assume is an affectionate pose, since one dove's head is tucked into the other one's neck. Either that or the dove is worried that the Good Shepherd in the Tiffany stained-glass window is going to drop the lost lamb smack-dab on top of him.

I crane my neck a bit farther and see what looks like two white bed sheets suspended from the ceiling.

"For the packing peanuts," Cecilia says as she steps up behind me. "When David kisses you, we'll release them. It'll be like sealing your vows in a fairy tale, all snowy and white."

Well, I have to agree that it will be like something out of a fairy tale, but I'm thinking more along the lines of the Brothers Grimm than the Disney version. I take a deep breath and plaster a smile on my face before I turn around to greet her, reminding myself that she did do me the favor of giving birth to the man I love.

"Is David here yet?" I ask.

"No, no. We don't need him until much later."

Of course not. All the groom has to do is show up.

"Did you find Jed to help with the air conditioning?"

Cecilia makes a face. "That man was no help at all.

He says the compressor's broken, and they can't get a part in until next week."

"Next week? You mean it's going to be this hot for the ceremony?" I'm about to crumple as it is. I can't imagine what it's going to be like under all that satin and Jeremy's photography lights heating things up another fifteen degrees.

"You'll be fine," Cecilia says, patting me on the shoulder. "I'm sure you've been through worse."

Well, yes, but not while wearing a six-thousand-dollar designer dress. It's not exactly like sweating through a pulpit robe on a Sunday morning.

"I guess I'd better get changed, then, so Jeremy can reshoot my portrait."

Cecilia frowns. "Actually, I could use your help moving some tables around for the reception in the fellowship hall. Are there more chairs anywhere? I don't think we have enough."

I glance down at my thirty-dollar manicure. It barely withstood my putting together the bouquets for my bridesmaids and me last night. "Can't Jed help you?" I ask.

"Please, Betsy," Cecilia says, dramatically pressing a hand to her forehead. "I think I have the beginnings of a migraine."

Why am I so nice? Or perhaps more accurately, why am I such a conflict avoider? I give in, of course, and for the next ninety minutes, I find myself fetching, carrying, and literally doing Cecilia's heavy lifting. Not exactly how I envisioned spending the hours leading up to my wedding ceremony.

Eventually, of course, more people begin to arrive. My bridesmaids. My father and Tracy with the twins in tow. The boys look as if they've been threatened within an inch of their lives. They barely move their lips when they speak. In fact, they're so sluggish I begin to wonder whether Tracy's reverted to her old habit of plying them with Benadryl, like she used to do when they were toddlers and she was too exhausted to keep up with them. I used to get really indignant about her doing that, but after last night's melee, I find myself willing to indulge in a conspiracy of silence if it will keep Matt and Corey from literally climbing the walls at my wedding.

Then my mother makes an entrance that would give the show-stopping Bernice a run for her money. She quickly hustles me into the bridal dressing room off the narthex and proceeds to pelt me with last-minute instructions.

"Don't slouch," she says while plugging in the steamer that's kept in the dressing room for touch-ups on wedding gowns and bridesmaid dresses. "And for heaven's sake, don't lock your knees either. The last thing we need is a fainting bride."

I don't know. Passing out looks like a pretty good option at the moment.

"Yes, Mother," I say with the resigned tone of the long-suffering.

"We have to get you ready quickly," she warns. "Jeremy wants to do some mother-daughter shots in the Garden of Prayer."

Great. That's possibly the only place hotter than the sanctuary at the moment.

"Couldn't we take the pictures in the shade somewhere?"

A few months ago our overzealous lawn-maintenance company came through the prayer garden and "topped" the trees, a bizarre local practice of whacking away limbs so that the result resembles a Q-tip instead of an oak or a maple. It's apparently a Nashville tradition, but I cry every time I see one of these pruning victims.

"Betsy, please." My mother presses a hand to her forehead, much as Cecilia did. At least they have that much in common. "Can't you be cooperative today of all days?"

Now that remark sends my blood pressure spiking. I think I've been a pretty good sport about this whole thing. I've even been agreeable and helpful about moving furniture on my wedding day, which quite frankly I expected to be all about me and not about overlooked logistics. So my mother's criticism really stings, and now I'm getting as hot under the collar as I am everywhere else.

"Look, Mom—" I'm ready to come out with both guns blazing when the door to the dressing room opens and Cecilia steps in.

"Oh, good. You're almost ready for Jeremy."

Almost ready? The stylist hasn't arrived to put my hair up, I don't have any makeup on, and I'm not wearing my wedding gown. Why in the world would she think I'm ready for Jeremy?

"Cecilia, I think it's going to be awhile before we can do the photos."

"Oh no. This is perfect." She places her hand on my upper arm and curls her fingers possessively around my sleeve. "We have to do the before pictures."

"'Before' pictures? What 'before' pictures?"

"Oh, didn't I tell you about that? We thought it would be great to have before-and-after shots for your bridal portrait. Sort of like a mini-makeover. So you're perfect, just like you are."

I wish that were true. I wish anyone involved with this wedding, including me, would think I'm perfect just as I am. And at that moment, it hits me—The Great Truth About Weddings. What the hoopla is really about. It all comes down to this: the bride isn't good enough as she is. No, she requires new makeup, new hair, new nails, new clothes, new shoes, and new jewelry. If she's overweight, she has to diet. If she wears glasses, well, better pop in to the nearest clinic for some LASIK surgery. Whatever the bride's flaw, she'd better get it corrected before the wedding, which is nothing more than a celebration of the girl's success in proving herself deserving of a groom.

My mother and Cecilia continue the conversation without me, debating the best locations in the church to do the before shots, but I'm like one of those people hit with a stun gun. I can barely move. Overcome by the intensity of this current revelation, I sink into a nearby chair.

Here I'd thought I could escape the contagion of wedding madness by ignoring it as much as possible. But I can't. Because no matter how indifferent you try to be, you can never escape that one intangible truth: the entire point of a modern wedding is to prove that the bride is good enough to deserve a man.

My stomach turns sour, and I'm regretting the venti latte. I'm regretting it even more a few moments later when I find myself on my knees in one of the stalls of the women's rest room, experiencing the latte for the second time. If only I could purge myself of my new-found knowledge as easily as I can rid myself of the contents of my stomach.

Chapter 20

After my rather dramatic dash to the rest room and subsequent illness, Cecilia dispenses with the whole idea of before-and-after bridal portraits. In fact, she's very sweet about the whole incident and is the one who brings me a cup of ice chips from the kitchen to spoon bit by bit into my mouth.

"All brides are nervous," she says in the most soothing voice she can. I'm reclining on the chaise lounge in the bridal dressing room, and I suddenly have more handmaidens than Cleopatra floating down the Nile on her royal barge.

My mother does her part too, deflecting the well-meaning attentions of my bridesmaids, who have arrived two hours early as instructed so that we can shoot the majority of the photos of the wedding party. The only pictures we're saving for after the service are photos that David and I are in together. I'm not particularly tied to tradition, but I don't want David to see me in my dress until I'm walking up the aisle on my father's arm. If there's going to be one moment of pure happiness for me amid all this fuss and bother, that's going to be it.

Eventually I recover from my bout of nerves. But I'm pretty numb when Angelique sweeps my hair into a sophisticated chignon. She places the veil on my head as if she's setting the Hope Diamond in Queen Elizabeth's crown, and then she plasters the whole thing into place with most of a can of hair spray. When the aerosol fumes finally dissipate, she goes to work on my makeup, transforming my natural look into a much more glamorous one. The last step, of course, is to get me into the dress. And even though I feel slightly sick with the knowledge that all of these efforts are done to cover my inadequacies rather than to celebrate my happiness, I can't help but be pleased with the reflection I see in the mirror as my mom fastens the last few buttons of my dress and the bridesmaids fluff out the train. At this point Jeremy's invited in to take some not-quite-candid shots of me "getting ready."

Finally, Cecilia shoos everyone out of the room—even my mother, which is quite a feat—so that she and I can have "one last chat." Quite frankly, I don't really want to be alone with her at this point, but I suppose she has some last-minute instructions for me on what to do during the ceremony so that Jeremy's photos will be fabulous. So I'll listen because I'm vain enough to want to look perfect in *Budget Bride* when it hits the stands next winter.

"You look beautiful," Cecilia says, taking my hands. There are real tears in her eyes, and I let my misgivings and resentments slip away. *This is how all weddings are,* I remind myself. You can't expect to enjoy the process. Just feel lucky if you make one or two good memories along the way.

"Thank you, Cecilia. I do appreciate all you've done." And I mean it, even though it hasn't been easy. If nothing else, I'm getting David out of this deal.

The tears trickle out of the corners of her heavily mascara-laden eyes. "Betsy, I do want you to know that I'm glad David is marrying you. You are much better for him than—" She stops herself abruptly, but we both know the end of that sentence.

"Thank you," I say. "I will be a good wife to him."

Cecilia leans forward and presses her lips against my cheek. "I know you will." She smiles, but there's as much sorrow as happiness in her expression. I guess it's not easy for her to have her only child make it official that another woman will now come first in his life.

She pats my cheek one last time. "Besides," she says, "you look much better in that dress than Jennifer ever did."

I don't know which of us makes the gasping noise that I hear, but I'm pretty sure I'm the one whose stomach plummets to the floor. "Excuse me?"

Several expressions fly across Cecilia's face. Panic. Desperation. Regret. "I mean . . . no, I didn't mean . . ."

But the words are out there and can never be taken back. My skin crawls at the voluptuous touch of Vera Wang's carefully crafted satin. Because I'm standing here, ten minutes away from the start of my wedding, in a dress that belonged to the ex-fiancée of my husband-to-be. Good thing I've already thrown up and nothing is left in my stomach to expel.

I teeter in my four-inch heels but catch myself before I topple over. My head's swimming, but one thought is very clear. David won't be surprised, astonished, and delighted to see me in this incredible dress. Because he's seen it before.

Then I have a horrible flashback to the time he told me about Jennifer's wedding gown. About how much it cost, even at a sample sale, but how Jennifer would be satisfied with nothing less than the best for her wedding. And so she got the Vera Wang dress. In addition to the Tiffany ring.

I look down at the eBay Easter-basket atrocity on my finger. I pluck at the skirt of the dress while Cecilia babbles on, trying to rescue the situation by saying things like, "Let's focus on the important thing here" and "We didn't mean to hurt you."

"We?" That pronoun somehow penetrates the heavy fog of pain that settles over me. "We? As in you and David?"

And suddenly I'm putting two and two together. Here I was worried that David was having lunch with Jennifer because she was trying to get him back, when it turns out that he was really bumming a slightly used wedding dress off of her.

A low, keening sound escapes my throat, one I've only ever heard at funerals. I've never had an experience like this when grief hits you like a Mack Truck in fourth gear.

"Betsy? Betsy?" Cecilia's voice seems caught in the fog of numbness too, so it sounds as if it's coming from far away.

"Is David here?" My voice sounds hollow in my ears. As hollow as the yawning emptiness in my midsection.

"Yes, of course. The music's started. He's with Reverend Squires and the groomsmen. They'll come out as soon as your mother and I are seated. Look, Betsy, it's not that important, really, in the scheme of things. It's only a dress."

"If you're not happy in the dress you're wearing, you won't be happy in the marriage." Edna's words swirl around me.

"I need to talk to David."

Now Cecilia's looking as desperate as I feel. "I'm not sure that's a good idea. Every bride has last-minute nerves. You can't panic now."

I'm not panicked, I want to say to her, but my lips don't seem to be responding to any of the signals my brain is sending.

"Betsy?" I hear my mom's voice from behind me. "Is everything all right?"

I turn, and the expression on my face must match the

devastation in my heart, because she rushes toward me. "What is it, honey? What's happened?"

"I need to see David," I manage to get out between sobs.

Mom presses a handkerchief into my hands and wraps an arm around my shoulders. "Of course, dear. We'll get him right away."

"I really don't think that's a good idea," Cecilia says.

"I don't care what you think!" My mom, in tigress mode, is as impressive a sight as it is rare. "Just get David," she barks, "and get him right now."

"Thanks, Mom," I whisper, and she hugs me tighter.

"You'd better sit down," she says, pulling me toward the chaise lounge, but I shake my head.

"It will crease the skirt." Although why in the world I'm concerned about the dress at this point is beyond me.

I hear Cecilia's heels tapping against the floor as she leaves the dressing room. And as she does, all of the doubts and misgivings that have been building up over the past few months crowd into the room with my mom and me. The tacky invitations. The wholesale flowers. The bridal shower I never attended. The horrible ring. The surprise engagement party. Never having a real courtship. Never really having time alone with David, period. By the time I hear more footsteps, I'm so deep in disappointment and resentment that I'm drowning.

"Betsy?" David's familiar baritone only makes me feel worse. I press the handkerchief to my carefully made-up eyes.

"I need to speak to him alone," I whisper to my mom.

"Of course, honey. I'll get rid of everyone else."

We turn around to see David in the doorway, flanked by his mother and the rest of the wedding party, expressions of deep concern on their faces.

"Are you okay?" he asks, when it must be apparent to everyone that I'm distraught.

"Please, Mom, make everybody leave."

"Sure, honey." She squeezes my hand. "I'll be right outside the door."

"David, you stay," she instructs him. "Everyone else, would you please step outside?" She says it like a question, but it's clearly an order.

A few moments later the door shuts and we're alone, but I can't look David in the eyes. I turn away, and then I see myself reflected in the enormous mirror. Was it only a few short weeks ago that Angelique and I were squealing with delight at that same reflection the first time I tried on the dress?

"Betsy, honey, what is it?"

David looks as white around the mouth as I do. I search his face for any sign of the guilt he must be feeling over pawning off Jennifer's dress on me.

"I can't believe you would do this to me." I can barely get the words out, they're so thick with misery.

When I see the guilty expression on his face, any hope I had of David denying knowledge of the dress's origin evaporates.

"I can explain about that," he says, but you know, I'm not particularly in the mood to hear his justifications. I mean, I've always known that David was cheap. I've known he could pinch a penny so tight that it screamed for mercy. I just didn't think that when it came right down to it, he'd think it was more important to be a tightwad than to respect me as a person. And while I've always thought that the pain of my parents' divorce would be the worst I would ever endure, I was wrong. Because this hurts more than anything I've ever experienced.

"How could you?" I'm shaking uncontrollably, and I feel the stems of my bridal bouquet snap in my clenched fingers. "How could you do it?"

For years I would have sworn that I knew David better than I know anyone on earth. And now I feel like I've never known him at all.

"It's not what you think," he says.

Oh, please. How stupid does he think I am? "What am I supposed to think, David? Did you or did you not know that this was Jennifer's dress?"

David flushes bright red as he always does when he's embarrassed. And while my heart might be willing to believe any excuse he made up right now just so I don't have to hurt this much, I can't deny the flaming color that covers him from neck to cheek to forehead.

David opens his mouth, then closes it again. "I did know, Betz. I won't deny it."

But it's more than just him knowing about the dress's origin. Maybe I could excuse that. But now I know why he had lunch with Jennifer. Because he was persuading her to donate her dress to Betsy's Budget Wedding. The

246

shame of that penetrates me to the core, a deep, private place I've spent the past fifteen years of my life trying to protect from being hurt this way again.

"Why didn't you tell me?" I wail, wishing that I wasn't falling apart, that I could do this without sounding like a shrew.

"You were so happy about the dress." He reaches for my hands beneath the bouquet, but I jerk them away. Hurt at my reaction etches his face, but I don't care. I'm the one who's been wronged here. This time I'm not going to be the one to make it all better by sacrificing a little piece of my soul.

"I don't care how happy I was about the dress. You should have told me. But you didn't, did you? Because you knew that if I found out where the dress came from, I wouldn't wear it."

"No, that's not it at all."

"Isn't it? You can quit lying to me now, David."

His spine stiffens, and I know I've scored a direct hit. "I never lied to you."

"No, you just never told me the truth."

"How could I? That night at your apartment, you were so excited about that stupid dress. What was I supposed to do? Take away the one thing in this whole mess that made you happy?"

You know, sometimes I can't believe how clueless he can be. "The one thing that made me happy? Are you kidding me? You think the one thing in all this that made me happy was that stupid dress?"

Confusion clouds his eyes. "Wasn't it?"

I wish I had something more substantial in my hands to whack him with than a crumpled bridal bouquet. "No, you idiot, the dress was not what made me happy."

Still, he looks confused. Clearly I'm going to have to spell it out for him.

"You, David," I snap. "You were the one thing in this whole sorry mess that made me happy. Knowing that at the end of all this ridiculousness, I got to go home with you. Forever. That's what made me happy."

David's expression is a mixture of joy and regret. "But you were disappointed about the invitations and all that other stuff. I wanted you to have one thing you could remember and enjoy about our wedding."

"Then you should never have let someone else pick out my engagement ring."

"You don't like the ring? Why didn't you tell me?" David asks, defensiveness creeping into his tone.

"Because you should have known that this is a horrible ring. The ugliest ring ever crafted by human hands. It's an affront to bubblegum machines everywhere."

Okay, that came out a bit harsher than I intended, but once the cork is out of the bottle, nothing's going to keep the contents inside. The hurt on David's face is finally starting to equal the pain in my chest.

"If it's that awful, maybe you should return it."

I shouldn't be surprised at this. From the moment Cecilia spilled the beans, I knew it was coming—one way or another.

"Maybe I should." I throw the bouquet to the floor and wrestle the ring from my finger. "Maybe I should never have accepted it in the first place."

How can David stand there looking at me as if I'm the one who's being cruel? But that's what he's doing, anger and pain chasing each other across his face. I thrust the ring into his hand, and he takes it automatically.

"If you'll give me five minutes, you can have the dress back too," I say, reaching up to snatch the veil from my head. Did it belong to Jennifer as well? I drop it like a hot potato.

"Betsy—"

"No." I hold up a hand to forestall any further attempts at excuses or explanations. "Enough. Just take all of Jennifer's things and get out of here."

"Betz—" He reaches for me, but I'm not about to let him get that close. Not when a single touch from him would send me to my knees.

"Just go, David. Just go."

He stands there for the longest moment of my life, looking at me as if I'm insane.

"I can't believe you're doing this," he says, which is pretty cheeky considering he's the one who just asked for his ring back. What in the world does he expect?

"I can't believe what you've already done," I snap, but my anger is starting to drain away, replaced by thick, heavy despair. "Just get out of here."

I can't look at him anymore. And I'm not sure I'll ever be able to look myself in the mirror again. I was so, so stupid. Just because I loved him. Just because I needed to make him happy. Just because I was willing to give up most of what I wanted so I could earn a place in his life, like some sort of bizarre emotional dowry offered to seal the nuptial deal.

Why won't he go? What's he waiting for? I look in the mirror and see his face reflected just over my shoulder.

"Fine." He looks horrible, like he's suffered a mortal wound. "Fine. I'll go."

And then the worst thing of all happens. Worse than the stupid dress. Worse than all the angry words. Because David does just what I've asked him to do. He turns on his heel and strides out of the room.

Then I do fall to my knees, dress and all, gasping for breath, because he's taken with him the very air that I breathe.

Chapter 21

When someone you love hurts you as badly as David has hurt me, you can't just forgive that person. I learned this lesson from my mother when I was fifteen and my father left us for Tracy and her unborn twins. My mother taught me this particular truth out of love—or so she claimed. She didn't want me to suffer the way she suffered. Or maybe she just wanted a partner in her ongoing drama once my father refused to participate anymore.

I guess it's ironic that I ended up in a profession with

the central tenet being forgiveness. Or maybe it isn't ironic. Maybe it happened out of desperation. Or simply an addiction to self-defeating behavior. For fifteen years a war has been going on inside me between the part of me that knew my mother was right and the part of me that knew a loving God was a better voice to listen to.

Somehow, despite the numbness in my fingers, I wrestle myself out of the Vera Wang. A few buttons pop off in the process, but I'm past caring. When the door closed behind David, I lost interest in maintaining any sense of decorum. The clothes I wore to church smell a little sour from my earlier furniture-moving efforts à la Cecilia, but does it really matter? I don't think runaway brides are judged on their fashion sense as much as their absence at the altar.

The handy thing about being married in the church you pastor is that you know all the escape routes. I take the back door out of the dressing room, walk away from the sanctuary, and wind my way through the education wing of the building. That's how I make my escape, unnoticed, from Church of the Shepherd.

Or should I say almost unnoticed. Because as I sneak toward the glass double doors beckoning me toward freedom, a shadow falls across my path.

"Preacher? Where are you going?"

"Booger! What are you doing here?"

"I asked you first."

We're both wary, but Booger's looking especially distressed to be caught lurking in the hallway.

"Booger? What is it?"

Lord, please don't let him have been stealing something. The prayer flies up instinctively, reflecting the automatic reaction of anyone who's worked with the homeless for any length of time. We've had a lot of things disappear from the church in the past year. A couple of purses. A TV-VCR combo. Even some of the gold-plated communion ware. How low is that when someone stoops to stealing the chalice off the altar? But I would never have suspected Booger. Not until this moment when we're both out here in the hallway while everyone else is safely tucked away in the sanctuary.

"I ain't up to nothin'," he says defensively.

Booger is a very bad liar. He's also hiding something behind his back.

"What's that?" I nod toward whatever he's concealing.

"Nothin'."

"Then why are you hiding it?"

Booger blushes, something I've never seen before. I've witnessed him being contentious, contrite, and even inebriated, but I've never seen him embarrassed.

"Booger? Show me." I sound like Tracy trying to get the twins to confess one of their many, many transgressions. My motherly tone must be effective, because slowly, reluctantly, he pulls the object from behind his back and extends it toward me.

"It's for you," he says.

The gift-wrapping isn't the work of a professional, to say the least. The bundle is covered in the Sunday comics, and the gold ribbon shows creased evidence of previous use. Extensive previous use.

"You didn't need to get me anything."

"Sure I did," he says. "I brought a present just like all the other folks."

Okay, now I'm feeling about three inches high, as well I should. Or maybe more like a rat. Or an amoeba on a flea on a rat. Booger pushes the gift toward me again, but how can I accept it? Booger generally doesn't get enough to eat. He shouldn't be using any of his money on a present for me.

"This is really sweet of you, Booger. But it's not necessary."

His eyes drop from mine.

"No, Booger. I don't mean it like that."

He still won't look at me. "I understand, Preacher. It's not like that other stuff in the fancy paper."

"No, no," I protest some more, then grab his arm when he starts to turn away. "I meant that you don't need to give me a present because there's not going to be a wedding."

Booger's shaggy white eyebrows rise to meet his hairline. "What do you mean?"

And at the question, I sag with exhaustion. I'm just not up to explaining it to anyone. I'm not sure I can even fully explain it to myself.

"Let's just say that new information has come to light, making the wedding an untenable option."

"A what?"

"David lied to me." There. That's the most effective short version anyway.

253

Booger growls. "Do I need to straighten him out?"

I thought I'd lost my ability to smile, but I haven't. "No, but I appreciate the offer."

"Another gal?" Booger asks, cutting to the chase and clearly ready to commiserate with me.

"Yes. No. Well, not exactly."

"What is it, then? Is he gay?"

I didn't think I could ever laugh again, but I do now. "No, Booger, he's definitely not gay."

"Well, if it's not another woman and he likes girls, what's the problem?"

Trust Booger to simplify the equation.

"He lied about the dress," I say.

"Huh?"

"The dress his mother sent me. The one I modeled at the mother-daughter banquet. David got it from his old fiancée."

"And he didn't tell you?"

"Nope."

Booger lets out a long, low whistle of sympathy. "That's a pretty dirty trick." He pauses, his eyebrows knit together like Santa Claus contemplating a Zen paradox. Then he looks up at me and smiles. " 'Course, we can teach him not to do that anymore."

I blanch. "I think that's what I'm doing right now. You don't need to do anything else."

"You're leaving?"

I hold up my purse and car keys, surprised he hasn't noticed them.

"Oh," he says.

"Don't tell anyone you saw me. Please."

"Sure," Booger replies. "Your secret's safe with me."

"Thanks." We're both quiet for a moment, unsure what else to say.

"I guess I'd better be going," I say.

"Yeah, guess so. Me, too."

But even though we both say the words, neither of us moves.

"It'll be okay, Preacher," Booger says. Of course, neither of us really believes that.

"Sure. Sure it will." I glance over my shoulder to see if anyone in my family has figured out that I've cut and run, but the dim hallway is empty behind me.

"Take this anyway, Preacher," Booger says, thrusting the awkwardly wrapped package into my hands.

"I can't, Booger."

"Please. I want you to have it."

Our eyes meet, one human being connecting with another, and I feel my fingers curl around the edges of the gift to accept it.

"Okay. Thanks."

Booger releases the gift to my care, gives me one last smile, and then slips away down the hall. I brush away the tears that spill down my cheeks and make my escape through the glass double doors and out into the parking lot.

Frankly, I've never done anything so irresponsible in my life, but I figure the least David can do in payment for his sins is to stand up in front of the congregation and tell everyone that the wedding is off. I'm unlocking my ancient Honda Civic when I remember Jeremy and the photo spread in *Budget Bride*. But I won't let myself feel guilty over that one either, since Cecilia is just as guilty as David. Frankly, I'm realizing what a lucky escape I've just made. Can you imagine spending the rest of your life with that woman for a mother-in-law?

I place Booger's gift in the passenger seat and then start the car, but I hesitate before shifting it into reverse. Where am I supposed to go? If I go back to my house, they'll find me in the next fifteen minutes. No, I need someplace to hide out for a little while. Someplace they'll never think to look.

Like a lot of other girls, I used to imagine my dream wedding. I was influenced by Barbie, *Little House on the Prairie*, and trips to the fabric store with my mother. When I was nine, my imaginary wedding involved a life-size Ken doll, twenty-two yards of tulle, and shoes with four-inch heels. When I was a teenager, I discovered *Seventeen* and Madonna, and my dream-wedding scenario evolved into a cross between an MTV video and Princess Di walking down the aisle of St. Paul's Cathedral.

In college I gave up any idea of getting married in favor of joining the Peace Corps and traveling to Botswana to teach sheep farming or something. The only husbandry in that scenario was of the animal variety. In divinity school, once I started looking at weddings from a theological point of view, I lost all interest in having one of my own. I recoiled at the idea of any bride, including me, being given away as if she were up for auction on eBay. And my newly minted sense of social justice rebelled at the amount of money spent on such vanities as corsages and cream mints.

Then I turned twenty-five and realized I had no marital prospects on the horizon. This happened at approximately the same time I graduated from Vanderbilt Divinity School and left for my first parish in a small county-seat town. It was also the same time David's fiancée, Jennifer, broke up with him. So I began forecasting wedding scenarios featuring David as the new and improved version of my childhood Ken fantasies. The fact that I'd been avoiding my feelings for David for three solid years in divinity school simply added fuel to the fantasy fires. When it comes to David, I have serious Jennifer envy. I guess this comes as no surprise to anyone in light of what just happened in the bridal dressing room at Church of the Shepherd.

So now, instead of all my fantasies coming true, I'm racing down Broadway à la Julia Roberts in *Runaway Bride*. And I'm wondering where a girl's supposed to go when she ditches her groom at the altar. I mean, cruising along in my Civic seems anticlimactic in light of the fact that I've left two hundred people sitting in the pews waiting for me to march down the aisle.

I wish I could tell you what I'm feeling at this exact moment. Seems like I should know—that it would be important to be in touch with my emotional core. But considering what my core just did, maybe it's better to be emotionally unavailable for the time being.

Somewhere around the Vanderbilt area, I figure out a place I can go where no one will ever think to look for me. That place, of course, is Harry Snedegar's swimming pool. If there's anything Harry loves more than tennis, it's swimming. He's got one of those half-swing, half-winch contraptions that lowers him in and lifts him out of his enormous kidney-shaped pool. The contraption is mounted where the tiki bar used to be—or so I've been told.

I have a swimsuit in the small suitcase I packed for my honeymoon, so I don't have to go home to get one. When I arrive at Harry's, no one is there but Maria, their housekeeper. I'm kind of surprised that Harry and Joann haven't returned yet from the wedding-that-wasn't, because I drove around for a while before heading over here. Maria, bless her, has seen pretty much everything in her thirty years of working for the Snedegars, so she doesn't bat an eye at my unexpectedly turning up for a swim at the exact time I'm supposed to be exchanging wedding vows with David.

"If anyone calls for you, are you here?" she asks in an impassive but not unsympathetic tone.

"I . . . I . . ." I burst into sobs, which she kindly takes for a no.

"How about I just take a message?"

"Thanks," I say between sniffles. I appreciate her protective manner as much as the box of tissues she extends to me.

"I'll keep an eye on you while you swim," Maria says.

I manage a watery smile of thanks.

That's how I come to be doing laps in Harry's pool when he arrives home from my wedding.

"Hello, Reverend Blessing." His bemused smile is as kind as Maria's words, but there's also a hint of disapproval around the edges.

"Hey, Harry."

He rolls his chair to the edge of the pool. "Do you need to talk or do you need to swim?"

I want to say swim, but we'd both know that was a lie. I wouldn't have come to Harry's house if I didn't need serious advice and counsel. Since I've never ditched anyone at the altar before, I'm a little out of my depth. And not just because I'm in the eight-foot end of the pool.

"I left a pretty good mess behind, huh?" I'm sure my fabulous chignon is plastered to the back of my neck, and if I have any mascara left after all the tears I've cried, that's probably slithering downward too.

"Yep." Harry rolls over to a rack of towels, plucks one off the top, and jerks his head, indicating for me to get out of the water. "But you're not the first person to wreak a little havoc and then make a break for it."

"Yes, but I did manage to do it rather spectacularly." I clamber out of the pool and catch the towel Harry tosses to me. He waits patiently while I dry off and wrap the enormous piece of terry around me. Trust Harry to have towels the size of Idaho.

Maria, on cue, appears with glasses of lemonade on a tray. Harry rolls up to one of the tables shaded by a large umbrella, and I take a seat next to him.

"Was it a huge scene?" Morbid curiosity on my part, I know, but I can't help asking.

"Your future mother-in-law was pretty entertaining. Looked like she couldn't decide whether to throw a fit or fall into a faint."

"What about my mom?"

"Crying." Harry's not one to spare anybody's feelings by soft-pedaling the truth.

"I'm sorry about that."

"Hmm."

"Well, I am."

"I believe you." But, again, there's that faint odor of disapproval hovering around us.

"I know it was wrong. But I was so mad. And I couldn't face them. How could I tell them the wedding was off?"

"Why was it?"

"Didn't David say? I figured he'd make an announcement to the congregation or something."

"All he said was that you weren't feeling well and unfortunately there wasn't going to be a wedding today."

"He didn't say we'd broken up?"

"No. He didn't even say you'd run out on him. At least not publicly."

"I didn't leave until after he broke up with me," I snap, because on this point I feel compelled to defend my honor.

"He broke up with you? He didn't mention that."

Now I'm confused. David's not the type to lie about something like that, even under duress. So if he didn't tell people he'd broken it off with me, then . . .

"I think asking for the ring back amounts to the same thing." I look down at my bare finger and, perversely, miss the weight of the old Easter basket.

"I suppose it does." Harry's manner lightens somewhat. "He didn't mention asking for the ring back either."

"You talked with him for quite a while, huh?"

Harry shrugs. "Not long. His mother had him pretty well cornered."

"What did they do about the photo shoot?"

Harry pauses, and his eyes don't meet mine.

"Harry?"

"His mom said they had to have photos for the magazine, so they . . . I guess you'd say they staged a wedding."

Even though I'm all dried off, my skin breaks out in goose bumps. "With David as the groom?"

"Yes."

"And the bride was?"

"Some brunette I didn't know. They asked the guests to stay for the photos. A few folks left, but most stayed. Either pretty kind or pretty curious."

Or both, I want to add, but I don't. "A brunette, huh?" And I bet I know just which brunette they got to pose as David's bride. That's what I get for agreeing to let him invite her to the wedding.

"It took them awhile to pin up the dress to fit her."

Hah! Well, at least I can console myself with my superior bosom. Although, frankly, it's not much consolation, is it? Funny how the things you think are important turn out to be really unimportant.

"So what are you going to do now?" Harry asks.

I take a sip of my lemonade, but my stomach's still sour from the events of the past few hours.

"I guess I'll go home eventually. Got to face the music sometime."

Harry's brow creases. "Before you go, I'd better tell you something I found out this morning."

I can't imagine what Harry would feel the need to tell me at a time like this, but he's been nice enough to hear me out and to let me take refuge in his swimming pool, so I say, "What's that?"

He twists the glass of lemonade on the table in front of him. It's not like Harry to avoid saying something, but it sure looks as if that's what he's doing.

"It's about the sale of the church," he finally says.

Okay, that's pretty much the last thing I expected to hear. And I'm getting goose bumps again.

"What about it?" The church sale is the one thing that's gone right in the past few weeks.

Harry takes a swig of lemonade and then wipes his mouth with the damp cocktail napkin his glass has been sitting on. "I found out why Corday and his backers want the church."

My heartbeat picks up. I can tell from the creases between Harry's eyebrows that I'm not going to like what he's about to say.

"You know the old warehouse area behind the church?"

"Yeah?" Of course I know it. That part of downtown has been an eyesore for years, but no one's ever figured out what to do with it.

"Well, the city's going to buy that land."

"So you think we undersold the church? Is the city going to develop the land for offices or something?"

Harry sighs. "The city's planning a new convention center, Betsy. Church of the Shepherd will be a prime location for a new hotel. Every upscale chain in America's going to be after that property. Hyatt. Marriott. Hilton. You name it. Church of the Shepherd is sitting on holy ground, so to speak. You undersold the church property by several million dollars."

Chapter 22

Just when I was hoping my professional triumph might compensate for the disaster that is my personal life, Harry's revelation sends the walls of that particular Jericho crashing down.

"A convention center?"

"The value of real estate within five blocks will triple once it's announced. Corday somehow found out about the city's plans before they went public. No wonder, as much time as he spends eavesdropping on the Planning Commission. When the church agreed to the sale, his speculation paid off."

"Excuse me, Harry. I think I'd better go." I bolt up out of my chair, and he quickly rolls toward me.

"Are you sure, Betsy? You're welcome to stay here with Joann and me."

"No, no. I'll be fine." I knew there would be music to be faced. I just hadn't realized it was going to be an entire symphony.

I scoop up my purse and my pile of clothes from the chaise lounge by the pool where I'd left them. "I'd better go home and start sorting through the mess."

Harry pats my arm. "I'll help in any way I can. You know that."

I bend down and hug him, struggling to keep the tears from starting back up again. "Thanks. I know you will." I move off toward the side of the house when I hear Harry call my name again.

"Betsy?"

"Yeah?"

"Making mistakes is part of life," Harry hollers across the yard. "It's what you do *after* you make a mistake that shows who you really are."

The sight of Harry sitting there in his wheelchair clamps down so hard on my heart that I think I might finally pass out. But Harry would misinterpret that as pity, so I steel myself against the wave of dizziness that threatens. I lift my hand in thanks, send him a weak smile, and turn toward my car.

And in that moment I realize I have no choice about what comes next. As Harry said, it's what I do next that will show the real Betsy Blessing.

The last person I expect to find waiting for me when I

walk into my apartment is Cecilia.

"You're okay!" she exclaims, leaping up off the couch.

"How'd you get in?"

She pulls back, uncomfortable. "David had a key. I talked him into giving it to me." She eyes my swimsuit questioningly but doesn't ask.

I look at the floor, then at the ceiling, then finally at her. "I have absolutely no idea what to say to you."

"It was all my fault," she says in response.

Okay. Those are the last words I expect to hear from Cecilia at this juncture. Especially as I'm standing in the middle of my living room in a damp swimsuit.

"Sorry?"

She smiles, but not really. It's the look of someone in pain who's attempting to be friendly.

"I should never have told you about the dress. It was wrong of me."

Huh? Surely she means that she should never have talked David into getting the dress from Jennifer to begin with. I set my purse and clothes down on the coffee table among the remnants of the bridal bouquet I fashioned so carefully last night.

"Actually, Cecilia, I'm glad you told me. It would have been worse to let me go through with the ceremony wearing Jennifer's dress without my knowing where it came from."

"But it's just a dress, Betsy. It doesn't determine your future. As long as you were happy with the dress, why should it matter?"

The fact that I feel clammy can't be accounted for by my swimsuit alone. "It matters because you both lied by omission. You knew I'd never agree to wear Jennifer's dress."

Cecilia flushes a little around the edges. "David said you'd be picky about that."

My stomach sinks a little more—who knew that was possible?—at this telltale sign of David's complicity in the whole deceit.

"I think any woman would object." I'm so exhausted by the trauma of the day that I can't even summon a modicum of anger.

Cecilia opens her mouth a couple of times, almost says something, and then doesn't. Finally, she says, "The truth is that the magazine's not just tightening its belt; it's in deep trouble. The winter issue was going to get a lot of buzz because it featured you and David. You know, the editor's son ties the knot, et cetera."

"I didn't know that."

"I didn't want you to. You or David. He's a good son. Has been every day since his father walked out on us. I didn't want to be a burden on David, financially, ever." Cecilia stops and swallows. "If the magazine goes under, I don't know what I'll do."

Just when I thought it wasn't possible to feel compassion for her . . .

"Why didn't you tell me all this?" I ask.

"We all have our pride."

Well, I couldn't disagree with her on that count.

"Did you get the shots you needed for the photo spread?"

"Enough to get the issue to print, but we won't be able to market it as we've hoped."

"Maybe you could spin it some other way and still generate the sales you need." I can't believe I'm comforting Cecilia at this point. Occupational hazard. Or habit.

"Maybe," she says.

I feel sorry for her, but she still doesn't regret what she's done. And while, as a single professional woman, I can understand her motives, I can't condone them. But there's one thing I do have to do, or else I'll end up as bitter and tense as my mother. I have to forgive her.

"Cecilia?"

"Yes?" She's looking at me with the kind of hope you see in a kid's eyes when you pass a Baskin-Robbins.

"I accept your apology." Even though I know she's never going to acknowledge guilt in the way I want. But I haven't been perfect in all of this either, and the only way anything is going to get set right is if we all bend a little. Or a lot.

She moves forward as if she's going to hug me, but I'm not quite ready for that. So I stick out my hand, which is about as far as I'm willing to go right now when it comes to bonding. She stops, pauses, and then takes my hand.

"I am sorry, Betsy."

"I know."

"You should call David."

"I will. When I'm ready."

Cecilia frowns. "Don't wait too long. David's like his father. His pride is important to him."

His pride? What about mine? "I just wish he hadn't been part of getting the dress from Jennifer."

"What do you mean?"

"David had lunch with Jennifer right before you sent the dress. Wasn't he doing your dirty work?"

Cecilia sighs. "Oh, Betsy. No. In fact, I was upset with him for trying to talk her out of handing it over."

Realization dawns. "You mean David *wasn't* trying to get Jennifer to *give* you the dress?"

"No. He had lunch with her to try to talk her out of it. Almost succeeded too."

Righteous indignation can be so empowering. You feel such a blissful combination of vindication and superiority. The only problem is when it turns out to be made of nothing but air, as it has at this moment in my life.

Cecilia leaves soon after that, since we don't have a whole lot more to say to each other. We part on fairly peaceful terms, and I don't mention all the things I've never gotten reimbursed for. The mismatched china. The DIY wedding invitations. I chalk those things up to what my father always called the Stupid Tax.

Sitting home alone in your apartment on your wedding day turns out to be pretty boring. After I've cleaned up the remains of my bouquet making, I move into the bedroom and actually make my bed. That leads to other general tidying efforts, and before I know it,

I'm in the bathroom scrubbing the tile grouting around the toilet with a toothbrush. I may well be single the rest of my life, but in my obituary, they can sing the praises of my pristine grout.

Or not. Because all this cleaning is just classic avoidance behavior. Wherever I go in the apartment, I'm keenly aware of where the phone is. The silent, non-ringing phone. I keep waiting for it to ring or for my mother to show up at the door, but there seems to be a conspiracy of silence. As late afternoon passes into evening, I unpack the small suitcase I'd readied for David's honeymoon surprise. And, really, I'm doing okay until I pull a small package from one of the zipper pockets. It's a small box wrapped in manly navy blue paper with a silver ribbon. My wedding present to David.

Just when I thought I was out of tears . . .

To be honest, the gift itself is nothing earth-shattering. A pair of modest gold cuff links for a man who's idea of black tie is chinos and a polo shirt. But when I picked them out at the jewelry store in the mall, they seemed like a very wifely sort of thing to give a new husband. They're engraved, too, so I can't return them.

Of course the moment I'm cradling those cuff links in my hand is the very moment the phone finally rings.

My dive for the handset is worthy of an Olympic medal. I flip over the phone, hoping against hope that caller ID will show David's number. Instead, though, it's a number I don't recognize. And in the space for the name, it says METRO GOV.

Now is really not the time I need some city employee telling me my water's going to be cut off while they do some work on the sewers.

"Hello?"

"Hello. May I speak to Reverend Blessing?" a female voice asks.

"This is she." The use of my title is the tip-off that the call is about more than my pipes.

"Reverend, this is Officer Stout of the Metro Police Department."

Those are words that will scare you into next week. Surely I didn't commit a crime by running out on the wedding?

"Yes?"

"I'm calling about one of your parishioners, Herman Jones."

"I'm sorry. Who?" The name doesn't ring a bell.

"Herman Jones. An older man. Resembles Santa Claus."

And then it clicks. "Oh, you mean Booger." You'll forgive me the wave of exasperation that floods through me. "What's he done now, Officer?" Frustration laces my words. I really don't think I can be Booger's pastor right now. I'm not up to tracking down a good bail bondsman on a Saturday night.

"Well, ma'am—"

"If he's been picked up for public intoxication again, he probably needs to spend the night in custody drying out." Booger himself told me that when he was sober. Said there was no point in bailing him out while he was still inebriated because he'd just go right back to the bottle once his feet hit the streets.

"I'm afraid that's not possible," the officer says.

"What does he need, then?" I don't mean to snap, but I've got one nerve left after all that's happened today, and it's frayed beyond belief.

"Actually, ma'am, we need someone to come down and confirm our identification."

My throat goes dry. "What do you mean confirm your identification? Didn't he already tell you who he is?"

"I'm sorry, Reverend. I should have been more clear. Mr. Jones was struck by a vehicle on Broadway late this afternoon. Unfortunately, he was DOA at the hospital. We found your name and phone number in his wallet to call in case of an emergency. We need you to come to the coroner's office to confirm his identity."

Dear God. Oh dear God.

"I . . . I . . ." My lips won't form any words. Finally, I manage to croak out, "Are you sure it's Booger?"

"Reasonably, ma'am. He looks like the photo on his ID card. But we need to be certain."

Certain they have the right dead body? My legs won't support me anymore, and I sink down on the couch. *Please let this all be a bad dream.*

"Can you get to the coroner's office this evening?" the officer asks.

"Yes." I have no idea how, since my legs have apparently quit functioning.

"Let me give you directions," Officer Stout says.

I forage around on the end table for pencil and paper.

271

Like an automaton, I numbly take down the directions. Somehow my legs start working again. I make it out the door with my purse and car keys. I slide into my old Honda, and then I see it—the Sunday-comic-wrapped wedding present lying on the passenger seat. With trembling fingers and a throat full of tears, I reach for it and rip away the wrapping.

It's a small painting, not new or expensive. Probably something he picked up at Goodwill. And then I realize what it depicts.

Church of the Shepherd.

I've seen this before in some of the members' homes, a not terribly professional ink wash of the front of the church, Gothic steeple soaring to the sky. I also find a card tucked into a corner of the frame.

For the preacher, it says. *To remember us by.*

"Hello. This is David. You know the drill." *Beep.*

I do know the drill, just like I know the message by heart, and given all that's happened, I guess I can understand why David's screening his calls. I've been doing the same thing myself, mostly to keep my post-nuptial contact with my mother to a minimum.

"Hey, David. We need to talk. Or at least I need to talk if you're willing to listen. Call me. Please."

My voice cracks on that last word. It's after midnight, so I'm pretty sure he's home. I can picture him lying there in bed, listening to my voice and not making the slightest move for the phone. Which, frankly, is starting to make me mad, because, although I may have been the one to make a break for it, his asking for the ring back five minutes before the ceremony started was certainly a contributing factor in my decision.

You'd think that after my trip to the morgue, this day couldn't get any worse. I threw up a second time after I identified Booger. The past few hours have made all that stuff about the dress seem as infantile as . . . well, as infantile as it really is. On the part of everyone concerned.

And David's silence is so loud it's deafening. Enough that my ears are ringing. Only I realize it's not my ears that are ringing. It's my phone.

"Hello," I say, tentative as a backslider trying to sneak into the last pew.

"Hey." David's voice sounds as flat and exhausted as I feel.

"Hey," I reply, not scoring any points for originality.

Silence descends. Then David says, "You wanted to tell me something?"

"I'm sorry for running out like that."

More silence. Finally, "Okay."

Okay? That's all he's going to say—okay?

I swallow hard and continue. "I should have stayed. But when I found out that you were part of the whole dress conspiracy—"

"I wasn't. At least, I didn't mean to be."

Okay, fair enough, but he still knew what was going on.

"Why didn't you tell me?" I think I've got a right to ask the question. He should have known I'd never freely choose to wear Jennifer's dress.

"I was going to, Betz, until I saw how excited you were about that dress. More so than about all the other wedding stuff put together. I know it was a sacrifice, letting my mom take over the wedding. I wanted you to have something in all of it that made you happy."

Again with missing the point, Reverend Dr. Swenson. When will he figure out that *he* is the one thing in all of this that my happiness depends on?

"David, I don't care about all that extraneous stuff—"

"Yes you do."

"What?"

"You *do* care, Betsy. You cared about every bit of it, even when you were trying to convince yourself you didn't."

"But . . . I . . ." And I realize he's right. Even while I was telling myself that the trappings and the superficial stuff didn't matter to me, I was seething and fuming over Cecilia's choices.

"But if you knew I was unhappy . . ."

"I didn't know you were unhappy enough to leave me at the altar."

"But you asked for the ring back."

"What? I did not."

"David, yes you did. You asked for the ring back."

"When?"

"When you said that if I didn't like it, I should just return it!"

His sharp bark of laughter hurts my ear. And then he's not laughing anymore. "That's what you thought? That

274

I wanted the ring back?"

"What else was I supposed to think?"

I hear David take a deep breath. "I meant that if you didn't like the ring, we should return it to whoever sold it to my mom on eBay. And we'd get you another one."

Oh. But wait a minute. "You left out the part about getting me another one."

He's quiet for another moment. "Yeah. I guess I did."

Over the past years, I've been pretty judgmental about all those brides and grooms I've worked with. I've made fun of their photo-op weddings, resented spending Friday nights cowing mothers-of-the-bride into submission so we could get through the rehearsals, and politely wormed my way out of attending as many receptions as possible. But now the tables have turned, and I'm the one whose life has been mangled by a nuptial train wreck.

Neither of us says anything for a while, but I can hear him breathing so I know he's still there. "David?" I say.

"Yeah?"

"What happens next?"

"I don't know, Betz. I really don't know."

Which isn't quite the answer I was hoping for.

Chapter 23

It's Sunday, and I should be in a honeymoon suite somewhere—or at the very least in a king-size room at a Hampton Inn enjoying my first full day of marital bliss. Instead, I spend it making arrangements for

Booger's funeral and sobbing into my pillow.

I forgot to tell David about Booger last night, and now I'd give anything to be able to go back to when David and I were just friends so that he could be here with me, telling me that everything's going to be all right.

A Sunday morning at home is a rare thing for a minister, but there's no way I can enjoy this one. I don't care about leisurely reading the paper, working the crossword puzzle, or watching the political talk shows while eating Pop-Tarts in my bathrobe. I had planned to take next week off for the honeymoon, but now there's no point. And I certainly don't want to spend the next five days wallowing in misery. So I decide that I might as well go back to work tomorrow.

Monday morning finds me standing in my office, knee-deep in wedding presents that have to be returned. I'd planned to spend this week luxuriating in David's company. Instead, the only guy I'll be getting intimate with is the UPS man who's coming by to pick up all these packages.

I sent David an e-mail yesterday.

To: pastorswenson@st-helga.org
From: blessingb@cotstn.org
Re: Forgot to tell you . . .

That Booger was hit by a bus on Saturday. His service is Tuesday at 3:00 p.m. if you want to come.

Just thought you'd want to know.

Betsy

When you have no money, as Booger didn't, there's not much choice but to be cremated. Angelique went down to the Salvation Army and looked through Booger's locker while I was wrapping packing tape around every empty box we could find in the church and filling out shipping labels. But her search turned up nothing in the way of a will. One of the funeral homes was kind enough to offer their services pro bono, even providing a small plot to bury Booger's ashes. The funeral is set for tomorrow with "visitation preceding," as they say.

Angelique posted a notice at several of the places where homeless folks gather or go for social services, and the church sprang for a notice in the paper. We're going to provide food at the visitation because I can't bear the thought of anyone going hungry at Booger's funeral. It seems like the least we could do. I'm a little nervous about the visitation, frankly. It's going to be an interesting mix of people. I only hope everyone will behave appropriately, especially the members of Church of the Shepherd.

I've finished boxing up the last toaster to be returned (David and I received three of them—so much for the efficacy of the modern bridal registry) when Angelique sticks her head around the door.

"Edna called," she says. "She needs someone to drive

her home from the rehab hospital."

Great. Just what I needed to make this day complete. Although it beats being summoned to help her hook her bra when she had that shoulder injury. And then I'm ashamed of myself for that uncharitable thought, since Edna was so supportive of my wrongheaded decision to accept Arthur Corday's offer. Which means that the only appropriate penance, of course, is to go get her and take her home.

"I'm on it," I say to Angelique, moving toward my desk to grab my purse and keys.

"Want me to finish wrapping up all these packages?" she asks.

"It's not your job," I say, demurring, when what I really want to say is, "I'll be your servant for life if you will."

"I don't mind." As usual, Angelique is my underpaid godsend. "Let's face it, Betsy. You can't return all these presents, prepare for Booger's funeral, and go see about Edna."

She's right, of course. But I feel guilty sticking someone else with a chore that's my responsibility.

Angelique dismisses me with a flick of her inch-long fingernails. "Aren't you the one who's always telling me we're a team? So go already, and let me do some teamwork with these wedding gifts."

"Thanks." I stop and give her a quick hug as I head for the door. "I appreciate it."

I guess when it comes to cleaning up my various messes, I'm going to have to break down and admit that sometimes I require a little help.

Edna's waiting in a wheelchair at the front door of the rehab hospital when I pull up under the covered driveway. An orderly is standing next to her, holding on to a rolling cart that's piled with the usual detritus from a long hospital stay—a couple of half-dead plants, one of those breathing-exercise things they give you to keep you from getting pneumonia, a plastic water pitcher, a half-used box of tissues, and several generic white plastic bags stuffed with Edna's unmentionables and other female paraphernalia.

"Good morning, Edna." I'm determined to be chipper and upbeat no matter how I truly feel. I've probably bared my soul a little too much to her over the past few weeks, but the heady experience of going from sworn enemies to secret-sharing friends seems to have pried loose more information than I would normally part with.

"Good morning, Betsy." She purses her lips. "You're late."

"Well, we'd better get moving, then," I say with a gee-whiz-golly-goodness smile as I unlock the trunk of my Civic. Fortunately, the brilliant design engineers at Honda have made it so that you can stuff an elephant in the back of this little compact car. Which is good, since Edna has roughly that amount of stuff to haul home.

Thankfully, the orderly helps me load both Edna and her belongings into the car. Edna turns out to be the trickiest item since my car is low to the ground and her new hip isn't. Her shoulder's better, though, so at least she has the use of both her arms.

I knew as soon as Edna called that I was going to have to tell her what Harry told me the other day. I've been sitting on that information since Saturday, vainly hoping, I guess, that some heavenly providence would drop out of the sky and fix the situation. Sadly, no such manna has put in an appearance, so I'm going to have to bite the bullet and start confessing to the members of the administrative committee. And since Edna has been the most vocal in her support, it seems only fair to start with her.

"Are you hungry? Do we need to stop anywhere on the way home?" I ask politely, perfectly willing to butter her up with some chicken salad from the Picnic Café or a carry-out plate from the Belle Meade Buffet.

"Alice will have something waiting," Edna says, referring to her housekeeper.

"Then home it is," I say.

Now that I'm sitting so close to Edna, I can see the tinges of gray around her lips. Surely that's not good.

"Are you feeling okay?"

"I'm perfectly well," Edna snaps. She twists her hands together in her lap in an uncharacteristic gesture of anguish.

"Edna? What is it?"

I'm pretty sure that if I turned toward her, I'd see tears in her eyes, but I also think I'd better not take my eyes off the traffic on Harding Road.

"It's nothing."

"Neither of us believes that," I say gently. "Please tell me."

"I'd rather have stayed in the hospital a few more days," Edna says, scowling.

"But I thought the doctor said you were well enough to go home. The physical therapist gave you his blessing."

"Humph. What do those medical people know?"

Considering that those medical people are the reason she can walk at all, I'd say they know quite a bit. But what parishioners usually complain about and what's truly bothering them are two different matters entirely.

"Well, you'll have Alice to look after you," I say, trying to be helpful.

"Because I pay her." Edna's clearly not interested in being told to count her blessings or think positively today.

"True. But she still cares about you."

"I guess."

And then I realize what's bothering Edna. I didn't think of it right off because of her prickliness, but the truth is that she loves being in the middle of things. For a long time she was in the midst of the proverbial stew at church. Since her fall, she's been the center of attention at the hospital. But now she's headed home, where it will be just her and one other person, and Alice will have her hands full with cooking, cleaning, and nursing. Socializing will be way down on her agenda.

"Edna, have you ever considered assisted living?" I

ask this with all the innocence of a lamb, but she's onto me immediately.

"Assisted living? I don't need assisted living. Some aide counting out my pills and asking if I've had a bowel movement?" She sniffs regally. "I think not."

You would think I asked if she wanted to moon a trucker out the passenger-side window of the Civic.

"It might make things easier, and you'd always have companionship."

"Companionship? More like busybodies sticking their noses into what doesn't concern them." She waves her hand as if she smells a foul odor. "No, thank you, miss. The last thing I need is to be dragged to bingo three nights a week."

"It was just a thought."

I sneak a sideways glance at her to see if she's truly as perturbed by the idea as she's making out, but I can't tell. At least maybe I've planted a seed. Mentioning assisted living to a senior citizen is generally met with the same hostility as when you inform a teenager that he or she might not be ready to take a driving test.

"So you left that Lutheran at the altar?" Edna asks, countering my assisted-living question with an equally uncomfortable one of her own.

I don't want to talk about my aborted wedding, but since I set a precedent by discussing the wedding details with her, I have to explain what happened. So I give her the speech I've been rehearsing, which bears some semblance to the truth without casting too much blame on either me or David.

"It's unfortunate that we canceled at the last minute,"
I say, "but we both realized we weren't ready to take
such a big step." That sounds much more mature than,
"I found out I was wearing his first fiancée's dress, and
then I thought he asked for the ring back, so I ran out
the back door." After all our discussions about the role
of the dress in the proceedings, I'm too embarrassed to
tell Edna how easily hoodwinked I was on that one.

Still, I see Edna's Arched Eyebrow of Skepticism out
of the corner of my eye.

"So you'll be rescheduling the ceremony for a later
date?"

"Mmm . . . well . . . I don't think that's been decided
yet." The passive form of the verb *to decide* comes in
really handy at the moment.

"Decided by you or by David?"

Why does she have to be one of the few who is per-
ceptive enough to pick up on that? Of course, that per-
ceptiveness is one of the qualities that has made her
such an effective agitator at the church all these years.

"We haven't discussed rescheduling," I say.

"He's not speaking to you?"

"Look, there's the Belle Meade Buffet. Are you sure
you don't want me to stop for some carry-out? They
have amazing chicken-fried chicken livers."

Edna ignores my question. "I was under the impression you were in love with that Lutheran."

Argh! "I am in love with 'that Lutheran,' as you put
it."

"Then do something about it," Edna snaps. "Before

it's too late." Her voice shakes on the last few words, and I shoot her another quick glance before putting on my turn signal and pulling into the left lane.

"Don't miss an opportunity you might regret losing," Edna says, and she sounds like the voice of experience. Tempted as I am to do some prying of my own to see what's behind her vehemence, I refrain. As I've so recently learned, some things are so tender they deserve the respect of being left alone.

I make a left onto Belle Meade Boulevard, the ritziest street in Nashville and the one Edna has called home for years.

"There's something I need to tell you," I say, and Edna listens without comment while I relay the abbreviated version of what Harry Snedegar told me on my wedding day.

When I'm done, Edna doesn't say anything. I pull into her driveway and stop beside the front door. It opens to reveal Alice waiting for Edna with a smile on her face—a fairly superhuman feat, if you ask me. Then it occurs to me that maybe Alice has been lonely these past weeks, rattling around in this big house all by herself.

I turn off the engine, still waiting for Edna to respond to my news. Alice comes out of the house and moves toward the car.

"Edna? Aren't you going to say anything about Arthur Corday?" I ask.

Slowly she turns her head toward me, and the look of pain in her eyes reminds me of that day I rushed to her house and found the paramedics loading her onto a stretcher.

"I'm sorry," I say, which has become my mantra these days. "I really thought selling was the right decision."

"It wasn't, though, was it?" Her voice isn't hostile, but it's still heavy with recrimination. Edna went out on a limb for me, which is pretty amazing considering that for most of my tenure at Church of the Shepherd, she has just wanted to get me fired.

"I supported you, Betsy, because you were gracious to me when I made a mistake. But, like me, you'll have to deal with the consequences of your error. Are you prepared to do that?"

My hands go clammy, and I try not to wipe them on my pants. "Do you mean I should resign?"

At that critical juncture, Alice opens the car door. "Hello, Mrs. Tompkins. It's good to have you home."

"Thank you, Alice." No hint of emotion shows in Edna's tone or face. She turns back to me. "You've already fled one difficult situation, Betsy." Her eyes pin me in my seat. "I hardly think running away a second time will improve matters."

Having said her piece, she turns back to Alice. "Well, don't just stand there. Help me out of this contraption."

Alice does so with her usual good grace while I get out of the car, open the trunk, and start unloading Edna's belongings. And as I do so, I think about how much I really, really hate it when Edna's right.

All the way back to Church of the Shepherd, I rack my

285

brain, trying to think of some way out of my dilemma. And later that afternoon, while I'm preparing Booger's funeral service and trying not to cry, Edna's words continue to haunt me. They aren't anything I didn't know already, but somehow hearing them from her makes the situation all the more real. And scary.

I got Church of the Shepherd into this mess, and now I have to get us out of it.

If nothing else, this problem gives me something to obsess about besides my disaster of a wedding and David's continued stoic silence. I haven't heard from him since that late-night conversation on Saturday, although I've had plenty of other people leaving messages on my machine. My mom. My dad. Tracy. Even the twins. Various rubbernecking parishioners. And, on a more sympathetic note, a nice message of consolation and commiseration from Reverend Squires.

By two o'clock Tuesday afternoon, I'm standing in the fellowship hall at church, greeting the folks who've come to pay their last respects to Booger. Edna's not here in person, given her limited mobility, but she spent the balance of yesterday on the phone, corralling members of the ladies auxiliary into providing food and drink for the visitation. This task wasn't as difficult as one might think, given all the unused food from my wedding reception still in the industrial-size refrigerators in the church kitchen. I recognize the fruit trays I picked up at Costco, minus some of the more perishable contents. What's more, my wedding cake has been dismantled into rows of individual cupcakes that line a faux-silver tray. Well, at least all that food isn't going to waste, but I don't have any more appetite today than I did on Saturday.

I was afraid that all of my parishioners would end up on one side of the room and all of Booger's homeless friends on the other, like the great gender divide at a junior-high dance. However, food, as always, appears to be the great equalizer. Bernice, The Judge, and Margaret Devereaux are standing elbow to elbow with several street people as they all pick and choose their tidbits from the refreshment table.

A man materializes next to me—someone I've never met.

"Preacher, I want to thank you for doing this for Booger." The stranger's greasy hair is matted to his thin skull. Bright blue eyes stand out against his leathery, tanned skin.

I force a smile in spite of the pain that Booger's name evokes and shake the man's proffered hand. "We're glad to do it. We're certainly going to miss him."

The man studies my face intently, and I shift from one sensible pump to the other.

"You mean that?" he asks.

"Yes, I do." It's nice to feel this little bit of certainty in the midst of all the chaos that has become my life.

The man takes a bite out of a giant strawberry from his plate. The juice dribbles down his chin and disappears into his thicket of a beard. "Booger appreciated what y'all did for him, ma'am," he says after he swallows the strawberry.

"We didn't do that much." What I want to say is that we didn't do nearly enough. I think of the Tiffany stained-glass window in the sanctuary and the Good Shepherd toting home the lost lamb. I wish we could have done that for Booger. Maybe if we'd tried just one more time to get him into rehab. Or if a church family had been brave enough to invite him into their home until he got back on his feet. Not that Booger would have taken anyone up on that invitation. He valued his independence just as much as, if not more than, any of us.

"I'd say you did right smart for him," the man says.

"I hope so." But my voice reveals my doubt. I need some consolation at this moment, some bit of comfort to carry me through the next few hours of being the one to console all the mourners and lead the service.

"Not many churches would have let ol' Booger be a member," the man says. "But y'all did. And Booger, he was as proud of being part of this church as anything in the world."

Tears sting my eyes, but I blink them back. They're tears of regret, of humility, of frustration.

"We were proud to have Booger as a member too," I say, even though it's a half lie, as much as I want it to be true. Not everyone around here was delighted when Booger plopped down next to them in a pew on Sunday morning.

The man contemplates me through bright blue eyes that reflect the weary weight of the world on his shoulders. "People think it's the big things that matter. Like a high-paying job or a mansion out on Belle Meade Boulevard. But, Preacher"—he pauses—"sometimes it's enough just to be able to pee indoors."

I have absolutely no idea what to say to that. And then I think of Booger sneaking into the church at night. I always thought he wanted a safe place to sleep, but evidently the real lure was the plumbing.

The man starts to move away before I realize I don't know his name. "Excuse me? I'm sorry. I should have introduced myself. I'm Reverend Blessing."

He smiles, a weary but peaceful expression, and nods at me. "Pleased to meet you properly."

"And you are?"

"Oh. Sorry, ma'am. I'm Jesus. Jesus Christ."

He's not the first homeless person I've met who thinks he's Jesus, but he's certainly the most calm about it. Since I've been at Church of the Shepherd, I've also encountered the apostle Paul, Mary Magdalene, and Noah. Given the percentage of homeless people who suffer from mental illness and how often that expresses itself in religious ways, that's not surprising.

What does surprise me is that, for the first time, I'm not entirely skeptical.

While the organ plays the prelude for Booger's service, I stare up at that stained-glass window. The Shepherd doesn't look unduly burdened by the sheep slung around his shoulders. I myself would be stooping and stumbling and generally grousing about the weight of the woolly lamb chop around my neck. But the Good

Shepherd bears his burdens with equanimity. I wish I could pull that off half as well.

The organ music fades away, and I step into the pulpit.

"Friends, we are gathered here today to remember our friend, Booger Jones, and to celebrate the good news of eternal life."

The familiarity of the funeral liturgy frees my mind to notice the details of the moment. The crowd is a respectable size, although it's certainly not the traditional gathering of doctors, lawyers, and Indian chiefs one finds in our sanctuary. We have enough bulletins, but just barely. And I think Booger would be amused to see Bernice and The Judge sitting next to the man who introduced himself as Jesus. And then, in the back row, I spy David. He slips in as I'm talking and nods encouragingly before settling into his seat. Despite our current awkwardness, I'm deeply grateful for his show of support.

As I lead the congregation through the service, I'm overcome by the familiar sense of being an instrument of a more powerful force, my personal grief notwithstanding. I don't mean that to sound too "woo-woo," but leading worship often takes me to a sort of transcendental place where I feel as if I'm simply a spoke in a much larger wheel. When we come together, we are something greater than the sum of our parts. It's the reason I always worry about people who say they don't need to be part of a religious community to practice their faith. I think they're missing out on one of the greatest gifts in life, even if those communities can often be a real pain in the neck.

My mind is chasing that particular rabbit while the congregation sings "Great Is Thy Faithfulness." It's one of those hymns I usually belt out on automatic pilot because I've known the words for so long. When you lead two services a Sunday for five years, you memorize all the hymns pretty quickly.

"Morning by morning new mercies I see," I sing along with the congregation. "All I have needed thy hand hath provided. Great is thy faithfulness, Lord, unto me."

At that moment the chancel rocks beneath my feet. I look around, surprised, but no one else seems to have felt it. The congregation just goes on singing, and then it's like I'm hit by one of those metaphorical lightning bolts God tends to zap me with when I'm not looking. Because in that moment I realize that my mistake in accepting Arthur Corday's offer isn't what I thought it was. You see, I thought I'd just goofed because I undersold the building and cost the church money. But as I look out at this odd assortment of personages gathered to remember a slightly smelly, kindhearted homeless man, I see that my mistake was in thinking that the church should ever be sold in the first place.

The thought disturbs and disrupts me so much that I don't move back into the pulpit when the congregation reaches the end of the hymn. They're all just standing there looking at me, waiting for the signal to be seated once more, and I'm standing on the chancel, looking out at them, my mouth most likely hanging open. I'm not supposed to be Moses after all. No, more like Nehemiah, the man God called to rebuild the walls of Jerusalem after all those long years of exile. But, frankly, I'd much rather be Moses any day of the week. Because however scary the unknown can be, it still has the advantage of brimming with novelty. And hope. And expectation. Whereas rebuilding something that's been broken down seems a far, far riskier proposition, haunted as you are by memories of the glory days.

How ironic, then, that when I do come to my senses, motion the congregation to be seated, and move into the pulpit, I begin to read an appropriate passage from Ecclesiastes.

"For everything there is a season, and a time for every matter under heaven."

Normally, like the hymn, I can pretty much recite this one by heart, but today my head is buried in my Bible as I read the words aloud.

"A time to break down, and a time to build up."

And that's the thing about the life of faith. So often it's hard to know which time it is. Take my wedding, for example. I thought it was a time to dance when it turns out it was a time to refrain from dancing. So to speak. I wish it hadn't taken Booger's dying to open my eyes to the living, but there you have it. Sometimes that's what has to happen. I think of his wedding present propped against the pile of commentaries on my desk, and I have to smile through my tears. Even though he's gone, Booger's not going to let me take away his church.

And that's the moment when I realize that God didn't put me in this position to achieve the kind of success that gets a preacher his or her own television show and a book deal. Maybe I'm not meant to be the permanent senior minister of this congregation, but I do know I'm supposed to fight the battle here, on this corner of downtown, in whatever capacity the church will allow me to serve. My mom used to have a little sign hanging in the kitchen when I was growing up: "Bloom where you're planted." I always found that sign annoying and simplistic. But now I see the point. Somehow, someway, Church of the Shepherd's going to bloom where it's been planted for a hundred years.

I feel a new energy in my heart, and it comes out in my voice. And as I deliver Booger's eulogy, I'm thankful that in death, as in life, he's made me uncomfortable enough, knocked me far enough off center, that I see a little glimmer of the Divine where I never noticed it before.

Chapter 24

In the days after Booger's funeral, I carry that framed painting of Church of the Shepherd everywhere I go. Since it isn't much bigger than the average day planner, it's pretty portable. And in some obvious but still rather spooky way, it has become my personal icon, an earthly object that serves as my window to the holy.

Or maybe I just feel less guilty about not doing more for Booger when I'm taking good care of the painting.

David and I haven't made any more progress in sorting out the aftermath of our non-wedding, but I can't worry about that this afternoon. The one advantage to having your whole life fall apart simultaneously is that you can only obsess about one aspect of it at a time. This afternoon's emotional energy has to be channeled into the administrative-committee meeting The Judge has called.

I was brave enough over the past few days to gird my loins and go to the committee members, one by one, to tell them the truth about the sale of the church. I spilled all the beans—how Arthur Corday hoodwinked me, the city's plans for a convention center, and the probability of the church becoming a high-rise hotel.

The committee members' responses were so predictable that I might have scripted them in advance. The Judge did not refrain from saying, "I told you so." Mac bemoaned how many more Habitat for Humanity houses we could have built with the additional millions. Bernice took the news with her typical flair for the dramatic, nearly swooning and then recovering herself to give a rousing speech of defiance à la Joan of Arc, one of the many roles she understudied. I even met Peyton downtown near his office for a cup of coffee. I'd hoped my mea culpa would bring him and his wife back into the fold, but it turns out they're already happily ensconced at a Methodist church—get this—out in the suburbs. So my experience with Peyton turns out to be the equivalent of the boyfriend who breaks up with you because he's not ready to commit and then is engaged to someone else within a month.

When I arrive at Edna's on Friday after work, everyone else is already assembled. Alice shows me up to Edna's bedroom, which is evidently where we're going to meet.

"Good afternoon, Betsy." Edna greets me coolly when I enter the room. Has her goodwill toward me fully evaporated in the face of impending disaster?

"Hello, Edna." I continue on around the room, greeting The Judge, Mac, Ralph, and Bernice. We still don't have a chair of the elders, so with Peyton gone, there's just the six of us. I perch on the little stool in front of Edna's dressing table. If worst comes to worst, I'm the closest to the door and can bolt before one of the others nabs me.

"I don't think there's any point in beating around the bush," The Judge says without preamble. "We have no choice, Miss Blessing, but to censure you at a minimum."

Ouch. Well, I can't say I wasn't expecting it, but it still seems harsh.

"I understand, Judge, but I'm not ready to give up hope yet."

"I don't see what we can do at this point," he says. "I spent the afternoon rereading the contracts. Corday's company will get Church of the Shepherd for a relative pittance." He pauses to scowl even more deeply. "Then they'll turn around and make a fortune."

I have to admit that even though it would rankle if The Judge were the one to bail me out of this situation,

295

I would gladly take it on the chin if he had figured out a way to void the contract.

"I guess it's a lesson learned," Bernice says, but she's obviously very sad, and not just in an emote-so-the-back-row-will-cry kind of way. As much as having the church move to the suburbs bothered her, the fact that it's a bad financial decision only makes it more difficult to accept.

"Surely there's something we can do," I say, trying to keep the desperation out of my voice but not really succeeding. "I really am very sorry."

But an apology alone isn't enough. I need to go on record here and fully accept responsibility. Bernice will take it down, and it will be in the minutes of Church of the Shepherd forever after. I must publicly admit how one Reverend Betsy Blessing, interim senior minister, led the congregation right over the edge into the ecclesiastical abyss.

"I let myself think this was all for the good of the church." I swallow hard. Even though I rehearsed this speech in the car on the way over, it still sticks in my throat. "But I have to admit that my own ambitions played a part in my actions."

Five pairs of eyes look at me in a way that reminds me of all the times I disappointed my mom and dad. When I didn't snag a sufficiently impressive prom date (Mom). When I failed to register for the LSAT (Dad). Only this moment is worse, really, because my falling short in this instance has a lot more impact. This time it's not just about me; it affects a whole community.

"I could have Hart look over the contract again," I say, trying to offer some atonement.

"It's a shame," Ralph says, vocalizing what everyone in the room is feeling. "After all these years—"

"To go out with a whimper instead of a bang," Mac says, putting it pretty succinctly. "It's more like dying than a fresh start."

"We can take the window with us, can't we?" Edna asks. "It's unique. Not Tiffany's usual subject at all."

Again, as during Booger's funeral, I'm struck by how much history will be lost when Church of the Shepherd comes tumbling down. Maybe we can save the Tiffany Shepherd and his lost sheep, but the beautiful Gothic steeple, the golden stone that shimmers in the heat of summer, the dark mahogany beams in the sanctuary that point the way to heaven—all of that will be lost. I guess in my dreams of the future, I forgot to value the past. But these folks haven't forgotten. I look around the room again and feel what I never wanted to acknowledge before—the weight of all the collective years of faith and love that are as much a part of the building as the stone and mahogany and Tiffany glass. I can preach about community all day long, but can I really live it? Can I trust my flock enough to admit to them that I'm no shepherd, but just another stray lamb in need of a ride home? Of course, the last time a congregation perceived any weakness in me, it fired me. Looks as if history may be about to repeat itself.

"As far as my future at the church goes," I say, "you all do what you need to do. If you want my resignation,

297

I'll tender it immediately."

Honestly, has anyone else in the history of Christianity lost a fiancé, her professional future, and most of the equity in a hundred-year-old church in the space of a week? "First, though, I'd like the chance to at least try and make amends for what I've done."

Really, it's too bad the congregation never got around to having the building put on the National Register of Historic Places before now. Then Arthur Corday wouldn't be able to knock it down. But, as Dr. Black told me when I first started working at the church, the congregation didn't want anyone telling them what they could or couldn't do with the building for the rest of eternity. And, of course, that's the only out Hart saw when he reviewed the contract.

It's a good thing I'm sitting on Edna's dressing-table stool, because just then an idea pops into my brain that makes me go weak in the knees. My head snaps up.

"What if we could get the church designated as a historic landmark before the sale goes through?" I ask, looking first at The Judge and then at the others.

"Why would that matter now?" Mac says. "Would that stop the sale?"

I'm reminded that not everyone in the room has read the contract. They agreed to the sale, at least a simple majority of them did, based on blind faith in me. A lot of good that did them.

"That's the out in the contract," I say. "If the building is designated a historic landmark before the sale goes through, then the contract is void."

The Judge scowls, but it's a thoughtful kind of scowl. "I guess we've fought that kind of designation for so long, it never occurred to me to use that clause to void the contract."

Bernice drops her pen onto her steno pad. "I used to be on the board of one of the historic neighborhoods. It doesn't usually take long to have a building designated a local landmark. We did that when someone started selling off bits and pieces of one of the historic homes—a door frame here, some doorknobs there. We had to act fast before the whole thing was gone."

"The only way they can turn a profit is to put a luxury hotel on the site," The Judge points out.

"Wait a minute," Mac says. "If Arthur Corday couldn't tear the church down, then neither could anyone else. We'd never be able to sell it after that. A lowball offer is better than no offer at all."

I squirm on my stool some more, clear my throat, and then speak the words I knew I was going to have to say at some point. I've known since that pivotal moment at Booger's visitation.

"What if we decided not to sell after all?" I say.

They're all looking at me as if I've sprouted horns and a tail—and am toting a pitchfork to boot. Bernice looks more confused than ever.

"But, Betsy, haven't you been telling us all along that staying put is a death sentence?" Bernice asks. "That we owe it to the church to give it a chance at a future?"

The thing about doing a public about-face is that sometimes it happens so quickly, it can give everyone involved whiplash—especially the one doing the one-eighty, which in this case is me. In my line of work, we call this repentance. Literally turning your back on something and heading off in the opposite direction. We also call it the prelude to a visit to the chiropractor.

"Yes . . . um . . . well . . ." I resist the urge to grind my toe into the carpet like a kid caught with her hand in the cookie jar. "Obviously I may have been in error about that whole relocation thing."

Ralph, who has until now been busily tapping buttons on his calculator, looks up from his computations. "We're still not in any better financial position than we were when we agreed to the sale. Within months we'll be dipping into the principal of the endowment. After that . . ." He shrugs his slumping shoulders.

The Judge frowns. "I know I fought you on this, Miss Blessing, but I'm going to concede that it would be better to cut our losses and take Corday's money. We should be thankful the situation's not worse than it is."

The face of Booger's friend Jesus—scraggly, strawberry-soaked beard and all—rises in my mind's eye. Now that I've got the committee thinking we have to leave downtown behind, how can I get them to change their minds again? All the empirical evidence is against me, and I don't think that telling them about my epiphany, brought on by contemplating a homeless man's need for indoor plumbing, will do the trick. That account just doesn't seem like a very persuasive moment of enlightenment. More like one of those stories people tell, thinking it's hilarious, and when you don't laugh, they say, "Well, I guess you had to be there."

No, I need a way to show them that it's not yet time to give up on downtown. That we still have a part to play in our community.

"Look, I know the last thing I should be asking for is another chance," I say, choking back my pride. I'm prepared to grovel, if necessary. Fortunately Edna's bedroom carpet is extra-thick pile, very accommodating to the knees. "But I've changed my mind about the church. I'd like a chance to change your minds as well."

"You mean you think we're going to have an influx of new members for no reason at all?" The Judge says.

I should know that he's not going to make this easy on me.

"Maybe this is a sign," I say.

"A sign?" Mac shakes his head, and his long, gray ponytail bobs where it's draped over his shoulder. "A sign of what?"

"I'll grant you that Church of the Shepherd may never be what it once was." I smooth the fabric of my skirt over my knees. "But maybe God's trying to get our attention. Well, my attention more than anyone else's, since I started this whole thing. But maybe this situation is a way of making us see something we've never been open to glimpsing before."

"Huh?" Ralph says.

Well, no wonder he's confused. After all, I'm only just working this out in my head as I go along, and it's not something I can show him by pushing buttons on his calculator and having all the numbers add up.

301

"Look, if we stay downtown, we know we can't go back to the glory days. We can't keep doing business as usual. But what if God's calling us to some new business? What if we're supposed to be moving into Phase Two?"

"Phase Two of what?" Ralph asks.

"Phase Two of whatever Church of the Shepherd is supposed to be."

"Miss Blessing, you are making no sense," The Judge says. "Could you be less cryptic?"

"Probably not," I say ruefully, "but maybe—"

"Maybe what?" Edna's looking curious and also hopeful.

Come on, Betsy, think. Think hard.

"I don't know what else we can do but what we've been doing for the past hundred years," Bernice says. "Can you give us an example?"

Unfortunately, I can't. While I'm pretty sure I'm onto something, I'm still at that intuitive stage in the process, when I can feel something swirling around in the mists, but it hasn't yet coalesced.

"I need some time," I say. But we all know there's not much time to spare. We've signed the contract, and the closing date is less than two weeks away. "Just forty-eight hours. If I can't come up with something by then, something more concrete to show you, then you can let the sale go through."

They're all looking cautiously optimistic. Either that or they just want to humor the crazy woman so she'll leave quietly.

"Bernice," I say, "can you get the process started for having the church declared a historic landmark?"

The Judge starts to interrupt me, but I raise a hand to head him off at the pass. "If I can't convince you, then we can let the matter drop. But if I do persuade you I'm right, then we'll be able to get the designation in time."

Bernice is taking notes like crazy. The Judge looks around the room. "Well? What do we think?"

Edna pounds the pillow next to her and then shoves it behind her back. "I say give Betsy a chance. We can't be any worse off than we are now." Not a ringing endorsement, but I'll take what I can get.

"I'll entertain a motion," The Judge says, and I let out the breath I've been holding.

"So moved," says Edna.

"Wait a minute, wait a minute." Bernice is scribbling as quickly as she can. "Somebody give it to me verbatim."

Edna harrumphs. "I move we give Betsy forty-eight hours to convince us that Church of the Shepherd should stay downtown and commit ourselves to historic-landmark status."

"Second," Mac says.

"Any discussion?" From the look on The Judge's face, I'd be surprised if anyone opened their mouth. It's clear he's ready to be done with this.

"Fine. All in favor?" he asks.

Everyone agrees, and I can breathe again. And then I can't. Because I have only forty-eight hours to come up with a compelling vision for the church's future.

No pressure.

303

It's too bad, really, that no one has ever figured out how to bottle divine inspiration so that folks could just uncork it and take a swig as needed. It would be nice if you could have access to the transcendent via FedEx or have the cute guy in the brown UPS uniform deliver mystical insight to your doorstep. Frankly, I think the market demand would make the jockeying for shares in Google's IPO look like small potatoes.

I'm in the market for a miracle myself after yesterday's meeting with the administrative committee. My job pretty much hinges on figuring out by the end of the weekend how to save the church from a demise decades in the making. Really, though, what I need is not a plan for plugging the leak in the dam. No, what I need is a whole new water-delivery system. Spiritually speaking.

I came into the office early this morning hoping that I might find the answer in the deserted tranquillity of a church on Saturday morning. So here I am at dawn's early light, wandering around the building. An empty church is both eerie and comforting. An odd combination, to be sure, but the church is, generally speaking, a whole bundle of odd combinations. Just look at the makeup of the administrative committee if you have any doubts.

Church of the Shepherd is large enough that it takes a while to roam the halls and rooms. I know that when you're the minister, you're not supposed to equate the building with the church per se. You're supposed to say that a church is really made up of its people, not the bricks and mortar. That's why a lot of places have signs that say things like "The Blessed Fellowship of the Lamb Meets Here" or "Our Lady of the Latently Hostile Gathers on This Site." Such a sentiment is either really good theology or way too self-aware. I'm not really sure which. Because the truth is that the building *is* the church—at least in part. I've never yet met a pastor trying to start a new congregation who didn't have his or her sights set on winding up in a structure of some sort.

Anyway, as I wander through the halls, stopping in some of the classrooms to wipe writing off the whiteboards—if you leave those dry-erase markings on there long enough, they get a whole lot less erasable—I acknowledge that I'm hoping to find inspiration somewhere in the building. What is the point of having one hundred thousand square feet devoted to God when we barely have enough folks in worship on Sunday to pay the light bill? Church life is steeped in tradition. Sunday school. Bible study. Committees and task forces. Prayer circles and women's meetings. All as predictable as the earth revolving around the sun. I mean, we're talking about an institution where people freak out when you propose going to a trifold worship bulletin or changing the color of the choir robes. A complete overhaul of the very nature of a congregation is not something one accomplishes on a whim.

But the truth is—and I acknowledge this as I wander from room to room, careful to turn off the lights behind me as I go—that the old reality of Church of the Shepherd, the rhythms of the life the people here have always known, is gone. It slipped away as family after family moved farther and farther from downtown. Maybe some of the older generation stayed, but the children headed for greener pastures where the waters weren't so still that you could see the algae growing on the top.

Finally, I find myself in the sanctuary, always an excellent choice of location when you're looking to commune with the Holy. Well, *usually* an excellent choice. I sink into the same pew where I found Booger sleeping the morning after my disastrous engagement party. The light streaming through the stained glass shines more brightly now since it's full summer instead of early spring. But otherwise nothing in the sanctuary has changed. And yet everything has.

I look up at the Shepherd in the Tiffany window. He's still carrying that stupid sheep. Doesn't he get tired of doing that? I mean, if you have a hundred sheep, you've got to figure that at one point or another, all of them are going to wander off. Why not just leave the stray to the consequences of its stupidity? But that Shepherd goes after the strays every time, leaving the ninety-nine to their own devices while he tracks down that one errant lamb. What a self-defeating story to base a religion on. Unless, of course, you happen to be the lost sheep.

I sit in the pew long enough to know that no inspiration is forthcoming. So, in the absence of any actual sign from God, I decide to head for the kitchen to see what kind of breakfast I can scrounge up. I left so early this morning that I failed to choke down my usual protein bar. Maybe some highly processed carbs will help me attain enlightenment.

The kitchen looks no worse for the wear and tear of my rehearsal dinner. Jed and company have cleaned the floor and countertops until they sparkle. I think about Earlene, who used to fry chicken for the staff once a month, and the knot that's been growing in my stomach since last night doubles in size. Who am I kidding? There's no way out of this. We should just be thankful that we're going to get at least enough out of the deal with Arthur Corday that the church can go on struggling. I'm not opposed to the struggling. I think you pretty much accept that when you decide to make ministry your career. But once you've had the promise of, well, the Promised Land, it's hard to go back to Egypt. Not to be too biblical about it or anything.

I proceed to open the cabinets one after another, looking for anything I can consume to ease the ache in my heart. Not much to choose from except baking soda and some cans of frosting that may actually be old enough to get a driver's license. By the time I've worked my way systematically around the kitchen, I've scrounged up nothing more than some stray Ziploc bags and a few dried-up Sharpies.

Then I spy the industrial-size refrigerator. There's got to be something in there. Alas, no. Not unless I want to do ketchup or mustard shots. I move to the freezer, willing to settle for microwaving one of those frozen sausage biscuits I used to feed Booger. Only to my dismay—and to my horror that I actually feel dismay about this—all the sausage biscuits are gone. The cupboard is truly, thoroughly bare.

Has this ever happened before in the history of Christianity? Has there ever been a truly empty church kitchen?

I stand in the center of the room, and I'm overcome with what a complete waste this kitchen is. Everything is top of the line, state of the art. You could run your own restaurant with a kitchen like this. Well, actually, since it's an institutional kitchen and not a restaurant one, you could run your own prison or hospital cafeteria. But you get the idea. This kitchen is designed to feed a lot of people. I think of the folks at Booger's visitation, people from all walks of life, rubbing elbows as they noshed their way down the table. It was sort of biblical, like that messianic banquet Jesus described in the Scriptures about the man who invited all the muckety-mucks to a feast, but none of them showed up. So the host sent all the servants out to invite all the street people to come eat the feast—and they did. And everyone had a great time.

I can never see an epiphany coming. And I sure don't see this one. But my mom might as well have pelted me upside the head with a cupcake like she did Cecilia. Because that's what it feels like when the thunderbolt strikes and, grabbing the island for support, I realize what needs to happen next at Church of the Shepherd.

It doesn't take me that long, actually, to set my plan in motion. All the pieces were already there; I just didn't see how they fit together. Suffice it to say that if the Israelites could flee Egypt on a moment's notice, pulling off what I have in mind should be child's play by comparison.

Next I turn my attention to the other disaster in my life that needs sorting out. If I can save Church of the Shepherd from the wrecking ball, surely I can do something to salvage my relationship with David. I decide that since the lion won't return my phone calls, I'm going to corner him in his den. Or his pastor's study, as it were.

I leave Church of the Shepherd right after lunch and head for St. Helga's because David always works on Saturday. The office entrance is open, but there's no one behind the small desk in the reception area when I enter. The door to his study is open too. I think about calling out to announce my presence, but I happen to know that his study has a back door that leads to the sanctuary, and I don't want to give him any advance warning so he can escape before I speak my piece.

I'm not much good at stealth, but I sneak up to his door without making a lot of noise. I peer around the door frame, ready to take the bull by the horns. Only there's no bull to take—by the horns or otherwise. He's not there.

I have two choices. I can give up and go home, or I

can go poking around the church to see if I can track him down. I opt for the latter.

Fortunately, St. Helga's isn't as large a building as Church of the Shepherd. I go through David's office and into the brand-spanking-new sanctuary. It's a marvel, really, and also a shame that they still can't use it. David's not there, though. Nor is he in any of the Sunday-school rooms. I'm about ready to start checking the men's rest rooms when I hear raised voices in the fellowship hall. I take a deep breath and move forward.

David and another man are standing in the empty fellowship hall, and they're arguing. Unsure of whether to stay or go, I hover in the doorway about fifteen feet away from them.

"We've done everything you asked and more. We don't have the money for anything else," David says.

"You won't be able to use the sanctuary until you can come up with it. The codes are very clear."

I've stumbled onto David's ongoing battle with the fire marshal. I'm about to spin on my heel and beat a hasty retreat when David spots me.

"Betz? Is something wrong?"

Okay, I didn't quite envision mending fences with my former fiancé in front of a civil servant.

"Um . . . I just had something I need to talk to you about."

David's torn. I can see that. Or else he's just mad at both of us and trying to decide who has caused him the most grief.

"Can it wait?" David asks. "We're in the middle of something."

And that's the problem, isn't it? David has been "in the middle of something" since the moment our relationship shifted from friends to romance. I never stood a chance against the fire marshal, the new sanctuary, or St. Helga's.

I look down at the fliers clutched in my hand and then thrust them at David. "I just came to ask for your help. If you could pass these out at any meetings tonight and put the information on your e-mail loop, that would be great."

David takes the fliers without even looking at them. "That's it?"

"Yes. That's it. Good-bye." Now I do spin on my heel and walk the other way.

"Betsy! Wait!"

You know what? I've waited long enough. For David to notice me. For David to recognize his feelings for me. And now for him to apologize. Well, I'm tired of waiting. When David gets ready to talk, he can come find me. Until then, the fire marshal can have him.

They say waitressing is like riding a bicycle—it all comes back to you once you climb back on, so to speak. Well, okay, I don't know if anyone actually says it's like riding a bicycle, but I'm hoping it's true.

It's Tuesday noon, a week to the day after Booger's funeral. I'm winding my way through table after table of patrons while balancing plates of pasta primavera up and down my arms. Back in high school, when I last practiced the world's second oldest profession, I worked at the SONIC drive-in and did this on roller skates, so this assignment should be a piece of cake. And it would be—if my whole professional future weren't hanging in the balance as precariously as the plates are resting on my arms.

"Waitress!" a familiar bearded man hails me from a table as I pass by. "Can I get some ketchup for this?" he asks, poking with his fork at his plate of primavera.

I'm not sure The Judge envisioned his signature dish coated in an "impertinent tomato-and-sugar-reduction sauce," but if I can keep him in the kitchen, he won't have to witness the horror.

"Sure, Jesus," I say. "Just let me drop off these plates, and I'll be right back." I do owe the guy, after all. I couldn't have pulled all this off without his help. I have the church connections, but he's the one who put the word out on the street.

"Could I get some silverware?" the distinguished-looking older man sitting next to Jesus asks with an apologetic smile. "If it's not too much trouble." His Italian wool suit would easily pay the church's electric bill for several months. When he first came in, I thought Hart must have brought him from his law firm, but as it turns out, he's a friend of Jesus. Evidently they have coffee together on a regular basis.

As I deliver the plates in my arms and then head back across the fellowship hall to the kitchen, I marvel at the turnout for the very first Pay-What-You-Can Café. If someone had told me four days ago, before that meeting at Edna's house, that we could pull this off on such short notice, I never would have believed it. But here we are, serving lunch to the most eclectic gathering of three hundred souls I've ever seen. Every part of the downtown community is represented: lawyers (Hart brought them in by the score), bankers (I see Harry Snedegar's influence there), and state employees who trekked over from the capitol and assorted other office buildings. We're also serving a number of people from St. Helga's and the other downtown churches. And then there's the homeless contingent, roughly a third of the crowd, sitting beside people who pull in six-figure incomes. Add a dash of tourists who've wandered in off the streets after spending the morning at the Country Music Hall of Fame, and there you have it. Our first step toward a new vision for Church of the Shepherd.

"It's fabulous," I say to The Judge as I swing through the kitchen door, snag a bottle of ketchup, and hide it behind my back. I grab a few rolls of silverware (we were up until one o'clock last night rolling knives and forks in napkins) and dash back out again. I deliver the requested items and then head back to the kitchen for more plates. But before I can pick up another load, The Judge steps in front of me and pulls me to one side.

"Miss Blessing, we need to talk."

You know, would it kill him to call me "Reverend"? Honestly, you'd think a man who uses his job title for a first name would understand the importance of addressing someone professionally. Or maybe he understands it all too well.

"Sure, Judge. Or should I say Chef?" I'm not averse to greasing the wheels of acceptance with a little flattery.

"I know I said I'd only help out this one time, but . . ." He stops and then swallows. Wait a minute—is The Judge *nervous?*

"Yes?" Surely he's not going to walk out on me halfway through lunch. The Judge didn't particularly like my idea of the Pay-What-You-Can Café, but he also couldn't resist when I asked him to be the head chef. You see, it's always helpful to know your congregants' weaknesses when you need to get them to do something, and their weaknesses usually have to do with what they love the most. The fact that The Judge is wearing an actual chef's hat and jacket at this very moment tells me I hit the nail on the head.

"If you're going to make a habit of this kind of thing, you're going to need someone for the long haul."

My shoulders are already stooped with exhaustion from my herculean efforts over the past few days. But at The Judge's words, gravity pulls them down a little bit farther. I was hoping the size of the crowd in the fellowship hall might bring him around.

"Could we just get through today before we pick this apart?" I snap. "Can we just enjoy a moment of hope?"

I look The Judge in the eye and, to my surprise, see hurt there instead of the usual disapproval and condemnation.

"You're saying this is a bad idea, right?" I ask. But I

can tell from the stricken look on his face that I'm missing something important here.

"Actually, no. That's not what I'm saying."

"Oh."

The Judge collects himself, willing away any trace of emotion from his face. "Actually, I was going to volunteer my services as permanent chef."

I'm stunned. "So you think this could work? That the café might set an example for what the church could be doing?"

"What I think, Miss Blessing, is that you've proven your point. If we can get three hundred people to come here on a weekday and eat lunch, then maybe our job downtown isn't finished."

"Really? You don't think it's too pie in the sky?"

"Of course it is. But that doesn't mean it isn't the right thing to do. If we sell out and move to the suburbs, then we're just another church following the lure of money and members."

I nod in agreement.

"But," he continues, "if we stay here, we'll have to become something else entirely."

These are the last words I ever expected to hear coming out of The Judge's mouth.

"I've always been a man who likes a challenge. You threw down the gauntlet, Miss Blessing, and I'm picking it up. I'll call a meeting of the administrative committee before the end of the week, and I'm going to recommend we finalize the historic-landmark designation."

Now I know how Moses felt when the manna fell

from heaven. Talk about your unexpected miracles.

"You're sure?" I ask.

"Well, I do have one condition."

Okay, there it is. The other shoe dropping.

"And that is?"

"That you submit your name for consideration for the permanent position of senior minister."

I was wrong. *Those* are the last words I ever expected to come out of The Judge's mouth.

"Seriously?"

"Miss Blessing, have you ever known me to be frivolous about anything?"

Well, he's got me there.

But I foresee one small problem. It's something I've come to realize since Booger's funeral. As busy as I've been, I haven't been too occupied to come to some important conclusions. Chief among them is that I'm not ready to be the senior minister of a congregation like this. A humbling moment of truth, to be sure, but I'm learning to accept it.

"I appreciate that, Judge, but if you'll allow me, I'm going to decline with thanks."

His eyebrows shoot up in surprise. "You are?"

"Yep." Just saying it aloud takes a huge burden off my back, and my aforementioned droopy shoulders rise a notch. "As much as I hate to admit it, you were right. I'm not ready to lead this congregation. But"—I pause—"I would like to stay on when you find a new senior minister. If he's agreeable to retaining the old associate, that is."

The Judge looks at me a little suspiciously, which I guess is to be expected. Not many people would turn down a promotion that is offered on a silver platter. But thinking back over the past few months, I realize that Arthur Corday could never have perpetrated the deception he did on someone like Dr. Black. A seasoned senior minister would have had more resources for checking up on Corday. I always made fun of the way the big-steeple preachers congregate at ministerial association meetings, but now I see the point. Their networking is as important to their jobs as it is to those of us who are second bananas. At this point I don't have the connections or the battle readiness to be what the church needs from its next senior pastor. Don't get me wrong; I plan to get to that place eventually. I guess I've just realized that, once again, my timetable and God's might be the tiniest bit out of sync.

"We'd be delighted for you to stay on," The Judge says. "I'll recommend that to the personnel committee."

"Great," I say.

"Preacher!" Jesus appears in the kitchen doorway. "This ketchup bottle's empty!"

I'm pretty sure the original Jesus never bellowed at the waitstaff in such a deafening tone.

"I'm on it," I call back, and The Judge frowns disapprovingly.

"Ketchup? On my primavera?"

"Love the sinner; hate the tomato-paste sin," I say, smiling.

And The Judge, reluctantly, smiles back.

Chapter 26

Of course, the one face I was hoping to see at the Pay-What-You-Can Café didn't turn up. The Reverend Dr. David Swenson was conspicuous in his absence, although I swear every one of his parishioners was here. I'm not sure what that means, but it's clear by the number of his congregants who came that David went to a lot of trouble to support me today.

Several hours later I'm the last one in the kitchen, drying and putting away the remaining pots and pans. I've reached that point of exhaustion when you can't stop, so I figure I might as well do the last bit of tidying up.

The fellowship hall is quiet once more, and even though I'm weary to the marrow of my bones, I can't help but feel good about what we've accomplished. With The Judge's support, the café can become a regular gig. And with Bernice's help, the historic-landmark designation shouldn't take long to finalize. Once that goes through, our contract with Arthur Corday will be null and void. Then, of course, the real work will start. The Judge was right. One event does not a new vision make.

Now, though, for the first time, things about the church feel right. Odd that in giving up what I thought I wanted, I found what really mattered. If only my wedding to David had worked that way.

"Ahem."

My head whips around so fast that the rest of my body has a hard time following. And there he is, standing in the kitchen doorway. My best-friend-turned-fiancé-turned-ex, looking as scrumpdillyicious as ever. Chocolate brown eyes. Lanky build. Devastating smile.

"Hey," he says.

"Hey," I reply.

So much for witty repartee.

"Looks like it went well," David says, leaning against the door frame. "My parishioners were singing the praises of the pasta primavera."

"People were great," I say inanely. "Thanks for encouraging your folks to participate."

"I hope they participated with their wallets and not just with their knives and forks," he says, a hint of a smile playing around the corners of his mouth.

"We more than covered our costs. In fact, we cleared a nice amount. Enough to buy food for the next time the café opens its doors. And a little for a marketing budget."

"I don't guess there will be many next times once the sale goes through, though, huh?"

"Actually, we've changed our minds."

"You're staying?" He looks surprised at first, and then he actually smiles. "Would you hit me if I said I told you so?"

The familiar teasing tone is back in his voice, and it's a particular timbre I haven't heard since before the night of our engagement party. One of the best parts of our friendship, barring recent history, has been when we harass each other.

"I do have a weapon," I say, brandishing the damp dishtowel in a threatening manner.

"Okay, okay." He holds up both hands in front of him in surrender. "I know enough not to provoke you when you've got one of those. Your aim is deadly."

In the past I probably would have happily popped him with the dishtowel and shown no remorse whatsoever, but now I'm feeling ever-so-slightly less sure of how he'd respond.

"So, did you come by to get a plate of leftovers, or did you want to talk?" I try to sound flippant, but I don't quite pull it off.

David pushes away from the door frame and comes into the kitchen. "I came to talk. If things go well, maybe I can convince you to heat me up a plate of leftovers."

Okay, that sounds promising. But it's also confusing. There he is. The love of my life. My ex-fiancé. The man who let someone else select my engagement ring off eBay and who failed to tell me I was wearing his first fiancée's wedding dress.

"I had a talk with my mom a little while ago," David says. "She told me to get myself over here pronto."

"Yeah?" I'm surprised that Cecilia would say anything to him that would bring him within a mile of me after all that's happened, but maybe her apology in my apartment the day of the wedding really was sincere.

"She said I had to come clean with you."

"Come clean?"

David moves into the kitchen and around the island, putting the length of the steel-covered countertop between us. "Well, there may be one or two things I should have told you."

My fingers have a death grip on the kitchen towel. The last thing I need from David is more startling secrets revealed.

"What should you have told me?" If the towel I'm twisting so tightly in my hand were someone's neck, the poor guy would be dead.

"Look, Betz, it's not that I ever lied about stuff."

Not an auspicious beginning.

"But?" I say, breathing deeply to ensure that my voice doesn't squeak or crack. *Calm. Calm. I will be calm.*

"I know we've been friends a long time, but there's something you don't know about me."

How can David possibly have any secrets at this juncture? Dread rises in me. He's gay. No, he's really a woman. Or worse, he has a secret thing for stuffed animals.

"Nothing sexual," he says, and I blush because apparently my expression gave me away on that one. "I think we've established that I'm pretty much a typical heterosexual male."

Well, he's got a point there.

"What is it?"

He takes a deep breath and places his hands, palms down, on the countertop. Then he leans forward. "I'm not really cheap."

"What?"

321

"Ever since you've known me, you've always teased me about being a skinflint. Or, as you so eloquently put it, 'tight as the bark on a tree.'"

"And?" I'm not seeing the connection here.

"The truth is, I have a problem with money."

"David, this is really no time for joking." I can't believe he thinks he can come in here, play a prank like this, and then we'll have a few laughs and everything will be back to normal.

"Betz, I'm serious." His luscious brown eyes underline his words.

"You're a shopaholic?" I am oozing skepticism.

He winces. "I didn't say that. It's not like I'm some woman who buys too many shoes."

"Then what is it like?"

"From the time my dad left when I was younger, I used money to ease the pain. Trying to prove I was 'good enough.'"

Honestly, I feel as if I'm caught in a really bad episode of *The Twilight Zone*. I didn't think it was possible for a man to be addicted to shopping.

"David, you've always been the cheapest guy I've known. I mean, look at the car you drive. That Volvo's almost old enough to have little Volvos of its own. And your apartment. If you own one stick of furniture you didn't assemble yourself—"

"That's because I got help. I made a choice to put an end to living that way." He looks down at the counter. "That's when Jennifer broke up with me. When I cut up my credit cards and changed my ways."

I drop the dishtowel. "You're kidding."

He raises his head, and the pain in his eyes floors me. I want to sink down beside the dishtowel, but I manage to remain upright.

"And in all the years I've known you, you never trusted me enough to tell me this?" Hurt flows through me, stiffening my legs and hardening my heart. "As close as we were, you couldn't confide in me?"

"I was ashamed."

His quiet words pierce me to the depths of my soul. And then things start to fall in place, like puzzle pieces that finally fit together.

"That's why Jennifer had the Tiffany ring? And the Vera Wang dress? Because you wanted to buy them?"

"Yes, although I don't recall her complaining when I spent so much money on her. Only when I wanted to stop."

And all along I thought it was her. That she was the one who was so bent on a lavish wedding with all the glamorous trappings.

"When we graduated from divinity school, I was sixty thousand dollars in debt."

"How could I have known you all through school and not have known this?" I feel like a prize idiot.

"Because I hid it from you. Spending money was like a drug. I'd get my fix, but I kept it a secret from the people I really cared about."

My mind's racing as I try to sort out this new information. "You never seemed like a big spender except when it came to the wedding."

"You know all those credit-card solicitations you get in college?" I nod my head. He half laughs, half sighs. "Well, I applied for every single one of them. Got 'em too. As a freshman in college, I spent thousands on stereo equipment and CDs."

I can't believe what I'm hearing.

"My mom was the one who ended up bailing me out when I graduated from divinity school. That's why she needs her job at *Budget Bride* so much. She cashed in her retirement, all her savings, everything to get me out of debt." He smiles, but there's not much humor in it. "With what I owed, I could have bought a new hood for the kitchen at St. Helga's."

That certainly puts Cecilia's actions in a new light.

"I owed her big time, and when she asked for the opportunity to plan the wedding, I thought it would work for everybody. Neither of us had the time to do it, Mom really wanted to, and we'd get to be together that much sooner."

"That's what your mother meant when she said I was so much better for you than Jennifer."

"When did she say that?"

I half laugh, half wince. "Right before she spilled the beans about the dress."

"I'm sorry about the dress, Betz. Really. I didn't say anything because you loved it so much."

"So Jennifer dumped you when you decided to stop spending money you didn't have?"

David winces now too, and then he stands up straight and crosses his arms over his chest. That chest where I love to rest my head because it makes me feel like everything will be okay.

"She let me know in no uncertain terms that she expected the best in life, and if I wasn't prepared to provide her with that, I could take a hike."

Anger at the sheer, grasping greed of the woman erupts inside me. "Correct me if I'm wrong, but did she not know all along that you planned to be a minister? Where did she think this money was going to come from?"

"I don't know." David drops his arms, and they hang forlornly by his side. "What I do know is that I lost the first woman I ever loved because of my inability to deal with money." He stops, clears his throat, and then looks me straight in the eye. "But I'm not prepared to lose the woman I want to spend the rest of my life loving over the same thing."

Okay, the good news here is that David just said about the most romantic thing I've ever heard him utter. And I'm assuming that, given his confession, he hasn't given up on us as a couple.

The bad news is that my beloved has been keeping a secret all these years. How am I supposed to respond to this information? That's the quandary I'm trying to sort out here in the middle of the church kitchen when a second man appears in the doorway.

Arthur Corday.

Well, at least this time I'm not covered in toner. I'm just having one of the greatest personal crises of my life.

"Hello, Mr. Corday." I'm impressed that my voice sounds so measured and even, given that I'm ready to run out the door screaming.

"Reverend Blessing."

He's really, really mad. I can tell from the way his neck seems to be welded to his spine. He can barely turn his head to nod at David.

"What can I do for you?"

"You may tell me, Reverend, why papers were filed yesterday to designate this church as a historic landmark."

That's not really what he wants to know at all. I'm betting he'd love to know how I found out about his duplicitous scheme. But he can't very well ask that, can he?

"Well, Arthur, I guess I'm invoking a woman's prerogative to change her mind. We've decided we don't want to move to the suburbs after all."

"May I ask why?" Now that he's not trying to win me over, his smarminess is oozing out all over the place. Jed's going to have to mop the floor all over again.

"You may certainly ask, but as that decision was made in an administrative-committee meeting, I'm not at liberty to tell you." I have no idea whether the discussions in those committee meetings are confidential, but it sounds good.

"I can block your filing, you know," he says with a smile that would be pleasant if his lips weren't as thin as razors. "A nice try, but ineffective in the long run."

"Really?" I'm wondering what David's thinking

about all of this, but so far he's just standing there, following the back-and-forth conversation like a spectator at Wimbledon. "You might be wrong about that, Arthur. I don't think you want to undermine our efforts."

"Because?"

"Because Bernice Kenton, one of my wonderful parishioners, has an entire media campaign outlined to discredit you if you do. Think how it would look in the *Tennessean.* 'Evil Real Estate Developer Defrauds Little Old Church Ladies.' Bernice has already rounded up the ladies auxiliary for a photo op of their emotional devastation." As I've said before, the woman doesn't have a flair for the dramatic for nothing.

"I can survive a little bad press."

"Really? I think Bernice mentioned something about chaining themselves to the sanctuary doors when the wrecking balls show up."

That's the moment when I see Arthur decide that it's not going to be worth the battle. Thank heavens for the ladies auxiliary.

"You might regret this, Reverend Blessing."

A sarcastic retort leaps to my tongue, but before I can launch it, David steps in. "I think it's time for you to leave," he says to Arthur.

Not for the first time, I'm thankful for David's imposing height. "I agree," I say. It's nice to have David in my corner, but I want to fight this battle myself. "Mr. Corday, you found your way in; I assume you can show yourself out."

His scowl might intimidate me if I wasn't accustomed

to regularly seeing The Judge's much worse one. Arthur's mouth opens and closes a few times without any sound emerging, and then he clamps it shut, spins on his heel, and strides from the kitchen.

"Thanks," I say to David. "I could have handled him, but sometimes it's nice to have backup."

David shoots me a rueful smile. "Sort of how you felt about my mother, too, huh?"

And I have to smile back. I'd never have thought I could have a sense of humor about my botched wedding so soon after the fact, but I'm finding that even when you're hurting, life can—and indeed does—go on.

"David, what you just told me, was that really why you wanted your mother in charge of the wedding plans?"

His smile slips from his lips, and I don't mean to give him a hard time, but I need a few more questions answered.

"Yeah." He grimaces. "I was afraid that if I got too involved, my old habits would get the best of me. I mean, geez, Betz, if I bought Tiffany and Vera Wang for Jennifer, there's no telling what I'd have spent on you."

And with that, I burst into tears. David moves around the island, and—hallelujah!—there's his solid wall of a chest, and I get to snuggle right up against it.

"Shh. It's okay." He wraps his arms around me and makes all the desired soothing noises. "It's all right."

And in the weirdest, most unexpected way possible, maybe it is.

"I never meant to hurt you, David," I say between sniffles.

"Same here." One of his hands is stroking my back, and I could just melt.

"It's just that—"

"Just that what?"

And I have to smile. "It's just that all I really wanted out of this was a date."

"A what?"

I lean back in his arms, reluctantly lifting my cheek from his chest so I can look at him when I say this. "That night at La Paz? All I wanted was a really good first date."

"Aw, Betz," he says in that growly, masculine way that sends shivers up my spine. "Why didn't you just say so?"

"David?"

"Yeah?"

"Shut up and kiss me."

And finally, at long last, I get just what I want.

Edna has made enough progress with her hip that a few days later we're able to have a meeting of the administrative committee in her living room. Alice has made teacakes, and since I no longer have to worry about fitting into Jennifer's wedding dress, I help myself to three.

"I'm glad you all could be here," The Judge says, looking around the room.

Everyone except Edna is perched on the edge of an

antique chair, balancing a cup and saucer on one knee and teacakes on the other. Reclining on a settee with a small table at her elbow, our hostess is trying to maneuver her coffee to her lips and then back to the waiting saucer. And while we all look a little off balance, I think we've finally found our footing again.

"And I want to thank all of you, too," I say. The Judge nods approvingly, and so I continue. "If it hadn't been for every one of you, we could never have pulled it off."

"Here, here," Mac says, raising his cup in a toast. "To Church of the Shepherd. Long may she stand."

I look around, afraid of clinking my cup against anyone else's given its fragility. So by silent consent, we all simply raise our cups to one another and then bring them to our lips.

"All's well that ends well," Bernice says before taking a bite of her teacake and then lifting her eyes to heaven in thanks as it melts on her tongue.

"But this is just the beginning," I say. "We have a lot of things to figure out now that we've decided to stay. We can't go back to business as usual."

That's my biggest fear, of course. That all of the lessons we've learned over the past few months will be set aside in our relief at getting out of the contract with Arthur Corday.

"Betsy, we'd like you to submit your résumé to the search committee," Ralph says, his accordion file of financial documents lying closed at his feet for once.

Tears quickly pool in my eyes. That's what I've dreamed of hearing the leaders of this church say. I've

330

been seeking that affirmation for a long time—maybe my whole life—and it feels wonderful.

"I appreciate that," I say, "but after careful consideration and a whole lot of prayer, I've decided not to submit my name."

Even though those words sting, I feel liberated. At ease. Lighter than I've felt in a very long time. Because what I've learned in the past few months is that if you want to be the leader of a community, you have to be a real part of that community first. You have to love it as much as the people who comprise it do. And you have to be able to be the strongest advocate for those whose welfare is in your keeping. I'm not quite there yet, but I'm definitely making progress.

"Betsy and I discussed this," The Judge says, "and I assured her that she'll have our full support for continuing on as our associate minister."

"What about when we bring in the new senior pastor?" Mac says. "Don't they usually want a free hand in selecting their staff?"

"I think that's our decision," The Judge says. "I don't see us hiring anyone who wouldn't be supportive of Betsy."

"Of course not," Edna says. "We'll want someone with the good sense to treasure her like we do."

"Well, then, we'd better appoint a search committee," The Judge says. "Edna? Would you be willing to head up the search?"

So, over more of Alice's fabulous teacakes, the committee finally begins to make plans for finding a new senior minister. And I sit there munching and sipping, exhausted but happy. A long while later—because forming a search committee can take about as long as it does to build an ark—I happen to glance at my watch.

"Is that the time?" I leap to my feet.

"Hot date, Betsy?" Mac teases, and I blush because he's right on the nose.

"As a matter of fact, yes."

"Then go on, dear." Edna makes a shooing motion with her hand. "Don't keep that Lutheran waiting."

I guess if Edna can accept my continuing involvement with a Lutheran, anything is possible. Even a whole new vision for Church of the Shepherd.

"I'll just be running along," I say, scooping up my purse. "Let me know if I can be of any help with the search process."

Alice is there to see me to the front door. She opens it and then unexpectedly leans over to give me a quick hug.

"You're going to be just fine, Reverend Blessing," she says.

"I know, Alice. I know." I hug her back and make a dash out the door for my car. Because I've got a first date in a little less than an hour, and I want to get ready properly this time.

David is worried that his admission about his money problems might make me feel differently about him. I just worry that I'll be tempted to exploit his weakness next time we're at Green Hills Mall. The only thing that's kept me from dropping wads of cash is that I've never actually had any spare wads of cash to drop. But if David can put up with my pathological addiction to conflict avoidance, I guess I can support him in a life of simplicity. Although I sure did love that Vera Wang. Except for the whole preowned part of it.

Despite getting home late from the meeting at Edna's, I'm ready when David rings the doorbell.

"Whoa!" he says when he sees me.

Okay, so I did buy a new outfit for the occasion—a little camisole top that you'd think came from the lingerie department, a floaty summer skirt that skims my knees, and, yes, a pair of the cliché strappy sandals. I don't plan to mention my little shopping spree to David. Right now that information is on a need-to-know basis, and he doesn't need to know.

"I'll take that as a compliment," I say.

He gives me a quick peck on the lips and then steps back to admire me some more.

"Maybe we should just stay home," he says, suddenly very solemn.

"Stay home?" Is he kidding? Then I see the twinkle in his chocolate brown eyes.

"Well, to tell the truth, Betz, I'm not sure I feel up to fighting off all the guys who are going to be ogling you tonight."

I snort with laughter, punch him playfully on the shoulder, and secretly wallow in the compliment. "C'mon, Swenson. I'm a growing girl, and I need my Mexican food."

Yes, we're headed back to La Paz. And this time it's just a date. And if David falls to one knee, or if anyone I know comes leaping out of the back room, I'm making a run for it, and I'm not stopping until I hit the Alabama border.

Rule for Women Ministers No. 6: Always have a good escape plan.

5